DEADLY TREASURE

DEADLY TREASURE

★ ★ ★ ★ ★

a novel

JILLAYNE CLEMENTS

Bonneville Books
Springville, Utah

© 2009 Jillayne Clements

The views expressed within this work are the sole responsibility of the author and do not necessarily reflect the position of Cedar Fort, Inc., or any other entity.

This is a work of fiction. The characters, names, incidents, places, and dialogue are products of the author's imagination, and are not to be construed as real.

"A Child's Prayer" copyright 1984 Janice Kapp Perry. Used by Permission.

ISBN 13: 978-1-59955-228-6

Published by Bonneville, an imprint of Cedar Fort, Inc.,
2373 W. 700 S., Springville, UT 84663
Distributed by Cedar Fort, Inc., www.cedarfort.com

LIBRARY OF CONGRESS CATALOGING-IN-PUBLICATION DATA
Clements, Jillayne.
  Deadly treasure / Jillayne Clements.
    p. cm.
  Summary: A young woman and her friends seek a lost gold mine in Utah's
Uintah Mountains.
  ISBN 978-1-59955-228-6
  1. Treasure troves--Uinta Mountains (Utah and Wyo.)--Fiction. 2. Mines
and mineral resources--Uinta Mountains (Utah and Wyo.)--Fiction. 3. Gold
mines and mining--Uinta Mountains (Utah and Wyo.)--Fiction. 4. Adventure
stories, American. I. Title.

  PS3603.L465D43 2009
  813'.54--dc22
                              2008047585

Cover design by Jen Boss
Cover design © 2009 by Lyle Mortimer
Edited and typeset by Melissa J. Caldwell

Printed in the United States of America

10 9 8 7 6 5 4 3 2 1

Printed on acid-free paper

ACKNOWLEDGMENTS

Thank you to my parents, extended family, husband, and children for your love, support, and encouragement. I love you all!

Thank you also to all who helped me with this book. I couldn't have done it alone. Thanks, Mom, for giving the okay with the love story; Jax, for amazing family history mystery and plot advice; Jen, for reading and giving feedback on all the versions of this story no less than nine times and still wanting a copy; Candice and Michelle, for great female input and support; my "girls" at YL for your feedback and encouragement; Jen Nielsen, for your expertise on editing and writing; Sylvia Harbor, for your editing and feedback; Jodi Evans, for awesome plot advice; my patient husband, Greg, for putting up with my nonstop talking about this "baby" and for encouraging me to finally "give birth to it" by sending it in; and to the staff at Cedar Fort, who helped this story see its potential.

CHAPTER 1

★ ★ ★ ★ ★

"Lexi, wait!" Ron's distraught voice shot through the warm air from the other side of the parking lot.

I threw open the trunk lid of my car, stuffed in the rest of my belongings from my second year of college, and darted to the driver's door. My ex-boyfriend sprinted toward me while I tried with trembling hands to open the lock. I couldn't talk to him right now, not after what had happened yesterday.

The lock clicked up, but before I could lift the handle, Ron grabbed my arm, whirled me around, and thrust a gorgeous bouquet of long-stemmed roses into my hands. "I'm sorry."

"I don't want your flowers or your apology." I threw the roses at his feet and blinked back threatening tears.

"Come on. I told you she means nothing to me. Why are you making such a big deal out of this?"

"It may not be a big deal to you, but it is to me." I jerked free from his grip.

"You're just upset about your grandpa. Give it—"

"His death has nothing to do with this, and you know it!"

Ron's face softened, and so did his voice. "You're right, I'm sorry. Just hear me out." He slipped his fingers over mine. Tears filled his eyes. It was the first time I'd seen this man with untamed sandy-blond hair cry. "Everybody makes mistakes, and I made the worst of my life. Give me another chance."

I rubbed the headache from my temples. How I wanted to turn back time and have the last twenty-four hours disappear, but I couldn't. "It's over," I said.

He flinched from the sting of my words. His jaw tightened, his fists clenched in tight knots, and angry veins bulged from his reddened forehead.

I backed into the car door and felt for the handle behind me.

"Please." His words were forced through pursed lips. "I can't go on if you're not a part of my future. I need you. I want you. Come on, can't you see you're breaking my heart?"

My jaw opened, and I stared in amazement. "You broke my heart." I grabbed the door handle and dropped into the sun-warmed seat of my car.

Before I could slam the door, he bent down and placed a kiss on my cheek. Instinctively, I scrubbed it from my face with the back of my hand. Tears dripped from my chin and onto my jeans. I sped out of the parking lot, leaving Ron, the roses, and hopefully the nightmare behind.

★　　★　　★　　★

How did I get into such a mess? I was supposed to be forgetting finals, daydreaming about my boyfriend, and planning my first week of summer break. Instead, I was fuming over Ron and mourning the death of my grandpa.

I glanced at my purse, sitting open on the seat next to me. My dead cell phone was tucked into the outer pocket, and my friend's wedding announcement peeked from the main compartment; a stamp of the Manti temple graced its cover.

I'd always dreamed of a temple marriage, but when I met Ron, I fell hard for his charm and rugged good looks. I knew that he didn't share the same eternal goals that I did, but I was sure there wasn't any harm in just one date. Before I knew it, I was in a relationship that was growing more and more comfortable, and I wondered how I'd get out of it, or even if I wanted to. But I never thought it'd end like it did.

Last night, Mom phoned to tell me that Grandpa Rhoades had passed away. He'd collapsed from a weakened heart after returning home and finding his place completely ransacked. Paramedics tried to revive him, but it was too late. He'd already slipped from this life to be with Grandma.

I was devastated by the news and ran to Ron for comfort. But I was shocked when an attractive girl answered his apartment door, wearing only the oversized T-shirt I'd given him for Christmas, and Ron lay in candlelit shadows inside.

He'd chased after me, apologized, and promised she meant nothing to him. I was the only woman for him; he knew that now. But I knew then and there that he wasn't the man for me.

Hadn't my parents tried to warn me about dating him? Hadn't I felt impressed not to pursue the relationship? I squeezed the steering wheel until my knuckles turned white.

I snapped out of my thoughts nearly two hours later, when I almost missed my exit. I darted between two cars just in time to take Park City's Kimball Junction exit. It was hard for me to imagine that the intersection had once been home to a lonely gas station and hotel surrounded by nothing but sagebrush-dotted hills. Now, this heavily traveled area had a Walmart, a grocery store, and the Tanger Outlet's numerous stores, strung together under covered walkways.

The road into the heart of Park City continued through hills and lush, green mountains, thick with colorful foliage. I was glad to be going home.

I turned into the cozy cul-de-sac that hid my house. Bugzy, the Whitman's poodle, still guarded the road from his favorite spot—the very center. He'd been there when I'd gone to Utah State last fall and was still there to welcome me home. I was forced to drive around him to enter the driveway, but it was something I was used to doing.

I clicked off the ignition and glanced in the rearview mirror. My deep-blue eyes were only slightly red and puffy, and I prayed that I could control my emotions while explaining Ron's lack of character to my parents. How could I bring it up without breaking down?

Mom and Dad, I have something to tell you. Ron and I broke up. It seems that he doesn't love me as much as he loves himself or that other chick. Yes, I'm fine; just give me a day or two to get over him.

After I had that little line memorized, I took a big breath, grabbed my bags, and stormed up the Columbine-lined walkway to the porch.

The aroma of Mom's famous lasagna made with whole-grain noodles and fresh garlic, oregano, and basil hit me the moment I walked through the front door. My stomach growled, but the appetite I'd been expecting wasn't there.

My silver-haired father greeted me with big, opened arms. I had complete control of my emotions until then, which was precisely when my eyes began to burn with tears. Dad pulled back, and his smile disappeared. "I'm sorry," he said. "Grandpa was a wonderful man. I miss him too."

I shook my head. "No, it's more than that." I took a deep breath and rehearsed the line once more. "Ron and I . . . ." but the rest of my sentence was an unintelligible slur of sobs, mixed with the few words I could muster out of my mouth.

Mom ran from the kitchen when she heard my blubbering. "What happened?"

"I . . . It's too horrible," I said.

Dad turned me to face him. "Let's go sit on the couch. You can tell us everything."

After we sat, it took nearly ten minutes before I could finally say, "Ron cheated on me."

Mom gasped, and her eyes widened. "Oh, sweetie," she said.

"But he wants me to take him back. He thinks that

Grandpa's death is getting in the way of my good judgment."

Dad stood. "I'm getting my shotgun. No one messes with my little girl."

I laughed right through my tears. "Dad, sit down. That's slightly illegal. I just can't believe he expects that an apology and a promise to break up with her will make everything all right." I swiped at fresh tears rolling down my cheeks. "I feel so awful. He said he loved me."

I buried my face in my hands and sobbed until my tears had dried and my emotions had stabilized. Though I'd somewhat expected my parents to restate their concerns of my dating him in the first place, there was nothing but sympathy for what I was going through at the moment.

For the next several minutes, we all shed tears for my breakup and for Grandpa.

Finally, Mom said, "Come have some dinner, you must be starving."

We got up off the couch, and Dad slipped an arm around me. "And after that, I can give you a blessing."

I smiled. "I'd like that."

Mom's meal was one of my favorites, but I hardly noticed the taste. After I managed to force down most of the food on my plate, I helped Dad with the dishes and plopped down on the fluffy couch in the living room. I stared up at the two-story, intricately laid brick fireplace. This couch had always been my favorite spot growing up while doing homework, reading scriptures, and pondering.

The phone's ring startled me, and Dad's hushed voice drifted from the other room. I didn't even have to guess he was talking about Grandpa. I strained to hear the words, "fingerprints," "suspect," and "strong." I thought Dad was supposed to be retired from his detective work. Had they found a suspect yet?

When he was off the phone, Dad brought in a dining room chair for me to sit on. "Are you ready?" he asked. He said nothing about the phone conversation, and I took it as a sign not to ask.

I sat on the chair, and the moment he placed his hands on my head, warmth poured through my entire body. Fresh tears seeped from my eyes, but they were tears brought by the knowledge that my Father in Heaven and also my Savior loved me more than I could comprehend. A literal weight lifted from me, a weight that I'd subconsciously carried since I'd begun dating Ron.

I couldn't recollect all the beautiful words my father said, but I remembered one part quite distinctly. He blessed me that I would feel comfort and peace in the trials I was facing, and they'd ultimately add to my character and strengthen my testimony.

Images flashed through my mind. Images buried deep in my subconscious of catching Ron "checking out" other women when he thought I wasn't looking. Rumors I'd heard accusing him of cheating on me but that I'd brushed aside. Recollections of conversations we'd had that left me wondering if his interest in my beliefs were merely to humor me. I felt that I could and should forgive him, but there was someone else for me. Someone who would treat me like the daughter of God I knew I was. I just needed to find him.

★ ★ ★ ★

Park City, Utah. I loved being home in this small town once known for its booming silver mining facilities, but now world famous for its powder-covered ski runs. I enjoyed the reprieve from the scorching heat that the Salt Lake Valley offered. Summer days seldom reached the 90s, and the nights always dropped to a crisp chill.

I awoke the next morning feeling light as a feather. The sun peeked over the horizon, pouring brilliant rays of gold on the tips of the highest mountains. I grabbed a T-shirt and jogging pants, laced my tennis shoes, and then stepped outside

and filled my lungs with refreshing air. I was long overdue for
a jog.

The low mountains our once-little subdivision was nestled
against, caught my attention. It had been at least a year since
I'd hiked them, so I jogged to the base and climbed the dirt
path through the trees.

The view from the top was amazing. It overlooked a good
section of the heart of Park City just as the sun cast its golden
rays on the rooftops.

My thoughts turned to Ron, like they had steadily for the
last couple of days. I was surprised that the anger and bitterness
had dissolved and was replaced with a new freedom. I still had
a long way to go before I could completely forgive him, but I
was hopeful that I could. At least he'd evolved from pond scum
to a toad in my mind, and with a little work and time, I was
sure he'd eventually become human.

When I returned home an hour or so later, I felt invigo-
rated both mentally and physically. I stretched along the way to
the kitchen and then gulped down a large glass of cool, filtered
water. Sweat trickled down my face and neck, and I dabbed
it with the bottom of my T-shirt. Not very lady-like, I know,
but I didn't want to use Mom's decorative kitchen towels.

My cell phone blinked on the counter, informing me that
it was fully recharged. It'd been completely drained of bat-
tery power for the last week, but I'd been so busy with finals I
hadn't taken the time to recharge it. I picked it up and flipped
it open to check for messages. Ron had called several times—I
wasn't surprised. A couple of friends had tried calling as well.
But the unread message that caught my attention was from
Grandpa, the morning before he collapsed.

I scrolled to his name and held the phone to my ear.

"Sweet pea, this is Grandpa." The sound of his voice
brought a lump to my throat. "There's something I need to
talk to you about. It's important, so give me a call as soon as
you get this message. Talk to you later. Love you."

Goose bumps climbed up my arms. What had he needed to talk to me about? I knew he was interested in family history as well as hunting and fishing, but that wouldn't explain the urgency in his voice.

I ran upstairs and handed the phone to Dad, who was tying his shoes on the bed. A crease formed between his eyes as he listened to the message. When he was done, he said, "Do you mind if I borrow this for awhile?"

"Why?"

"Oh, I just think some of my friends might be interested in hearing it." I knew from the tone of his voice that "friends" meant his buddies at the Park City Police Department.

His answer sent chills down my spine, but I hesitantly nodded in agreement.

CHAPTER 2
★ ★ ★ ★ ★

Mom and I stood on Grandpa Rhoades' front porch. Neither of us dared open the door, afraid of what we'd find on the other side. The exterior of the historical mansion looked just as it always had (except for the smashed-in windows and police tape)—old brick that was cracked in a few spots, front steps that had been redone to pass current code, and enormous shade trees towering overhead. Finally, I turned the knob and pushed it open.

Mom and I both gasped. Papers, books, and garbage were strewn all over the hardwood floors in the main hallway. Glass shards and scattered wood were all that was left of the mirrored desk that had once stood in the hall. The doors to the formal living room were ripped from their hinges, and the antique sofa was slashed, its insides pulled out.

Bookshelves were knocked over in the family room; and in the kitchen area, the little dinette—at which I'd eaten so many times—was flipped on its side. An unbelievable stench came from the rotting food scattered all over. Nothing could describe the intense feelings of frustration, anger, and sickness that swirled inside of me.

Mom handed me a large garbage bag and some gloves. "How someone could do such a thing to a kind, old man is beyond me." She turned to face me. "Are you sure you want to do this?"

I nodded. "Let's get to work."

We started in the kitchen, filling garbage bag after garbage bag with rotting food, junk, and papers. Next, we worked in the living room and then took a short break. Mom decided to next work in the bedroom on the main floor while I did the upstairs room and attic.

A steep, narrow, hardwood staircase led to the attic from one of the bedrooms on the upper level. Dusty light filtered through the attic's small bay window and landed on the built-in bench directly beneath it. I remembered the times as a child that I'd sat on that bench, reading books or looking for nests in the branches that hugged the window.

Boxes of old clothes and blankets had been ripped open, their contents spilled all around. Ancient fishing and hunting supplies were dumped, and papers and albums from an open trunk lay everywhere. I began sorting what could be salvaged into piles.

The work went fairly quickly until I started reading some of the papers that'd been tossed to the floor. I was in a family history buff's heaven. I picked up an aging photo album, sprawled upside-down on the ground. My fingers flipped through its yellow, breakable pages, straightening what pictures they could.

There were a handful of pedigree charts as well as one-to-two-page life histories of some of my ancestors. I followed one chart, which dated back to my great-great-great-great-grandpa, a man named Thomas Foster Rhoades. From a compilation of life histories, I gathered that he was a farmer, a trapper, a prospector, and that he could also translate and communicate with the Ute Indians. But his life changed when he discovered maps on the murdered bodies of a group of Spaniards. He followed the maps and found gold in Utah's mountains. Before I could read more, Mom's voice broke my concentration. "Are you alive up there?"

"Yeah, I'm just . . . reading." My mind's eye could see the

look on her face. It wasn't friendly.

I stacked the rest of the papers and albums into the trunk and then started sorting out the old blankets. The dust in the room was so thick I could taste it, and it was very unpleasant. I waded through stacks to the window and tried to lift it for some fresh air, but it was stuck. I made sure it wasn't locked and tried again. It still wouldn't budge. Finally, I stuck my knees on the bench, jabbed my elbows into my stomach, and lifted with all my strength.

Crack!

I gasped and searched all over the window for a break but couldn't find anything.

Crack! Crack!

My knees sank lower, and I jumped off the bench just before the lid collapsed to the floor with a thud.

"What was that?" Mom called from downstairs.

"I, uh . . . just broke the bench."

There was a pause. "Can you fix it?"

"I'll try."

I grabbed the lid to the bench, careful to avoid the old nails poking through the edges, and lifted it out. A couple of marbles, an old toy car, a locket, and an old leather diary lay under dusty cobwebs on the floor. I reached through the webs, grabbed the items, and tossed them into the trunk. I slid the bench lid back in place, and with a few whacks of an old boot, it was repaired.

Mom's footsteps approached me from behind. "Dad and Uncle Joe are here. Are you ready to call it a day?" She pulled off her gloves and wiped sweat from her dirty brow.

"Absolutely. Does anyone have claims on the family history stuff?" I motioned toward the trunk.

She smiled. "Your dad does."

"Great." I couldn't wait to read more.

★　　★　　★　　★

The morning of Grandpa's funeral, I hopped out of bed, got ready, and dashed downstairs. I still had a half hour before we needed to leave, which was close to a miracle, and I planned to spend most of it digging for treasure.

The old trunk sat in the family room, and I opened its heavy, dusty lid. I picked up an aging photo album and flipped through the delicate pages. The young faces of Grandma and Grandpa Rhoades stared back at me.

The knowledge that death is only a temporary separation from our loved ones touched me. I knew I could live with my family forever, even my future family, if I chose to marry in the temple. How could I have been so wrapped up in a guy that I nearly forgot how important that was in my life?

I pulled out the leather diary. It was fastened tight with a metal lock. I wondered whose it was and what family history it contained. In another album, a cracked and aging picture of a family caught my eye. It wasn't so much the people in the photo that intrigued me as much as where it had been taken. Small trees dotted the neatly manicured front yard, and the mansion in the background looked almost new. But there was no mistake they were sitting in front of Grandpa's home.

The gentleman was middle aged, wore a tall hat, and had a curled, dark mustache. Children, ranging in ages from young adult to infant, stood and sat around his wife. The woman's gray-streaked hair was pulled up in a bun; a beautiful locket encircled her fancy, high-collared dress.

The locket I threw in the trunk!

My hand plunged into the trunk and felt its way through stacks of memorabilia. When I couldn't find it, I took out a large stack of journals and set them gently on the floor.

"Lexi, phone," Mom called from the next room.

I plunked the journals back in the trunk and closed the lid. The search for the locket would have to wait.

"Hello?" I said when I reached the phone.

"Hi, it's me, Ron."

"Oh."

"How've you been?"

"We're just about to go to Grandpa's funeral." He'd only met Grandpa once, so I couldn't imagine he'd feel much remorse.

"So, do you want to go out later on?"

The intake of air into my lungs was audible. "I'm not going out with you anymore."

I could almost hear a pin drop. "I'll do whatever you want. I'll be the man you've always wanted. I'll change."

"Don't change just for me," I said. Mom tapped at her watch.

Ron sighed. "Just give me another chance."

"No, I can't. I won't." I hung up before he could reply.

★   ★   ★   ★

Grandpa Rhoades left many people mourning at his passing. The chapel was packed with family and friends who'd come to pay their respects. It was a beautiful ceremony, with talks given by some of Grandpa's children and grandchildren, followed by his bishop. A group of some of his great-grandchildren sang, "Families Can Be Together Forever," and there wasn't a dry eye in the building. More than ever I wanted to make sure I lived my life the way I needed to, so I could be worthy to receive the blessings of an eternal family.

After the burial, we returned to the meetinghouse for a luncheon. I sat at a table next to a cute elderly lady with white hair and a friendly smile.

"You're Jonathan and Sharon's daughter, right?" she asked.

I nodded.

"I'm Aunt Ethel. I'm your grandpa's baby sister, although I'm not a baby anymore." Her gray eyes searched me. "The last I saw you, you came to my knees and wore curly, blond pigtails. You're such a pretty young thing. I bet you turn a lot of heads." She chuckled at the shocked look on my face. "I used to turn a lot of heads when I was your age, but now the only heads I turn are too stiff with arthritis to move much."

I laughed. Already, I felt comfortable enough with her to ask a question that'd been nagging my mind. "Aunt Ethel, before Grandpa died, he said he had something important to tell me, but I never had a chance to talk with him. I wondered if it has anything to do with family history or the gold mines. Do you know anything about them? Are they real?"

"Why? Are you planning to hunt for gold?"

"No, of course not," I said. "I'm just curious."

"Well, I'm glad you're not planning to look for gold. It can be mighty dangerous and even deadly, and I wouldn't want you to get hurt. But, if you get me some more water, I'll tell you what I know."

I grabbed a glass of water for us both and quickly headed back to the table.

"Thanks, dear," she said when I returned. "There're really two ideas about how it all started." She took a swallow and then continued. "First idea began way back when the Aztecs lived in Mexico and were being conquered by the Spaniard, Cortez. Some say the Aztecs traveled to the Uintah Mountains and placed all their valuable gold bars and other treasures in some mines and caves to hide them from the conquerors. The Spaniards then followed to find the gold. The other idea is that the Spaniards found the caves of rich gold and silver ore, smelted it, and compiled their gold bars in a cave until they had enough to take to the coast and sail it home to Spain.

"But no matter where the gold came from, it's up there in the Uintahs just as sure as I'm alive. And it's also cursed."

"Cursed?" I hadn't heard that before and didn't know if I believed it, either.

"Yes, cursed. Depending on the legend you believe, some say the Aztecs placed a curse of death on the gold, death to come to any that greedily take it. Others say it was the Spaniards who placed the curse, and others think it was the Utes. Lots of people talk of Indian spirits that protect the gold. But that's not all." She wet her mouth with another sip of water. "Many Spaniards were killed by the Utes. The Indians believed that the mines were sacred, especially a very valuable one, the Carre-Shin-Ob Mine. It's rumored that the Ute chief was the guardian of the sacred mine, and men and spirits watch it constantly. No one could go near it, or any other mines, except Thomas Rhoades."

I couldn't breathe. "Why? What was so special about him?"

A wrinkled smile formed across her lips, and she looked me in the eye. "He was friendly with the Utes, he knew their language, and the chief knew he wouldn't take more than he needed."

"Wow," I said. The hairs on my arms straightened. "So do you really believe in the curse?"

"Well, whether or not there's really a curse, I don't know. But I believe the gold is protected. For what reason, I'm not sure. But there've been many, many deaths in those mountains, and anyone who's ever tried to take or find the gold in greed ends up dying or disappearing. It's not a coincidence."

I leaned in closer. "Dying and disappearing? Like who?"

"Enoch Rhoades."

I was startled out of the conversation by the gentle pressure of two large hands on my shoulders. I jumped and whirled around to see Dad laughing at my reaction. "You ready to go?" he asked me and then spoke to Ethel. "It's good to see you again. Thanks for entertaining my daughter."

"Bye, Aunt Ethel." I stood and gave my newfound friend a squeeze. "Thanks for all the information. Hope to see you around."

"Take care. Don't break too many hearts." She gave a wink.

★   ★   ★   ★

When we returned home, I was still full from the luncheon, but I headed straight for the trunk in the family room. I lifted the lid and searched for the locket, but came across a crispy, yellowed handwritten letter from Enoch Rhoades, to Thomas Jr., his brother. "July 7th, 1885. Dear Brother . . ." I read a few lines and smiled at his unique handwriting and the personality that jumped from the pages. Under the letter was a pedigree chart stating that Enoch had died in September of 1884 at the age of twenty-three.

Wait a minute. This letter, written in his own handwriting, was dated after his supposed death. *Could the official records be wrong? Did Enoch write the wrong year on his letter?* Whatever the case, I gathered from the letter that it had been written while he was in the mountains looking for gold, and he had anticipated his return home in the fall. Suddenly, this short letter took on a much greater meaning.

A mental image of the locket flashed through my mind, and I plunged through the trunk of treasures. I pulled out large stacks of papers and dropped them to the ground, until the entire trunk was empty. But it was gone. I sighed.

"Is something wrong?" Dad asked. He sat behind me on the couch and picked up a newspaper.

"Not really. I just can't find the locket I put in here."

"I think your mom put it in with the other jewelry from Grandpa's house. Try checking on her dresser."

I jumped up and ran for the door.

Dad cleared his throat. "You're welcome."

"Thanks, Dad," I called over my shoulder.

I sprinted up the stairs to their room and found the jewelry box on the dresser. I studied its unique craftsmanship: the faded mahogany, the oxidized brass fastener in the front, and the design carved into its top. I lifted the lid and found an assortment of old jewelry. My fingers ran over several old necklaces, bracelets, and an old watch. The jewelry sat in velvet-lined trays, which could be lifted to reveal another layer of jewelry underneath. I sorted through the ancient stuff, some of which was surely valuable and other pieces that were simply costume jewelry from the sixties. There was a ruby necklace, an old ring, brass keys, and . . . the locket!

It was about the size of a silver dollar and was made of black, oxidized silver. An eagle with its wings spread and talons just touching the tip of a rock was delicately engraved on the outside. Inside were pictures of the gentleman and his wife who I'd seen previously in the album, only many years younger. I closed the locket, fastened it around my neck, and smoothed it over my breastbone.

The leather diary came to mind. *What information was locked in its pages? When and how did Enoch really die? What had Grandpa wanted to tell me?* I was determined to find the answers.

CHAPTER 3

★ ★ ★ ★ ★

The weekend after the funeral was Brandi Manning's wedding reception. She and her twin had been my best friends growing up, but we'd lost touch with each other since starting college.

Before I could attend, I needed to buy a gift for the new couple and a dress for me. After all, I'd be seeing people at the reception tonight that I hadn't seen in a few years, and I wanted to look my best. Luckily, I worked at one of the many Tanger Outlet stores, and I was sure I'd have no problem finding what I needed.

During my lunch break, I walked the aisles of a bed and bath store and searched for just the right gift. I was trying to decide between bath towels or scented candles when I overheard a conversation between two women the next aisle over.

"Did you hear about what happened in Price?"

"No, what?"

"Someone broke into the museum and totally demolished part of it. The police are looking for a guy named Chet Strong—at least, I think that's his name. Anyway, the police . . ."

Chet Strong? I know I've heard that name somewhere.

I would've put more thought into the matter, but I was having a hard enough time deciding what gift would be best for the new bride and groom. Procrastination, coupled with waiting for payday, had led me to put off shopping until today, just a few hours before the reception.

Finally, I decided to get both bath towels and scented candles, and I waited in line for what seemed like hours to purchase my items. I glanced at my watch. My lunch break was nearly over. I'd have to look for a dress after work.

I had planned to attend the reception that night with my parents. However, after working extra hours to fill in for a recently vacated position and purchasing a new outfit after work, I didn't get back home until they were heading out the door.

"Sorry," Mom said. "We'd wait for you, but we've got to leave right now. Dad's got a meeting tonight."

"That's all right." I took a moment to admire what a cute couple my parents still were. "I don't want to hold you guys up. I'll meet you there in a little while."

I ran upstairs to my room and donned my recently purchased outfit. I was lucky to have found a midnight-blue satin top with coordinating knee-length chiffon skirt and a pair of dressy sandals at the first store I went to. I freshened up in the bathroom and glanced at myself in the mirror.

The freckles of my youth had faded to a small sprinkle on my slightly upturned nose, and the blouse's color brought out the deep blue of my eyes. I'd once thought the stubborn ringlets in my long golden hair were a curse, but eventually came to accept them.

I was anxious to see my friend Brandi, but my thoughts constantly drifted to her tall, dark, and handsome older brother, Derek, who I'd heard was still single. It was amazing that I was even thinking about other guys after breaking up with Ron. Maybe I just wanted to fill the void I felt not having a significant other in my life, or maybe I was genuinely interested in moving on.

I glanced at my watch. Wow, I'd spent far too much time in front of the mirror. I'd already missed part of the reception, and I wanted to arrive before the receiving line ended. I grabbed my already-wrapped wedding gift off of the kitchen counter, along with my car keys and wallet, and ran to my car parked in the driveway.

But I stopped in my tracks when I saw the deflated tire on my car's front left side. Had I hit something in the gutter when I drove around Bugzy? I rubbed my forehead. If I waited for Mom and Dad to return, the receiving line would be over.

I grabbed the tire iron out of the trunk, but when I tried to loosen the bolts, they were stuck. I tugged and pulled on each one, even pressing with my body weight, but they wouldn't budge. I threw the tire iron back in the trunk and sighed.

Then I remembered Dad's SUV was parked in the garage. I sprinted to the closet where he kept his keys, but it was empty. He must've taken them with him. I felt a little panicked and wasn't exactly sure what next to do. I ran back outside, hoping something would come to me.

Then I had a thought. I'd just walk, even if it would take twenty minutes. I picked up my gift and started down the street. After a couple blocks, my feet started to notice the pinch of my new shoes. I glanced at the shiny black pickup truck driving slowly down the road and was half tempted to hitch a ride. Then I heard a horn behind me.

"Sister Rhoades, do you need a lift?" Brother Whitman said. He sat in the driver's seat of his blue sedan and was dressed in Sunday attire. His wife carried a neatly wrapped gift on her lap.

"Yes, are you going to the reception?"

"Sure am."

"Thank you." I lifted the door handle and hopped inside.

"We've missed you the past couple of years on our campout at Strawberry." Brother Whitman's middle-aged eyes glanced at me through the rear view mirror. "Are you coming with us this year?"

The handful of families, whose yearly tradition was to

camp and fish together, would be expecting me. Ron was supposed to come with me this year, but now I'd be alone. I could just hear all the questions I'd be asked.

"Where's your boyfriend?"

In Logan.

"You broke up?"

Yes.

"Why?"

"He's a toad!" Whoops. Did I just say that out loud?

Sister Whitman turned around to look at me. Not one bleached hair in her stiffly sprayed hairdo moved, but she seemed to know what was on my mind. "Everyone has experienced a break up at one time or another. If you're having doubts about going, just remember that it may be nice for you to get away and think about things."

I had to admit she made a good point. Besides, I really could use a vacation.

★   ★   ★   ★

I had always loved Deer Valley, which stood majestically overlooking Park City's south side. How fortunate that Brandi's family happened to live there in a home no smaller than a spacious mansion and could use their breathtaking backyard for the reception.

I stepped under a trellis of flowering vines and onto a stone path that wound its way through a mini-forest of aspens and flowers at the base of a hillside. Trickling water and the soft murmur of laughter and voices filled my ears even before I completed my journey through the aspens.

The stone path led me to an elegant table draped in lace and decorated with a lovely picture of the bride and groom, as well as a guest book and pen. Morgan, Brandi's sister, was sitting at the table dressed in yellow chiffon. Her long, dark hair was draped atop her lovely head.

She greeted me with a hug and a warm smile. We talked

and reminisced awhile before she found an usher to take my gift. I strolled to the end of the long line of guests, who eagerly waited their turn to congratulate the bride and groom. Unfortunately, the throng of people obstructed my entire view of the receiving line and any sign of Derek.

I turned around to take in the beauty around me and glanced at the guests conversing at lace-topped tables as they ate their refreshments. I looked for Mom and Dad but couldn't see them anywhere. They must've already left.

My eyes wandered to the food table and the abundance of chicken salad croissants, fruit platters, veggie trays, and choco-late-dipped strawberries. My stomach growled so loudly that it caught the attention of the people standing next to me.

Then I spotted Derek, wearing a black tux, which set off his dark hair and tall, muscular frame. He filled his cup from the silver punch fountain at the end of the food table. When his cup was full, he guzzled it down, and then held it under the pink waterfall again.

Other than filling out a little, he'd hardly changed since I'd last seen him. My heart skipped a beat. I wondered if he'd even notice me; he never had before. Then his eyes locked onto mine, and for a moment I couldn't breathe. But instead of striding toward me and sweeping me off my feet, he merely smiled and began to fill another cup. My lips drooped.

Suddenly, he looked up at me again, this time with a dropped jaw. His overflowing goblet dropped to the table and landed on its side. He didn't notice. Instead, he strolled over to me. I wiped my wet palms on the sides of my chiffon skirt. It wasn't very absorbent, but it helped.

"Lexi Rhoades, is that you?" He gave me a hug and then stepped back to look at me. His honey-colored eyes seemed to like what they saw. "What've you been up to?"

"I just finished my second year at Utah State. Right now I'm working at the Tanger Outlet for the summer." I was relieved I didn't stumble all over my words. "What about you?"

"I started my own business. Maybe you've heard of it: 'Sew What Embroidery and Design.' I used to run it here in Park City, but I've since moved it to Lindon in Utah County. I have an apartment down there now."

"Sew What Embroidery and Design?" I asked. I couldn't picture him sitting in a rocking chair with an embroidery hoop in one hand and a needle in another, designing pillowcases. He must've noticed the look on my face.

"It's not what you think. I spend most of the time on the computer, digitizing and designing the work. Then it's fed into the computerized embroidery machines, which do all the work. We put logos on lots of things like hats, golf bags, shirts, and the like. We even do heat pressing on uniforms and other things; it doesn't crack like silk screening . . . Hey, last I heard you were dating someone pretty seriously."

"Actually, we broke up," I said without as much as a lump in my throat.

"That's too bad. I was engaged, but it didn't work out. Looks like we're in similar boats . . . I have to get back in the receiving line before Brandi kills me for taking so long. Maybe we can get together sometime and talk."

"I'd enjoy that." My smile was wide.

"Good. I'll give you a call. See you later." He winked then squeezed my arm and disappeared out of vision.

Did he just say he was going to ask me out? I tried to suppress a giggle, but it came out anyway. Luckily, only three people gave me strange looks.

From that moment on, I was in a total daze. I worked my way down the line, but I had no recollection of speaking with Brother and Sister Manning, or the parents of the groom. I only assumed I must've shaken their hands and spoken with them when I found myself standing in front of Brandi.

We greeted each other with a big hug; we hadn't seen each other in such a long time. I was supposed to be filled with joy for her on her happy day, but I just couldn't believe the warm reception from Derek. *Poor Brandi and her new husband—what's his name?* Hopefully, they couldn't tell I was only pretending to listen to what they were saying.

"Hi again," Derek said when it was my turn to greet him in line. We shook hands, but instead of releasing mine, he kept it in his. "Is your number in the phone book?"

"Yes, under Jonathan Rhoades."

"Great, I'll give you a call." He gave my hand one last squeeze before he turned to the people behind me in line. My heart was about to jump right out of me.

I extended a hand toward the attractive guy next in line, but he didn't take it. Instead, he took me in his muscular arms. Before I had time to contemplate why he would give me a hug, and an affectionate one at that, he spoke. "Lex, it's been way too long."

"Brad?" I recognized the voice of Brandi's twin brother, though it was deeper and more mature. I pulled away and strained to find any resemblance between the man before me and the lanky, thick-glasses-wearing Brad stored in my memory banks. There was none. "What happened?" I asked. The words poured from my mouth before I could stop them.

He laughed and pointed to his eyes. "I had laser surgery, and I filled out a little on my mission." Usually when a missionary says he's "filled out," he means he put on a few extra pounds of fat, not muscle.

"So, when did you get back?" I asked.

"A few months ago, from Taiwan."

"Taiwan?" I imagined his sun-streaked hair and aquamarine eyes must've stood out in the crowd.

"Yes." His eyes lingered on my features before he said, "Maybe I'll see you around. Catch up on old times."

"Sounds like fun." I turned around and greeted the rest of the line, then found the refreshment table. After I'd gotten a plate of a chicken croissant, fruit, veggies, and a couple chocolate-dipped strawberries, I took a seat at a vacant table.

I bit into my sandwich and was startled when Brad straddled the chair beside me. "I need a little break. Mind if I join you?"

"No, not at all." I broke off another chunk of sandwich and stuffed it in my mouth.

"I'm sorry about your grandpa. How've you been doing?"

I shrugged. "It's weird. I thought I'd feel better and better every day, and generally I do, but sometimes I just break down."

"It's not weird. I think that's normal. I did the same thing with my grandpa." His eyes shifted to my collar. "Your necklace is nice. Is it an antique?"

I glanced down at the locket. "Yes, I found it when I was cleaning out my grandpa's attic. It looks a lot nicer now that I've polished it."

A loud whistle broke our conversation, and Brother Manning spoke. "It's time for Brandi to toss her bouquet to all the eligible ladies."

Brad nudged my arm. "Does that include you?"

"No . . . I mean, it does. I just don't want to."

"Why not?"

I swallowed a gulp of water. "I'm not looking for marriage right now, and I'd rather eat."

"Come on, I'll save your dinner. You should go out there." He practically pushed me from my seat, and when someone else tugged at my arm, I finally relented.

I met up with the herd of females in Sunday dress and waited for the bouquet. Brandi looked over her shoulder and smiled at me, then dipped low and flung the flowers over her head. They sailed through the air toward my arms.

The blur of a hefty girl flashed in my peripheral vision. Before I could even think, she bowled right into me, and everything went black.

"Wake up, Lex. Are you okay?" Brad patted my cheek with his hand.

My eyes fluttered open. I was lying face down in the grass with the bouquet just inches from my fist. A crowd of people whispered around me.

"Is she okay?"

"What happened?"

"Someone trampled her."

"She must've really wanted that bouquet."

Derek shooed people away while Brad and the female linebacker responsible for my aching jaw helped me to my feet.

"I think you need to sit for a minute," Brad said. He handed me the bouquet and led me by the arm to the nearest table.

I blinked the stars and dots from my eyes and rubbed the ache in my jaw.

"How's your jaw?" he asked.

"It hurts, but I think it'll be okay after awhile." I brought the fresh flowers to my nose. "I love flowers."

"You must. Even unconscious you wouldn't let her take them."

I laughed. "I don't remember catching them, or even wanting to."

"Maybe your subconscious took over before you blacked out completely."

Derek rushed to the table with a glass of water and set it down in front of me. "Are you okay?" he asked.

"I'm fine."

He scooted out the chair next to me and was about to sit when Brad said to me, "You still look a little pale. I think I should take you home. I'd be worried about you driving."

"I'll take her home," Derek said before I had a chance to reply.

Brad's eyes didn't move from his brother's. "Aren't you on the car decorating committee?"

"You can take my place."

"Actually," I said, "I hitched a ride with the Whitmans when I found out my car had a flat tire."

Just then, Derek's fellow committee members approached him from behind and dragged him off.

Brad's eyes looked over my features. "I can take a look at your tire."

I looked behind me. Derek was about to cover Brandi's car with a roll of toilet paper. "Okay," I said. "You can look at my tire."

"Good, I'll go talk with the Whitmans."

When he returned, he led me to a beautiful sports car. Its metallic flecks shimmered in the gold sun. "Wow, when did you get this? It reminds me of a Porsche."

He beamed. "I picked it up last week. It took me awhile to save the cash for it and to wait for just the right deal when it came. But it's only a year old and hardly has any miles on it." He opened the door and helped me into the passenger seat.

"It's a year old? It looks brand new." I looked around to admire the interior.

"It looks brand new, but it doesn't depreciate like it's brand new. I find I can get a better deal on a slightly used vehicle, yet still have a nice car."

"Your folks didn't buy it for you?"

He chuckled. "No, Mom and Dad have always had us work for our own things." He stood just outside the driver's door, removed his tux jacket and tie, and tossed them into the backseat. "I don't know about you," he said after he climbed into the driver's seat and started the engine, "but I'm starving. I could've eaten the whole tray of those little chicken things, but I only had four. Do you want to get a bite to eat?"

"I'd love to."

After we'd entered The Eating Establishment on historic Main, we took a seat by the window and ordered. I was only a little hungry so I ordered a salad and water, but Brad ordered a huge sandwich with a side of fries and coleslaw.

"What was your mission like?" I swallowed a bite of the salad, which was large enough to fill three famished people.

"It was a lot of hard work. There were a lot of Buddhists. Their beliefs are so different from ours that it was a challenge to explain the gospel. But the most frustrating part was that although people were interested, they seldom were baptized because of the repercussions. Like families disowning them and job demotions."

"Oh, that's awful. I couldn't imagine how hard it would be to know that if I was baptized my family would disown me."

There was a moment's pause in the conversation, and he looked thoughtfully at the condensation running down the side of his drink. "I could almost say it was the best two years of my life."

"Why almost?"

His look into my eyes was sobering. "I found that someone I cared a great deal about was in a serious relationship."

"Who, me?" I knew he'd liked me—even adored me—in the past. His younger sister, Morgan, had revealed that little piece of information when she'd taken a shower and found, "Brad + Lexi" written in the steamed mirror. But that was years ago. I never thought it'd carry over into his mission.

"So, are you still dating that Rob guy?"

"You mean Ron? We broke up, and our relationship wasn't that serious."

"That's not what I heard."

My eyes shifted from his to the handful of tourists walking Main Street, then to my plate. I tried to stab a little tomato with my fork without it hopping onto the table. "What've you been doing since your mission?" I hoped to take the attention from my relationship with Ron. Plus, I was curious.

His eyes scoped me for a second before he answered. "I've been going to BYU, business major. Right now, I'm doing construction here in Park City to earn some cash for school."

"So that's why your hair's lighter than what I remember."

He smiled. "Yes, I've spent a lot of time outside lately. What about you?"

"I'm studying history at Utah State, and I'm working at the Tanger Outlet during the summer to earn extra money."

Brad looked serious for a moment and asked, "What happened with Ron, anyway? If you don't mind me asking."

My eyes couldn't meet his, and I went back to my salad. This time it was a cucumber that I wrestled with. "I didn't intend on dating him seriously, but he was a lot of fun. Before I knew it, I was starting to fall in love with him. I thought he felt the same for me, but . . . he was dating someone else." I was impressed I didn't get emotional.

"I'm sorry you had to go through that." He placed his hand over mine and gave it a squeeze. A smile crossed his face, and he looked at my lips. "Looks like you have a little bit of salad dressing on the corner of your mouth. Here, let me get it for you." He grabbed a napkin and began to wipe.

How embarrassing. He moved the napkin to my cheek, my cheekbone, and finally wiped my forehead. I set down my fork and smiled. "Okay, the joke's up. Do I really have salad dressing on my face?"

He flashed a white smile. "No, I just wanted to see the look on your face."

"Was it worth it?"

"Every moment."

★　　★　　★　　★

We enjoyed a pleasant conversation on the way home. Although I was still in a bit of shock over the changes he'd gone through, the comfort of our friendship wrapped around me like a warm blanket. I felt light and happy—feelings I hadn't experienced in ages, but they were short-lived.

When we turned the corner into my cul-de-sac, the flicker of red and blue police lights lit the night sky in front of my home. Brad darted around Bugzy, and had almost come to a complete stop when I jumped out of the car. Mom and Officer Reynolds, Dad's good friend, were standing by the police car, talking. I couldn't see Dad, and I didn't like the look on Mom's face.

"Where's Dad? Did something happen to him?"

"Lexi!" Mom threw her arms around me.

I was vaguely aware of Brad's hand on my shoulder. "Where's Dad? Is he okay?" I asked.

"Dad?" Mom seemed puzzled. "He's inside on the phone trying to find you."

"Me?"

"Where have you been?" Mom's stern look made me feel like a young child again.

"I was at Brandi's reception. Brad offered to take me home, but we stopped to get something to eat. What's going on?"

Just then, Dad came out of the house. Relief washed over his face when he saw me. He dashed over and gave me a big hug. "Thank goodness you're home! We expected to see you at the reception but never did. Then when we came home and found your car tires slashed and you nowhere in sight, we thought something happened to you. Are you okay?"

"Wait a minute, did you say my tires are slashed?" I'd been so worried about Dad that I hadn't even looked at my car. Sure enough, there were four flat tires, although in the dark they looked more like black puddles oozing from the wheels.

I spoke in quiet words. "When I left there was only one flat tire. I couldn't change it, so I rode to the reception with the Whitmans." I leaned down and felt the long, angry slits etched in one of the tires. Goose bumps formed along my arms and legs.

"Who did this?" I asked.

The crease between Dad's eyes deepened, and he stared at the pavement. "We'll find out, sweetie," he said. But there was something odd about the shift in his eyes and the tone of his voice. I had a feeling he knew more than he was telling me.

CHAPTER 4

★ ★ ★ ★ ★

To say I had a peaceful rest that night wouldn't be truthful. Between the dreams of Derek, the chill of someone slicing my tires, and the fact that it was an unusually hot night, I hardly slept at all. It was nearly dawn when I finally unwound enough to sleep, but a repetitive noise kept me from sleeping as soundly as I would've liked. It was the phone.

I pried open my eyelids and wondered who would call so early on a Saturday. I pulled the pillow around my ears. Why hadn't anybody answered the phone? I glanced at the clock beside my bed: 7:00 AM. Mom and Dad had gone to an early morning session at the Salt Lake Temple. I squeezed my eyes closed and buried my head in my pillow. I was sure that whoever it was would give up, but the phone wouldn't stop. I dragged myself out of bed and padded into the den to reach the phone. "Hello?" I said.

Silence.

"Hello?"

Still silence.

I hung up the receiver, shuffled back to my room, and climbed back into the inviting covers. I was completely exhausted and had little trouble getting back to sleep. I don't remember what I dreamt, but at least it wasn't a nightmare about my car tires being slashed.

Then the constant, steady ring of the telephone woke me again. I tried to shut it out, to pull my pillow tight enough around my ears to block out the noise, but it still rang.

I climbed out of bed a little quicker this time—7:24 AM. Why would someone call so early on Saturday, after I'd had little to no sleep? Didn't they know?

"Hello?" I asked.

Silence.

"Hello!" My voice sounded more like a dog barking than a human. When there was no answer, I hung up the phone and wandered back to bed, mumbling something negative about telemarketers.

I must've dozed off again, because the next thing I remembered was the phone ringing again. This time, I was determined to give whoever it was a piece of my mind. I ripped off my bedcovers, stomped to the den, and grabbed the phone. "What!"

"Uh . . . Lexi? This is Derek. Did I, uh . . . get you at a bad time?"

The intake of air into my mouth was audible. "I'm so sorry. I thought you were someone else. You didn't by chance call a few minutes ago, did you?"

"No, I didn't want to call before nine."

"Nine?" I must've slept later than I thought.

"I heard about what happened to your car last night. Are you okay?" The concern in his voice was a welcome sound.

"I'm fine. I just hope tire slashing is counted as a road hazard under my insurance policy."

"Right. I know this is short notice, and I don't know if you'd be up to it, but I was wondering if you were free tonight to go do something."

"I'd love to." I did a silent jig.

"How's 6:30?"

"Great, I'll see you then."

I hung up the phone and started dancing back to my room

when I was startled with the realization that I needed to be to work in twenty minutes. I set a new world record for getting showered, dressed, and out the door with an apple and a blueberry muffin to eat on the way. Dad's SUV would be my transportation since my car was slightly incapacitated at the moment. At least I had his keys.

When I opened the door that led to the garage, I froze. In the darkness, the interior light glowed from inside the vehicle. My heart pounded. Had my tires not been slashed the night before, the sight of the dome light on wouldn't have frightened me, but now it did. Someone could've recently opened the door. They could be in the garage with me at this moment. I thought about calling the police, but I could just picture the looks on their faces when I called in a panic saying, "Help! The dome light is on in my SUV! Come right away!"

I decided to wait to see if the light turned off. If it did, then I would know that the door had recently been opened, and I could start to panic. If it stayed on, then the door didn't get shut all the way the last time it was opened, which could've been a couple of hours ago. My eyes stayed glued to the dome light for the longest minute of my life, and I was relieved when it stayed on.

I grabbed my keys and poked one key through each space between my clenched fingers, to give a mean punch if needed. My heart pounded so loudly I could hardly hear the birds outside. I ran to the vehicle, did a quick check of the interior to make sure no one was hiding in the back, and left marks on the garage floor from pealing out in reverse.

On the way to work, I chided myself for being so paranoid. I realized that Dad sometimes kept his wallet in the glove box in the SUV and would have needed it for the temple. I'd let a silly thing panic me, and I was determined to not let it happen again.

By the time I pulled into the parking lot for work, my breathing and heart rate had returned to normal. But when I dashed toward the building and nearly crashed into the black pickup truck circling the parking lot, my heart rate was higher than ever.

"Sorry I'm late," I said after I'd entered the store.

Ashley, my manager, always wore her dishwater-blond hair pulled into a ponytail and had a permanent tan line from her sunglasses. If she was perturbed at my lack of punctuality, she gave no sign. "Hey, Lexi, this is Kirsten. She's our new girl." She nodded toward the woman I'd noticed standing near her.

"Nice to meet you." I extended my hand toward hers, but it was hard not to notice her long, silky brown hair and striking looks.

"You too."

Kirsten was a natural when it came to helping customers and working the cash register, and since we'd been short a person the past couple of weeks, it was nice to have her help. She quickly became chummy with Jessica, a coworker of mine, whose shoulder-length blond hair stood in contrast to Kirsten's. I let Jessica take over the training, and the two of them chatted endlessly and took special interest in all the eye-catching male customers.

After lunch, I found it increasingly more difficult to concentrate on work. My thoughts were consumed with the events of last night and this morning. I thought of the tire slashing. Why would someone slice my tires? Was it merely because my car was conveniently parked in the driveway? It wasn't as if it had a sign taped to the back that read, "Come slash my tires, I need new ones anyway." Or was it more than that?

I couldn't believe Derek actually asked me out. I guess part of me expected him to think of me as that pre-adolescent girl with knobby knees and freckles who—

" . . . on sale too? Hello? . . . Miss?" A short, middle-aged woman waved a pair of jeans in front of my face. She looked a little perturbed. "Are these jeans on sale too?"

"Uh, yeah. They're 20 percent off." My face grew a little warm. How long had she been trying to get my attention? I looked at my watch and was relieved to see I only had thirty minutes left until it was time for me to rush home and get ready for my date. I wondered what the night would hold.

★   ★   ★   ★

I flew into the house at 6:25, waved to my parents, and ran upstairs. I had five minutes to freshen up before my date. I threw on my silver and charcoal speckled blouse, put on a fresh layer of deodorant, combed through my hair, brushed my teeth, and dabbed on some perfume. The doorbell rang at 6:30.

I dashed to the top of the stairs and then curtailed my speed when I heard Derek's voice. I strolled downstairs to find Dad and Derek conversing at the front door. I snuck up beside Dad and slipped an arm around him. "I didn't have a chance to tell you, but Derek and I are going out tonight," I said.

He smiled at me and then narrowed his eyes toward Derek. "Yes, he mentioned that, but I didn't get a chance to ask him where you're going and when he'll have my daughter safely home."

Derek straightened his casual, pale green, button down shirt. "We're going to Texas Red's, and then we're going down the Alpine Slide and playing a round of miniature golf at the Park City Mountain Resort. I'll have her back by 11:00."

Derek handed me a bouquet of roses he'd held by his side. "These are for you."

"Oh, thank you. They're so beautiful." I brought them to my nose and took in their scent. "Mmmm, I'll go put them in water."

When I returned, Mom entered the room and shook Derek's hand. "I'm glad you two are going out. I know Lexi must be thrilled." She turned to me and winked. I needed to call the fire department to put the flame in my cheeks out.

Derek led me out to his new, silver BMW. "You look really nice; you even match my car," he said to me when he'd opened the passenger door. I glanced down at my blouse and sure enough, the color was remarkably similar.

"Thank you," I said.

We chatted about a variety of things on the drive to Park City's historic Old Main, where we'd find Texas Red's. Okay, maybe our topic of conversation didn't vary much from the weather, sports, and the weather again, but it was still interesting.

Parallel parking in front of the restaurant was packed, and we ended up with a two and a half block hike to the place. Fortunately, the little walk was quite enjoyable, and the evening temperature was perfect.

Once we were seated at our checker-clothed table, the time passed quickly before we were served our meals. The tantalizing smell of BBQ ribs nearly made me drool in front of my date. I took several bites of my dinner then decided to ask Derek something that'd been on my mind since Brandi's wedding.

I sipped my water and cleared my throat. "You mentioned that you were engaged. When was that?"

He wiped his face with a napkin and studied it after he'd placed it on the table. "A couple months ago." His honey-colored eyes searched me before he opened his mouth and shut it again. Finally, he said, "Truthfully, I was nervous about getting married. Sometimes we didn't get along very well, and I have a lot of friends who've already been married and divorced. I didn't want to end up like them." His eyes wandered over my face. "But enough about me, I can't get over how much you've changed."

I dropped my fork. "Changed? Good or bad?"

"Good, of course." He studied the outline of my hair and face. "Really good."

I choked on my food. "Oh, thank you."

He reached across the table and squeezed my elbow. A warm sensation emanated from his hand and climbed up my arm. I couldn't believe this was happening to me. A couple weeks ago I had thought my life was over. Now it felt like it was just beginning. I needed to send Ron a thank-you note.

When dinner was finished, Derek helped me out of my seat and then led me through the hungry patrons waiting by the door. I followed close behind him and had nearly made it to the exit, when someone bumped into me from behind. I stumbled into Derek, who looked back at me with a patient smile. A glance behind my shoulder didn't reveal anyone who looked guilty for ramming into me.

We started our evening of recreation playing miniature golf. Derek must've been a pro golfer, scoring at or under par at each hole. I felt a little "golfing-challenged" in comparison, but he was very patient with me.

Throughout the course, my skills improved. Toward one of the last holes, we had to hit the ball up a hill and into its hole. Derek held the club between his hands, aimed, and hit the ball with a little more force than he'd used before. He made a hole in one.

I did my best to mimic what I'd just seen in order to get the ball somewhat close to the hole. I took my time, brought back the club, and hit the ball. It rolled partway up the hill then came back down again.

Derek stopped the ball with his club and handed it to me. "Why don't you have another try?"

I tried again, two more times, but the ball refused to cooperate.

"Try hitting it a little harder this time. You can do it." He patted my back and stepped aside.

I positioned the ball, brought back the club, and whacked it hard. The ball whizzed through the air. Derek ducked out of its way, but the innocent bystander several feet behind him wasn't so lucky. It nailed him in the chest with a thud.

My hand flew to my mouth. "I'm so sorry," I said.

The tall, angry-looking man with shaggy black hair, a goatee, and sunglasses just opened his mouth and closed it again. He picked up the ball and threw it back at me with such force, it burned my hands for several minutes afterward.

After we'd finished the last hole and returned our clubs, we walked to the tram for the Alpine Slide. It looked like four long, cement snakes twisting and turning down the mountain's side. I watched the people in front of us board the lift that took them to the top of the slide and was reminded, by the knot in my stomach, of my fear of heights.

I wiped my hands on my pants and climbed aboard. I was relieved that I'd had no major incidents with boarding the lift, like when I was thirteen and bent to latch a ski-boot and was smacked in the behind by the tram. But as my feet grew farther away from the earth below, I began to feel the signs of my fear of heights. My hands grew moist, my breathing became more rapid, and I held onto the thick bar across me like my life depended on it.

I tried to enjoy the scenery and happened to glance behind us. The man with the shaggy black hair sat two seats behind us on the tram. He didn't look too happy, but there was something familiar about his hair.

"Are you okay?" Derek motioned toward my white knuckles that gripped the bar across us.

"I, uh . . . I'm fine."

"You're sure?"

I could feel a vibration in the tram, and I wondered if it was from my trembling. "Actually, I get a little nervous in high places."

He placed a hand over mine. "You'll be fine. We're almost there."

When my legs touched solid ground, I was greatly relieved. We each grabbed a sled and walked the tree-lined path to the slides. We took the two slides on the far right and mounted our sleds at the same time. After we'd listened to the instructions on how to use the brake, I turned to Derek and mouthed, "Do you want to race?"

The shocked look on his face was priceless. "You're on," he said.

We both took off down the hill, slower at first, but then more quickly as we gained momentum. The wind blew through my hair, streaks of trees flew past me, and I was filled with a rush of adrenaline.

I glanced over to see if I could place him and found that I was slightly ahead. A bend in the track was coming up, and I needed to use a little more caution. I pulled slightly on the brake and looked again for Derek. I couldn't tell where he was, but I was able to see black, shaggy hair on the slide not too far behind me. I leaned forward and let off my brake.

I looked again for Derek. He was ahead of me, but I gained on him when I straightened. I neared a sharp turn and pulled back on the brake again. I didn't want to jump the track, which I'd heard happened a time or two when caution was ignored. Derek's head was visible from the next track over, but I also noticed the shaggy-haired man getting closer behind me.

When the track straightened out again, I rode my sled full throttle, partly for fun and partly because of the creepy man who was now just inches behind me. I went airborne on a jump, something I'd never actually done before, and leaned forward to make myself as aerodynamic as possible.

The final turn was just ahead. I didn't dare ride the corner without applying the brake a little, but the thoughts of "Shaggy" right behind me caused bravery I didn't know I had. I squeezed my eyes shut; I knew I was going to fly off the track, and I didn't want to see it happen. Moments later, the track straightened out, and I was still on it. I opened my eyes. I was near the end and had just passed Derek.

I slowed to a stop, dismounted, and had just grabbed my sled, when Derek pulled to a stop.

"I can't believe I beat you," I said. "How did I get ahead of you?"

His smile was wide. "I thought I had you beat, but toward the end, you flew past me. I've never seen anyone ride that fast."

"Actually, some rude guy was egging me to go faster than I would've liked around that last turn." I looked to the slide I'd dismounted, fully expecting to see Shaggy coming to a stop and was surprised to see instead, a gentleman with a little girl in his lap.

"Was he the guy egging you on?" Derek asked.

"No, the guy I saw was the one I pelted with the golf ball . . . but he's gone."

He looked at me then at the slide. I didn't know what was running through his mind, but I wondered if he was beginning to think his date was loony. "Hmm. I don't see anyone. . . . Shall we go?" He extended his arm.

I took his arm and looked along the mountainside. There was no sign of Shaggy anywhere.

The rest of the evening was uneventful. Derek and I talked at a park, and when it was time to go home he walked me to the door. The sun had long disappeared behind the mountains, and a chill filled the night air. He took a step closer and smiled.

"What is it?" I asked.

"I still can't believe how fast you came down that slide. I've never seen anyone fly like that before."

"Well, it helps to have a weirdo behind you giving you added momentum." I ran my hands over the goose bumps on my arms. I didn't think to bring a jacket.

"Would it be all right if I gave you a hug good night? You look a little cold." He placed his arms around me and my shivers faded, but my mind started to race. Who was Shaggy, and where had I seen that hair before? It kind of looked like professor Snape's hair in Harry Potter, but a little bushier. It was almost like . . .

"Johnny Lingo!" I yelled. I was surprised to hear the name jump from my lips.

He pulled away with a confused expression. "Excuse me?"

"Sorry, I was just wondering where I'd seen the shaggy black hair before. I figured it out. It's like Mahana's dad's hair in the original *Johnny Lingo* movie. I used to make fun of those awful wigs in seminary. The man with the shaggy, black hair was wearing a wig!"

"That sounds odd. Why would someone wear a wig down the Alpine Slide?"

"I don't know. Maybe he's bald or something. Or maybe he was upset that I hit him with the golf ball and wanted to give me a piece of his mind."

Derek smiled. "He did look a little upset. But are you sure you saw him on the slide? We never saw him get off."

My brow furrowed. "Hmm."

He took my hand and gave it a squeeze. "I had a really great time tonight. We'll have to go out again."

A grin spread across my face. "I'd love to."

He walked to his car and drove away. Goose bumps climbed my arms again. I'd finally figured out that Shaggy's hair was a wig, but there was some other place I'd seen it, and it wasn't the movie *Johnny Lingo*. It was Texas Red's.

CHAPTER 5

★ ★ ★ ★ ★

I'd never looked forward to the Sabbath and the rest I hoped to receive as much as I did the next day. After church, I went to my room and crashed on the fluffy pillows that covered my bed. Images of Derek, Grandpa Rhoades, Shaggy, and my tires bounced around my mind until I fell into a fitful sleep.

A soft knock on my bedroom door awoke me sometime later. "Are you up?" Dad whispered. "Brad's here."

My eyes popped open. "Brad?" I stopped by the bathroom mirror and gasped at my bloodshot, mascara smeared eyes, and the reddened three-dimensional imprint of a blanket on my left cheek. I wiped the mascara smears from under my eyes, pulled my hair over the mark on my cheek, and darted downstairs.

Brad's smile faded when he saw me. "Did I wake you? I can come back another time."

"No, I was just getting up anyway. So what's going on?"

His slacks and blue dress shirt rolled up at the sleeves brought out the color of his eyes and the darkness of his lashes and brows. Had they always been like that?

". . . who did it yet?"

It took me a second to realize he'd been talking to me. "Sorry, what did you say?"

"I just wanted to see how you were holding up after your tires were slashed. Have the police found who did it?"

"They haven't caught them yet, but they think it's just some neighborhood kids. There's been an increase in vandalism around here since school let out for the summer."

"Dinner's ready," Mom called from the kitchen.

Brad looked at me. "I really did come at a bad time, I'd better go."

"Why don't you stay for dinner?"

"Nah, I shouldn't. Besides, I'm not that hungry."

Mom's voice drifted from the kitchen along with a delicious aroma. "You're welcome to join us, Brad, there's plenty."

"Well, that settles it," I said. "You just got here so you can't leave yet, and I just happen to know that you're always hungry, so you can't use that as an excuse."

He shrugged. "I never could turn you down."

After dinner, Brad and I strolled into the backyard through the gated, wooden fence. The yard wasn't overly large, but it was nicely landscaped. A porch swing was placed in the back corner on a stone patio edged with flowers. Tall aspens provided shade from the west sun.

We strolled to the porch swing and had a seat. Orange and gold lit the sky as the sun made its descent behind the mountains.

After several minutes of peaceful silence, Brad spoke. "What have the police found out about your grandpa?"

"Just that they figure when he came home and saw his place . . . it was too much for his heart."

His hand covered mine in a sympathetic squeeze. "I really am sorry. I wish I could've been there for you when it happened."

"You're here for me now." I returned the squeeze.

He withdrew his hand but studied me with his eyes. "Did you find anything else at his place besides the locket?"

"Lots of family history stuff, pictures, photo albums, a

diary. Apparently, my ancestor had maps to some gold mines in the Uintahs."

"Really? Thomas Rhoades?" He placed a foot on the swing and shifted to face me.

"Yes, have you heard about him?"

"Yeah, he got a bunch of gold from mines in the mountains, but died with the knowledge of their whereabouts still secret. No one has ever been able to find them since."

"Where did you learn so much about my ancestor?"

He shrugged. "I just remember hearing something about it. I wondered if you were related but never thought to ask."

"Before my grandpa died, he said there was something important he needed to tell me. Only he died before I could find out what. It's been driving me crazy."

"Did you find anything interesting in the family history stuff? Maybe there're some clues to the mines."

I scrunched my nose. "I doubt it; I was thinking more along the lines of family history."

"What about the diary. Did you read it?"

"I can't, it's locked, and I have no idea where to even look for the . . ." I sat up straight with widened eyes. "The key, I think I know where it is!"

"Where?"

"In a jewelry box from my grandpa's place. There's a set of old keys, and some of them are tiny enough to fit that lock. Come on, let's go!"

He held onto me so I couldn't move and said, "Wait, I'll race you."

"That's hardly fair." I struggled to free myself, but a smile played across my lips.

"Okay, I'll give you a head start." He let go, and I plummeted to the ground.

He tried not to laugh while extending his hand to me, but he wasn't successful. "Are you all right?"

"I'm fine." I tried to pout, but my smile was too big. While he was looking over me to make sure I wasn't injured, I turned and rushed toward the house. "You said I could have a head start!" I yelled over my shoulder, but in three strides he had passed me and sprinted through the gate.

When I ran to the gate's opening, I expected to see him heading for the front porch, but he was nowhere in sight. I jogged to the front door and opened it. Only the ticking of the clock and Dad turning the next page of his book pierced the silence in the living room.

"Did Brad come in here?" I asked.

Dad glanced up from his book. "No, no one's come in here. Why?"

"Just wondering," I said. I stepped back onto the porch and scanned the yard that was growing darker by the minute. His car was still in the driveway, but he wasn't in it. "Brad, where are you?"

There was no answer.

"Come on. I'm waiting for you."

There was still no answer, so I retraced my steps toward the back gate. A faint noise in the shadows of the dark trees caused my heart to beat a little faster. I tiptoed through the gate and into the backyard.

"RAHR!" Brad yelled and grabbed me from behind.

I screamed so loud that several dogs, including Bugzy, began to bark throughout the neighborhood. "Oh! You . . . You scared the bajeebies out of me!"

He doubled over and clenched his stomach in laughter. "I scared what out of you?"

"The bajeebies."

He laughed even louder. "What are bajeebies, anyway?"

"I don't know, but I don't have them anymore."

"I'm sorry, Lex. I forgot how fun it was to play tricks on you." He stood and wiped tears from his eyes. When he could finally see the serious face I was pretending to have, he tried to stop laughing, but it only worked for about thirty seconds.

I stalked away. He chased me, put his arms on my shoulders, and turned me to face him. "Are you mad? I didn't mean to scare your bajeebies. I was just having fun."

I looked into his teasing eyes, and then to his lips that twitched in the corners in an effort to suppress a smile and be serious. Bubbles of giggles and laughter caught in my throat. I tried to swallow and keep them there, but they burst out of me, and we both spent the next several minutes doubled over in laughter. It wasn't until our stomach muscles ached so much we couldn't breathe that we finally calmed down enough to go into the house.

I led Brad to the trunk in the family room and pulled out the diary. He tried to find a keyless way to open it, but it was impossible to do so without destroying it.

"You say you know where the key is?" he asked. His eyes didn't move from the diary.

"Yes, I'll be right back." I dashed upstairs to the jewelry box and grabbed the little ring of keys. I returned moments later, slightly out of breath. He handed me the diary, and I tried each key that was small enough to fit into the tiny lock. The last one opened the lock and the book.

I turned to the front page and read, "Diary of Wilton Rhoades."

"Wilton Rhoades? Do you know who he was?" he asked.

I looked up and said, "I have no idea."

"What else does it say?"

I flipped to the first page. It was dated July 24, 1887. " 'Tonight I went to a dance in celebration of the Saints coming in Utah. I met a lovely young lady whom I intend to court. Her name is Rachel. We had a wonderful time.'

" 'August 1, 1887—Rachel and I met for a picnic and a stroll around—' "

"Skip into the book more. What does it say?"

I thumbed through several more pages and read,

" 'November 24, 1887—I met Rachel's family and was pleased that her father seemed to take a liking to me. My nerves about asking him for Rachel's hand in marriage have eased somewhat.' "

Brad coerced the diary from my hands. "I didn't think it'd be a romance novel. Is there anything else in here?" He flipped through the pages. "They got married, they had a kid, and another . . ." He flipped through more pages. "Oh, he went hunting for winter meat . . . had another kid . . . hmm."

"What is it?" I asked.

He closed the diary and handed it back to me. "I was just hoping it'd have some gold hunting stories or something."

"Well, I happen to think the love story's cute." I skipped to the end of the diary and read through a few lines. "But if you're interested in gold hunting, you might like this. 'October 10, 1895, went poking around the mountains a couple weeks ago while I was hunting. I knew I was close to where the cave was supposed to be, but it must have been well-hidden.' Then a little lower it says, 'August 15th, 1903—I finally found the cave. It's completely indescribable. Rachel and the kids shall not want for the rest of their lives.' "

"What else?"

I skimmed through more lines and read, " 'December 5, 1906—My secret has been discovered. I can no longer keep it safe without threat to my life and that of my family's.' "

"What's next?" He leaned closer.

"That's the last entry."

"You're kidding." He moved in even closer and examined the last page himself. A hint of cologne drifted to my nose.

"I wish I was," I said.

He looked up from the diary and held my eyes for a moment.

"Hey, kids, I hope I'm not interrupting anything." Dad walked into the room and took a seat with a newspaper.

Brad stepped back and checked his watch. "Wow, I didn't

realize it was that late. I need to get going."

I looked at the dark windows and knew he was right. "I'll walk you to the door."

He said good-bye to Dad and thanked Mom for dinner before we walked to the front door. When he'd opened the door, he paused. "Do you want to go to the library after work on Tuesday? I'm sure there're some books on the Rhoades Mines."

I smiled. "Are you interested in my family history or are you just intrigued by hidden treasures?"

"Maybe a little of both. Want me to pick you up at 6:00?"

"Sounds perfect."

"I'll see you then." He balled his fist, gave me a gentle nudge on the shoulder, and walked out the door. No hug, no handshake, just a nudge.

"Alexia, will you come in here for a minute?" Dad called from the family room where I'd left him.

I entered the room and plopped down next to him. "Yes?"

"Where did you get this?" He held the diary in his hands.

"I found it while cleaning out Grandpa's attic. Why?"

His brow furrowed. "There's something I've needed to tell you but haven't yet." He played with his silver mustache, something he always did when he was deep in thought. "Grandpa's death wasn't an accident."

I gasped. "What?"

A single tear rolled down his lined cheek. "He was home when the burglary took place. There was a struggle . . ."

"Why didn't you tell me this earlier?"

"I had my suspicions from the beginning. But I didn't want to tell you until the autopsy results were in and I knew for certain."

"But who'd want to hurt Grandpa? He never harmed

anyone." My throat was tight, and the formation of tears clouded my vision.

"Police are looking into the possibility that it might be Chet Strong." He motioned toward the newspaper he'd been holding. A black and white photo of a man with a shaved head and scowling face stared at me.

"But why?" My eyes plead with Dad for answers.

"I don't know for sure, but I'm wondering if it might have something to do with this diary."

My mouth gaped open, and I just stared at Dad.

"Be careful, Alexia," he said. His voice was barely above a whisper. "Be very careful."

CHAPTER 6

★ ★ ★ ★ ★

I thought Tuesday would never come, and when it did, it dragged. I was starving and couldn't wait for my lunch break at noon. I'd been keeping my eye on a cute pair of jeans for the past couple of weeks and planned to buy them with a new paycheck and an employee discount. The fact that I could wear them on a date that I hoped Derek would ask for had nothing to do with my decision; at least that's what I told myself. I just needed to try them on during lunch to make sure they fit properly.

At noon, I checked out, folded the pair of jeans under my arm, and slipped into the dressing room near the front of the store. I unbuttoned my pants and worked them to my ankles, but my left pant leg caught on my sock. I shook it to work it loose, but it did no good. I lifted my leg in the air and tugged at the bottom of the pants to work them free.

Kirsten's high heels clopped outside the dressing room followed by her hushed voice. "Jessica, did Lexi go on break?"

"I think so. Do you need her?" Jessica said.

I half turned the doorknob and was about to make my presence known when Kirsten continued. "If I tell you something, can you promise to keep it secret?"

"I love secrets." Jessica's voice was quiet.

I knew I shouldn't eavesdrop, but it was nearly impossible

not to. I just hoped they couldn't see my crumpled pants and trembling foot under the dressing room door.

"Well, last night when I was closing, a guy came into the store. He asked a bunch of questions about her."

"Who was he?"

"I don't know; some redhead that had a bad case of acne at one time."

"What did he want?"

"He wanted to know all sorts of different things about her, lots about her personal life."

"What did you tell him?"

There was a pause. "I told him to get lost."

"Does Lexi know?"

"No, I don't feel very comfortable talking to her. She seems a little. . . . Here comes somebody. We'll talk later."

Who was the redheaded, acne-scarred man, and what things did he want to know? My leg ached and trembled so hard that I knew it was only seconds away from giving out on me. I leaned against the door for support, but the door swung wide open, and my body hit the floor outside the dressing room with a thud. I looked at Kirsten and Jessica's stunned faces and couldn't tell if they were more surprised that I'd fallen out of the dressing room or that I'd overheard their entire conversation.

I stretched my shirt as low as it could go, and with hot cheeks, a cheesy grin, and a little wave to our latest customer, I hopped back into the dressing room. I could've won an award for the most embarrassing moment ever.

The front door opened, and Kirsten spoke. "Derek, what are you doing here?"

Derek?

"Oh, hi, Kirsten. Actually, I'm looking for Lexi Rhoades. Does she work here?"

"Yes. She's getting dressed," she said.

I threw on my pants, shoved my shoes in place, and stepped

out of the dressing room. Derek stood by the front door, and
Kirsten stalked to the back of the store with a scowl on her
face.

"Hi," I said when I saw him. I hoped he wouldn't notice
my flushed face.

He looked handsome in his tan button-down shirt and
dress slacks. "I had to deliver some jerseys to a client in Park
City and thought you might like to go get some lunch."

"I'd love to—let me get my purse."

When I returned, he escorted me to his car. "Did you hurt
your leg? You're limping."

"Oh, I just bumped it on something." I didn't mention
that it was the floor.

"I hope you're okay."

"I'm fine. It'll be good as new by the end of today," I said,
but I couldn't get over the fact that he knew my coworker.
"So, you know Kirsten?" I asked, once we were seated in his
car and on our way.

He looked to me then back to the road. "Yeah, we went
out a couple of times. Where did you want to eat?" he asked.

"I don't have a whole lot of time, so we can just go to one
of the fast food places close by."

"Sounds good."

I dove into my salad and had just taken a big bite when
Derek said, "I'm going to be in Park City this weekend. Would
you like to go out on Saturday?"

I suppressed a squeal. "That'd be great," I said. "What
brings you to Park City this weekend?" But before he answered,
someone entered the restaurant.

I shouldn't have been so shocked to see Brad waltz into a
fast food joint with some of his buddies on a work break, but
I definitely wasn't prepared for it. His dejected face from years
ago flashed in my mind. A face saddened by the knowledge
that I preferred his older brother to him.

I suddenly needed to locate something of great importance

in my purse. I ducked my head and searched for . . . it didn't matter as long as my head was down. While I fumbled around in my purse, it slipped from my grasp and landed on the floor with a crash, its contents spilled everywhere.

I scrambled to pick up my things with Derek's help and noticed Brad's feet walking towards the table.

"Here," Derek said, handing me a lip balm and a feminine product.

"Thanks." If I kept this up, I'd be so stuffed with humble pie I wouldn't have enough room for lunch.

"Hey, you guys." Brad's smile seemed genuine.

"Hey," was all Derek said.

Brad's eyes bounced between Derek's and mine, but he spoke to his brother. "You coming up for the weekend?"

"Wouldn't miss it."

"Good." Brad's eyes shifted to me. "See you tonight, Lex."

I swallowed hard. "All right," I said, hiding my hot cheeks behind an enormous forkful of salad.

Derek stopped chewing his burger and narrowed his eyes at his brother.

"Well," Brad said, "the guys are saving my place in line. Talk to you later."

Derek's eyes met mine, but he said nothing. I tried to read his face, but I wasn't very talented at the face-reading thing. Finally, I said, "We're going to the library to do some research about the Lost Rhoades Mines in the Uintahs. I'm a descendant."

His face relaxed. "Really? How are you related?"

"Thomas Rhoades was my great-great-great-great-grandpa on my dad's side. There're a lot of books written about him and the mines, and I want to find more information."

"And Brad's going with you?"

I nodded and checked my watch. "I'm going to use the restroom before we leave. I'll be right back."

A few minutes later, I pressed on the door to exit the

restrooms and stopped when I heard Brad and Derek conversing. Their tone was anything but brotherly.

"What about Li Shan?" Derek said.

There was a slight pause before Brad spoke. "What about her?"

"You know what I mean."

I swung the door closed and stayed inside until I heard footsteps leave. *Who was Li Shan?*

I returned to the table and was relieved that Brad and his friends were nowhere in sight. Derek and I left the place, and he hardly said a thing in the short drive back.

When we pulled into the crowded parking lot at the Tanger Outlet, Derek killed the ignition. "Do you know how to play racquetball?" he asked.

I had played it once and was nailed in the throat with the ball after it rebounded off the wall. "Sort of. Why?"

"I thought we could go to the Orem Recreation Center on Saturday. We could play a little racquetball, run around the track a few times, and soak in the hot tub."

"Great. I don't have to work that day. Do you want me to meet you down there?"

His handsome eyes bounced between mine. "No, I need to come up anyway. I'll come pick you up at two. Does that work?"

"Two's fine."

"Good." He climbed out of the car and let me out. "Thanks for going to lunch with me today. I hope your leg feels better by Saturday." He gave me a one-armed squeeze and left.

★　★　★　★

Later that evening, I answered the door and took a step back; the GQ model of the month was posed on my front porch wearing a dark, cotton-knit top over his broad shoulders. Wait, it was just Brad.

"You ready?" he asked.

I swallowed the unexplained dryness in my mouth. "Um, sure."

He led me to his car and held the door open for me. I dropped to the seat without warning. My legs were a little stiff inside the new jeans I couldn't wait to wear. I never did get to try them on before I bought them.

"I have a little surprise for you when we're done with the library tonight," he said after he started up the car. The tires squealed from his take-off, and I had to peel my head from the headrest.

"What is it?" I asked.

"Wait until dark." His smile was mischievous.

I tried to pry an answer out of him the entire drive. Every time, he blatantly changed the subject to the weather, sports, school, and a host of other topics. When we pulled into a parking stall, I finally gave up.

At the library, we found several books on the subject of the Rhoades Mines, including a couple of books written by a distant relative. All of them were very intriguing.

I flipped through the pages and read several accounts of lost treasure, clues, copies of maps, and meanings of symbols. Luckily, my years of studying Spanish proved to be helpful in deciphering many of the foreign words I came across.

In one of the books, I read of the murder of Enoch Rhoades. Once again, the year of his death was stated as 1884. He was a young, adventurous man, interested in the mines. His half brother, Caleb, knew of their locations and was going after them all the time. Enoch begged Caleb to show him a mine or let him come until Caleb finally gave in.

On the way to a mine in the Currant Creek area, Enoch was hit with an arrow but didn't die right away. He made a camp and tried to recover enough to ride out. One night, a couple braves snuck in his tent and shot him in his sleep. The wives of the two braves tried to save him the next morning, but he died shortly after.

Tears literally filled my eyes as I read the sad story, some of which had been gathered from the wife of one of the braves who had shot Enoch. But a sob erupted from my throat when I learned that he was engaged and was planning to marry upon his return.

"What's wrong?" Brad's concerned voice broke my concentration.

"Nothing."

"Your eyes are all red and puffy, and you're sniffling so loud the librarian almost had to hush you, but you're telling me there's nothing wrong?"

"Here, read this." I handed him the small book and watched a crease form between his eyes.

When he finished, he looked at me and said, "I'm sorry."

"It's all right. I don't know why I get so emotional." I wiped my cheeks. "Have you found anything interesting in the books you've been reading?"

"I did. Have you ever heard of statues of animals in the Uintahs?"

"No, why?"

"Well, apparently there are stone and wood carved statues in various parts of the mountains. They were built to guard or show the way to gold."

"Really?"

"That's what a couple of these books say. But that's not all. What was your grandpa's name again?"

"Henry Rhoades, why?"

"That's what I thought." His voice dropped low. "According to this book, your grandpa had a map to one of the mines."

"What?" Several people made shushing sounds around the room. "What?" I said more quietly.

"He found a map hidden in a diary of one of his ancestors. He used it to search for a mine and finally found it. He told no one except a couple of close friends and relatives, but somehow the word got out, and he felt threatened. He tore the map into three pieces, gave one to a cousin, the other to his close friend, and kept the third for himself, hidden."

"You can't be serious, Grandpa didn't mine."

"That you knew about. Did he go on fishing or hunting trips?"

I chewed my lip. "Well, yeah, but that doesn't mean . . ."

"This book was written by an old friend of your grandpa's. According to a newspaper article, this guy had a falling-out with your grandpa and the two he trusted most. He gives names and locations of both the cousin and the friend that were given the other two pieces of the map."

"Who and where?"

"An Albert Jordan from Price and Maxwell Rhoades from Tabiona. You know of the robbery in Price recently."

I nodded. "At the museum."

"Guess where Albert Jordan worked?"

My mouth opened. "The museum?"

"Right. And your grandpa's home was burglarized just before that. Do you think it's just a coincidence?"

I massaged my temples. "I don't know. I still need some time to think about all this."

"Well, if I'm right, we'll be hearing about another burglary in Tabiona."

"If you're right then wouldn't the police have surveillance all around the Rhoades guy in Tabiona?"

His eyes searched mine. "Maybe they do." His voice was just a whisper.

Someone brushed against my shoulder, and I jumped. "Library closes in five minutes," the middle-aged librarian whispered. I placed my hand over my chest to settle my heart.

Brad chuckled.

"What?" I said.

"Nothing."

"What?"

"It's nothing." He chuckled even more and was attracting looks from others.

"What's so funny?"

He squeezed his lips together to keep from laughing. "Just how high you jumped when the librarian touched your shoulder. You're pretty jumpy."

"You would be too if you had strange people following you."

His smile vanished. "What strange people?"

"No one, nevermind."

"Who?"

"No one."

"Alexia Susanne Rhoades, whose been following you around?"

I sighed. "I don't know who they are."

"They? How many people are following you and where? And when?"

The lights above us began to turn off. "Let's check out some of these books, and I'll tell you. But not here."

The moment we stepped out of the library, Brad began again. "So what's going on? People—"

I cut off the remainder of his words with my hand. "Let's go somewhere else, and I'll answer your questions."

Brad took my hand from his mouth. "You promise?"

"Promise."

We drove through the streets of Park City. Brad took us to a quiet park where we could talk and where he could give me the surprise. On the way, he told me about the Mandarin language and its five different tones. The same word could have five different meanings depending on which tone was used. When he spoke a couple of sentences it almost sounded like singing. He shared with me his Mandarin name, given to him in the MTC, which was as phonetically close to Manning as possible.

He took his eyes from the road and glanced at my face and hair. A smile emerged on his lips. "Mae Jin," he said. It was pronounced somewhat like "May Jean" minus the tones.

"What?" I asked.

"Mae Jin. That can be your Chinese name."

"It doesn't sound very close to Lexi."

"Sometimes people have names that have meanings. That name has a meaning."

"What does it mean?"

"*Mae* means beautiful." He turned to me again. "You are beautiful . . . and *Jin* means gold, for your golden hair. It's a good name."

I stared in unbelief for a full minute before I realized my mouth was gaping open. He'd told me a few times before that he thought I was beautiful, but we were only twelve then, and I didn't want to hear it. For some reason, I didn't mind so much now.

It was nearly dark when we pulled into the parking lot of a secluded park. "Okay," he finally said, "no one could've followed us here except by car, and I don't see any other vehicles besides ours. So . . ."

"I know, I know. You want to know who's been following me. It started on Saturday night when I went to . . ." I paused. "Park City Mountain Resort."

"With Derek?"

I hesitated. "Yes. There was a man there with a black shaggy wig, a goatee, and sunglasses. I accidentally hit him with my golf ball. He followed us up the lift for the Alpine Slide and practically ran me over with his sled going down. Then he just disappeared. I haven't seen him since."

"What do you mean he just disappeared?"

"He never came off the slide. He was right on my tail one minute, and the next he was gone. I don't know what happened to him."

"Maybe his wig flew off, and he had to hop off and get it."

I laughed. "I think he may've been getting even with me for hitting him with the ball."

"Maybe. Have you seen him anywhere else?"

I shrugged. "Just at Texas Red's earlier that evening."

Brad played with his clean-shaven chin. "You mentioned there was more than one person following you. Who else?"

"I don't really know if you could say the other one was following me, but today at work, I overheard one of my coworkers say that a man with red hair and acne scars came into the store last night and asked questions about me."

"What kind of questions?"

"Questions about my personal life," I said.

He didn't speak for a long time but finally did. "Have you told your dad?"

"I told him about Shaggy, but I haven't seen him today to tell him about the redhead."

"I think I should take you home."

"You can't take me home yet, what about the surprise? Besides, they were just isolated incidences. There's nothing to worry about." I subconsciously batted my long lashes.

It must've worked, because he opened the glove box and fished around for awhile. Finally, he pulled out a pack of Wint-O-Green Lifesavers and handed it to me.

"Lifesavers?" *Was my breath stinky?*

"You don't have bad breath, if that's what you're thinking," he said, and I wondered if he could read my thoughts. He got out of the car and opened my door. Large overhead lights lit the park, but dark shadows loomed in several spots. He led me down a set of cement stairs. A pavilion, with several picnic tables, overlooked a playground, complete with slides, jungle gyms, and swings. On the far left was a little fenced-in area for dogs to play. I had to smile.

I followed him to a pocket of complete darkness on the other side of the cement pavilion wall. He unwrapped the pack of Lifesavers and popped one in his mouth. "Watch," he said.

I looked at his mouth. Tiny blue-green sparks filled it with each crush of his teeth on the Lifesaver. He handed me a few, and I crushed them between my teeth. We both laughed as we crushed and sparked our Lifesavers, until the last one was gone.

Total silence filled the air, and stars twinkled like diamonds spread across the night sky. It was breathtaking. "I've always enjoyed Park City's starry nights," I said. "Of all of God's creations, I can't think of anything more beautiful than these stars, tonight."

"I can." His voice was serious.

I glanced toward him, but it was nearly impossible to see his face in the dark.

BANG! A deafening blast rang in my ears, and cement dust fell on my head. Brad pushed me to the ground and hovered over me.

"Are you all right?" he asked. His voice was quick.

"Yes. Are you?"

"I'm fine."

Car tires squealed from the parking lot above.

"What just happened?" I may have split my new pants.

"Someone took a shot at us."

"Why would anyone want to kill us?"

"They could've killed us if they wanted, but they didn't. I think it was meant as a warning."

CHAPTER 7

★ ★ ★ ★ ★

Saturday morning I awoke with the birds. My spirit longed to go for a hike up the mountains, but my body stayed put in the safety of my home. For three very long days I hadn't exercised outdoors, afraid of what might be lurking in the shadows.

Nothing out of the ordinary had happened since the incident at the park on Tuesday night, but that didn't mean I was safe from becoming someone's clay pigeon. Every morning, I hugged the walls of my home before darting to my car, crouched to half my size and using the car as a shield for imaginary bullets.

At least I'd be going to the Orem Recreation Center with Derek and would get a chance to run. Somehow, the thoughts of leaving Summit County and the danger here filled me with great pleasure.

Before I got ready for my date, I decided to go online and do some family history mystery solving. I logged on and went to FamilySearch.org where I looked up Enoch Rhoades. There were a handful of entries, but they all showed that he died in September 1884. It wasn't what I wanted to see. Next, I checked newspaper articles for information on the museum robbery in Price. Chet Strong was a major suspect.

I glanced at the clock and realized I'd been on the Internet for nearly two and a half hours, and I still needed to get ready for my date. At 2:00 sharp, Derek showed. He greeted me with a smile as white as the T-shirt he wore. He held my door while I climbed in his car, and we were soon on our way to Utah County.

We conversed about sports through the streets of Heber, but when there was no more to discuss about his favorite basketball team and whether they'd ever win a championship, an awkward silence filled the car. I tugged at my earlobe. Several topics ran through my mind but they either seemed silly, or we'd already discussed them. Finally, something came to mind. "Why did you need to come to Park City this weekend? You never had a chance to answer."

He glanced between the road and me. "Well, there're two reasons, actually. One, I needed to run a sew-out to a client of mine for work, and the other, my family's having a big, 'meet Li Shan dinner' tomorrow night."

"Who's Li Shan?" I did my best to pronounce the name. It sounded somewhat like "Lee Shawn."

"Brad didn't tell you about her?" The look on his face said more than his words.

"No, should he have?"

"Well, I just thought he would've."

"Is she from Taiwan?" I asked, though I was sure I already knew the answer.

"Yes, Brad met her and her family on his mission, but since then they've kept in touch by email."

"So she's in America, now?"

"Right. She's staying with us for awhile."

"How long will she be here?" *Maybe it was just for the weekend.*

"I believe . . . indefinitely."

Indefinitely? Why? What else didn't I know about this mysterious woman? And why did the mention of her name cause my stomach to turn? I wanted to ask more questions but was afraid of the answers. The car was so quiet I could hear myself breathe.

"What was I going to say?" I asked, just so I didn't have to listen to nothing.

Derek looked at me and smiled. "I don't know. We were talking about Li Shan. Was it about her?"

"No." It came out with more force than I intended. "It wasn't about her."

"Was it about school?"

"Hmm. No, it wasn't about school." I tried to think of a topic that I could say yes to if he asked.

"Was it about my work?"

"Uh, yeah," I said. "What's a sew-out anyway?" I sincerely wanted to know.

"Well, after I digitize something on the computer, I make an embroidered sample of it to show to my clients. They can either say go ahead with the order, or they can look at it and make any necessary changes. That way I don't waste a hundred items running off a logo someone doesn't like."

"That makes sense." I found his business interesting, and it turned out to be just the topic we needed to keep the conversation alive until we reached the "The Rec.," as Derek called it.

Racquetball was actually enjoyable this time around. Not once did the little blue ball incapacitate me, and Derek seemed impressed with how well I played for only my second shot at the sport. I managed to hit the ball with the racquet on most attempts and pelted him with the ball only once. Thankfully, it was nothing serious.

The run around the track was invigorating. I'd longed for a run all week but had hidden away in my home with a big purple bruise on my right thigh. Now that it was nearly healed, all of the pent-up energy I'd stored worked to my advantage. I had tremendous endurance and enjoyed myself so much that I didn't listen to my muscles when they told me it was time to quit.

I eased myself into the hot tub's steaming water in the over-crowded swimming area. My muscles welcomed the liquid heat, and I basked in the hot steam.

"You're a pretty good runner. Do you do it often?" Derek asked.

I looked at him through dense steam. "Almost every day but Sundays, weather permitting."

"I should be more dedicated to my workout routine, but sometimes . . . actually, most of the time, I'm too busy."

"I know the feeling," I said. "Some days I just have to skip it because there're too many things going on. But then I regret it. I need that energy and stress outlet."

"You must've had a lot of stress to relieve today, the way you were running."

I smiled. "Yes, fearing that I'll be shot at every time I leave the house has had a stressful effect on me."

Derek flashed his brilliant grin and then was silent a moment. "You know, when my mom told me that someone had shot at you and Brad, I felt sick. The thought of losing either of you . . ." He paused. "I'm just glad you're both okay."

"Me too."

We enjoyed the swirling bubbles and jets of the hot tub for several minutes before Derek said, "Have you worked up an appetite? If we get out now, we can beat the Utah County Saturday-night-dinner rush."

The rumble in my belly almost answered before I did. "I'm ready to go when you are."

The blow of a whistle made me jump. "Move away from the floating object!" the lifeguard yelled. "Move away from the floating object, until we can retrieve it!"

Floating object? A floater? I didn't think the lifeguard would make a big deal about retrieving a child's inflatable arm device. That left only one other explanation for the "floater" that I could think of, and I didn't want to see him reel it in, especially just before going to dinner.

We climbed out of the hot tub, and I looked at the wall until Derek tapped my shoulder. He pointed to the "floater" and I gasped. On the surface of the pool, floating inches from the grasp of the lifeguard's long-handled net was a shaggy, black wig.

★　　★　　★　　★

I couldn't believe it had only been a week since the embarrassing dressing room incident and the gun shot at the park. My life felt like a roller coaster ride, one minute seemingly perfect and the next, threatened into nonexistence. Then, just when I felt that maybe the bad guys had given up and my life was becoming peaceful again, something else would happen; something like the shaggy black wig floating in the pool.

Had Shaggy been at the pool watching us? Or did the wig belong to some guy who was trying to cover up a thin spot for a date? On second thought, no one would purchase a wig like that to impress a date. It had to have been Shaggy's.

The incident gave me the creeps and put me on edge for the rest of the evening, but not so much that I didn't enjoy our scrumptious dinner at Applebee's. Too bad we forgot about the leftovers, which we had placed on top of the car and only remembered them when they slid down the hood and into the intersection at the first stoplight.

Work was a nightmare because Kirsten was upset with me. I presumed it was because Derek had taken me to lunch, and truthfully, that was a part of it. But it was also because the police had stopped by and questioned her about the scarred redhead. For some reason, perhaps because my dad was in cohorts with the police, she blamed me for the whole thing.

In addition to my problems with Kirsten, I hadn't heard a word from Brad. Did it have anything to do with that Li Shan woman? Why did the thought of him liking someone else bother me?

"Lexi, phone," Jessica said, and I was thrown back into

reality. She brushed past me to help someone who'd just walked in.

I finished ringing up a purchase and ran to the back to answer the phone. "Hello?"

"Where is it?" The man's voice was hardly more than a raspy whisper.

My hands trembled, and my throat went dry. "Where's what?" I asked.

"Don't play dumb." He mumbled something that I couldn't understand and hung up.

I stared at the receiver clutched in my hand for a full minute before I finally set it down.

I mentioned the incident to my manager, and we checked the call back. It was an unknown number.

Several minutes later, Jessica called me to the phone again. I hesitated before answering. "Hello?" I asked in a small voice.

"Hi, Lexi, it's Derek."

Relief washed over me. "I'm *so* glad to hear your voice."

"Really? I'm glad to hear yours, too. Are you free to go out again on Saturday?" he asked.

I smiled. "Of course, but I've been thinking. You've planned all our dates thus far. Why don't you let me take that burden off your shoulders this week?"

"It's not a burden, but you're welcome to plan it if you let me pay."

"It's a deal." I played around with a few different ideas in my mind. "Wear something casual."

"All right. What time do I pick you up?"

"Six, and come hungry."

He chuckled. "You're sure about this?"

"Of course I'm sure. It'll be fun."

For the remainder of the workday, different date ideas flitted around my mind and replaced the fright I'd experienced from the phone call. I liked to come up with creative dating ideas and finally decided we would go bowling in Heber, even if I bowled much better with the bumper pads in place. By the time I had the evening planned out in my mind, it sounded like it could be a lot of fun.

★   ★   ★   ★

I was awakened early Saturday by my thoughts. Derek and I did a lot of fun things together, and I was beginning to wonder if he liked me. But I still had a hard time imagining that he could think of me as anything more than a little girl. Then again, several times I'd caught a glimpse in his eye that told me otherwise.

Brad was so much fun to be around, and the few times I'd seen him since Brandi's wedding had renewed, and even deepened, our friendship. But I'd hardly seen or heard from him since the mention of Li Shan. I didn't want to think his absence had anything to do with her, but unfortunately, I couldn't find any other explanation. It was like I was suddenly dropped from his world, and I didn't like it one bit.

In some ways, the past week had felt like a whole month and in other ways, it had whizzed by. I'd been so busy I hadn't had time for family history searching. I planned to ask some of my living relatives to help me out with the mystery surrounding Enoch's death. The first person I thought of was Ethel. After I'd exercised, showered, and dressed, I decided to give her a call.

I tapped at the paper, scribbled with handwritten questions, with my pencil and dialed her number.

She picked up after a few rings. "Hello?"

"Aunt Ethel, this is Lexi Rhoades. Do you remember me from my grandpa's funeral?"

"Sure I do, dear. It's hard to forget a pretty young thing like yourself. How are you doing?"

"I'm fine. I was wondering if you knew when Enoch Rhoades died. I have a letter in his handwriting dated July 7, 1885, but most of the records I've found show he died in September 1884."

"Hmm. That's odd. I don't think he'd have written it after he died. Let me see. . . . My records show him dying in 1884, too. Have you tried Aunt Margaret? She does a lot more genealogy than I do. Give her a call and see what turns up."

"I will. Thank you."

I called Aunt Margaret, and she, not having any information other than 1884, gave me the number for someone else, who in turn gave me a number for someone else. I dialed the last number. An elderly woman answered, and I explained my question.

"No, I don't have anything different than what you've already found," she said. "Maxwell would've known, though. He knew that story well."

"Maxwell Rhoades? Was he your husband?"

"Yes, but he died a couple of years ago."

"I'm sorry to hear that." A question popped into my mind, and my curiosity won over congeniality. "Did he ever say anything about a map before he died?"

There was silence on the other line for nearly a minute, and I wondered if I'd made a mistake in asking the question.

Finally, she spoke. "Yes, someone approached him one day. Physically threatened him with his life if he didn't hand it over. He resisted at first but finally let him take it. Poor Maxwell never recovered. He was weak physically and felt sick emotionally for giving in to the threat. It eventually took his life."

A pit formed in my stomach. "I'm so sorry to hear that."

"Yes, but at least they found the guy who did it and locked him up, but the map was gone."

"Who was he?"

There was a pause. "Chester, I think. Chester Strong."

The hairs on my arms stood up. "Thank you so much for your help." I hung up the receiver and rubbed at the chills on my arms. I needed to talk to Dad when he got home.

That evening, I took special care getting ready for my date

with Derek. I wore a nice pair of jeans and a dark blue blouse that enhanced the color of my eyes. As always, he was punctual, a trait I personally struggled with. However, I made sure I was ready when he showed up.

I answered the door and noticed how nice he looked in jeans and a simple button-down shirt. I grabbed the picnic cooler and blanket I'd placed by the door earlier.

"Let me get that for you." He took the cooler from my arms and carried it to the back trunk of his car. "What are we doing tonight, anyway?"

"You'll see."

He opened my door and walked around to the driver's side. "So where to? It's weird not knowing where we're going for our date."

"Well, first of all, I packed us a little picnic, so we just need to find a park. There's one in Heber."

"Heber?"

I grinned. "Yes, that's where we're going."

We drove the twenty-minute distance to Heber and found a park. Derek grabbed the cooler and blanket out of the back of his car, and we found a cool spot of grass under a tree.

I opened the cooler and took out a pan of layered bean dip, a bag of tortilla chips, and a container of guacamole. Last, but not least, I brought out a fun bottle of sparkling apple cider, complete with two clear plastic goblets.

His eyes widened. "You went through a lot of trouble for this date. I had no idea."

"It's not trouble, it's fun," I said. I opened the container of guacamole and chips.

Derek took two chips and scooped a large portion of guacamole. "Mmm. This is good guac. Where did you get it?" He scooped more guacamole with another chip.

"I made it."

"You made it? This is better than anything you can get in a restaurant. Do you just buy one of those little season packets at the store and mix, or is it more complicated than that?"

I laughed. "It's more complicated than that. It's a secret family recipe including fresh organic ingredients blended in just the right way. I could tell you, but then I'd have to do away with you."

It took a second before he realized I was joking, but he still only gave a slight smile. We conversed about sports and the weather throughout the picnic and even branched off to the topic of cars before we packed everything up.

We entered the crowded bowling alley a short time later. Several men were using a pool table. A handful of people sat at the snack bar, and a jukebox played a lonely country song. While we waited for a clear lane, we were fitted for bowling shoes and picked out our bowling balls, but the selection was picked over. I had a choice between ones that weighed more than I did, or a pink kiddy-style with small finger holes and a chip on its surface. I chose the latter.

Derek bowled first and got a spare. When it was my turn, my fingers got stuck in the ball's holes, and I went down the lane with my ball. By the end of the evening, I had a decent score if you counted the three strikes and five spares I received with the help of the bumper pads.

Before we left, I noticed my grimy hands. "I'm going to wash up," I said to Derek, who waited at the counter to return our shoes.

I entered the women's bathroom and lathered well with a dirty bar of soap, then scrubbed until they looked clean. I was grateful when I found a paper towel to dry my hands. When I exited the restroom, examining my hands, I bumped into someone going towards the men's room.

"Sorry." I stared into the face of a man with red hair and acne scars.

His eyes penetrated my soul. "Be careful." His icy fingers wrapped around my forearm.

I broke free and fought the crowd to Derek. "Let's go," I

said, looking back at the restrooms, but "Scar" was gone.

"All right."

Goose bumps lined my arms and got even bigger the moment we stepped outside. I scanned the darkened parking lot for any sign of Scar, but there was none.

"Are you cold?" Derek asked.

"Yes." My teeth began to chatter.

He helped me into the passenger seat and took his place behind the wheel. "Is something wrong?"

I checked the parking lot one more time as we left it, then looked at Derek. "Last week a man with red hair and acne scars came into the store where I work and asked a bunch of personal questions about me. I think it may have something to do with the Lost Rhoades Mines. I just saw him in the bowling alley."

"Did he see you?"

"Actually, I kind of bumped into him outside the restrooms. I apologized, and he told me to be careful. . . . Hmmm."

"What?"

"I was just thinking about what he said. 'Be careful.' It can be taken two ways. One, to watch where I'm going so I don't bump into another unsuspecting person, or two: a warning."

His eyes studied mine for a moment. "Have you told your dad about this guy?"

"Yes, the day it happened."

"Well, I don't really want to do this, but I think I should take you straight home."

I didn't want the date to end either, but I knew he had made a good point.

When we turned into my little cul-de-sac, emergency lights flickered in the night sky from the ambulance parked in our driveway. E.M.T.'s loaded a stretcher into the ambulance with Dad lying on its top.

I leapt from the car and ran to my mother's side. "What happened?"

"I came home from the store and found him unconscious at the bottom of the stairs," she said. Her face was pale.

"Is he going to be okay?" I looked into Mom's face but feared the worst.

She wiped tears from her cheeks. "I don't know. I just don't know. We're on our way to the hospital. They'll run some tests and see." Mom gave me a hug, jumped into the ambulance, and disappeared behind closed doors.

I whirled around to Derek. "I've got to go!"

"Do you want me to take you to the hospital?"

I fished for keys in my purse. "No, that's all right. I don't know how long I'll be or if I'll even get any sleep tonight, but thanks."

"Are you sure?"

I nodded. "You go on home. I'll talk to you later."

He placed a hand on my shoulder. "Thanks again for tonight. I'll give you a call tomorrow." He gave me a quick hug and helped me into my car, where my chin began to quiver.

CHAPTER 8

★ ★ ★ ★ ★

Mom and I paced the hospital floors for what seemed like hours. Finally, a middle-aged man clad in medical attire pulled us aside. "Mrs. Rhoades, I'm Dr. Michaels."

"Do you know anything about my husband? How is he?" Mom asked.

Dr. Michaels wiped weariness from his eyes. "He's had a lot of internal bleeding and a moderate amount of trauma to the head. We were able to contain the bleeding, but he may not regain consciousness for a few hours or even days. Right now, he's stable and resting."

"Can we see him?" Mom tried to hide the shakiness in her voice.

"He should be in his room, you may go ahead if you'd like."

When we entered Dad's room, we found him bandaged up and lying in a clean bed. Mom pulled a chair to his side, taking his hand, and I collapsed in a chair nestled against the wall. I glanced at my watch: 1:36 AM. No wonder I was so tired.

I tried to find a comfortable position to lay my head but didn't succeed. I closed my eyes and tried to find rest anyway. Visions of Dad falling down the stairs played over and over in my mind and left me feeling uneasy. The steady beep of machines and Mom's voice as she conversed with my sister by phone finally lulled me into a light sleep.

"Honey, can you hear me?" Mom's voice jolted me awake.

Dad pried his eyelids open like they weighed forty-seven pounds each. "What happened? Why do I hurt so much?" he said.

Mom and I exchanged looks. "We were hoping you would answer that for us," Mom said. "I came home from the store and found you at the bottom of the stairs. Do you remember what happened?"

Before he could answer, Dr. Michaels entered the room and walked to the bed. "Great. You're awake. How do you feel?"

"Like I've been run over by a truck."

Dr. Michaels chuckled. "That good, huh? Do you remember how you got into this predicament?"

Dad's eyes closed and the lines between his eyes deepened. "The last thing I remember was saying good-bye to my wife . . . everything after that is blank."

Dr. Michaels looked at his chart. "It may take awhile for you to remember exactly what happened. On the other hand, it's not uncommon for some to permanently block out the passage of events preceding an accident or traumatic experience. Time will tell. Now what you need is a lot of rest."

Good idea, I thought. I knew I needed a lot of rest as well, or at least some. I looked at the chair and thought of how to make it most comfortable.

"Lexi, why don't you go home and get some sleep," Mom said. "There's no reason both of us need to be sleep deficient."

Though my mind fought the idea of leaving, my body readily agreed. I said good-bye to my parents and headed home.

★   ★   ★   ★

Bird chirping awoke me at dawn. I pulled my pillow over my head to quiet their singing and to shut out the light that squeezed through my closed lids, but it was my mind that wouldn't let me sleep further. I wasn't so sure that Dad's trip down the stairs was an accident, but I wasn't able to convince Mom, his friends at the police department, or anyone else that it was for lack of concrete evidence.

I made a call to Mom and Dad at the hospital, then studied my scriptures and attended church. Afterward, I changed clothes and headed back to the hospital. Dad was doing fine, but Mom looked like she was about to pass out. I stayed awhile and gave Dad a kiss before I kidnapped Mom. She slept the entire way up Parley's Canyon, and after we arrived home we both had a bite to eat then took a long summer's day nap.

Later, I was awakened by a loud crack of thunder. The sky was dark and rain poured in torrents upon the roof. I tiptoed near Mom's room. I didn't want to wake her if she was still sleeping, but she wasn't on her bed. I called her name. There was no answer.

"Mom," I said while I descended the stairs.

When I entered the kitchen I found a note on the counter.

Lexi,

I couldn't sleep and didn't want to wake you. I'm going back to the hospital to be with Dad. I'll call you later with any updates. There are leftovers in the fridge.

Love,

Mom

The phone rang. I quickly picked up the receiver, anxious to hear an update from Mom.

"Hello?" I asked.

"Hi, it's Derek. How's your dad?"

I smiled at his voice but not at the thought of my dad.

"Well, he's had a lot of internal bleeding and a bad head wound."

"When can he come home?"

"The doctors want him to stay in the hospital for a couple of weeks. But at least he's expected to make a full recovery."

"How are you holding up?"

That was a good question. "I'm fine. I took a nap and feel a lot better now."

"Good." He paused. "Last night I never got a chance to tell you I bought a couple of tickets to the Stadium of Fire this weekend. I was going to see if you'd like to go but then your dad . . ."

Images of the large fireworks show exploded in my mind. "I'd love to go. What time does it start?" I asked.

"Actually, I was thinking we could do some things before-hand. Would it work if I picked you up at three?"

I thought a moment. "I have a sister who lives in Springville that I haven't visited in awhile. I can stay there for the week-end, so you won't have to come all the way up to Park City."

"Really? Are you sure? I mean, I can come up if there's a problem."

"Let me talk to my sister and make sure it's all right with her. If there's a problem I'll let you know." I gave him the address and directions to my sister's home, and after saying our good-byes, we hung up.

I dialed my sister's number. We talked for a number of minutes on Dad's condition before I said, "Lydia, I have a favor to ask."

"Sure, what is it?"

"Do you remember Derek Manning?"

She was silent for a half second while she thought. "Of course—you gushed over him twenty-four-seven when you were younger. Why?"

"He's invited me to the Stadium of Fire this Saturday, and I was wondering if I could stay the night at your place so he doesn't have to drive me back home so late."

She squealed. "I'd love to have you stay over. So after all these years, he's finally asked you out. You must be totally excited. Is this your first date with him?"

"Actually, we've been out a few times before."

"And?"

I could tell she wanted to know some juicy details, only there weren't any. "And . . . he's very nice and a perfect gentleman."

"Has he kissed you?"

"No," I said a little too quickly.

"Well, I'm happy for you, anyway. What time should I expect you?"

I thought a moment before I answered. "My date's at three, but would it be all right if I came down earlier? That will give me time to see you and your kids before he comes."

"Sounds good."

When I got off the phone, my growling stomach told me it'd been neglected. I rummaged through the fridge for the leftovers: vegetable stew and homemade, sprouted-grain French bread. I warmed up the stew, toasted a thick slice of bread, and topped it with a helping of butter and fresh apricot preserves. It hit the spot.

CRACK! Thunder and a bolt of lightning hit so close it shook the house. I'd been so engrossed in my phone conversation, only my subconscious had been aware of the dark, thunderous storm outside. I flicked on the lights and wiped the counters.

When I'd finished, I looked around for the diary. I hadn't had a chance to read through it since the other night, and I had no idea what Dad had done with it. I started my search in Dad and Mom's room, then in Dad's dresser. I didn't find the diary, but I did find the combination to his safe. Of course!

I bounded down the stairs to the family room where the safe was located. Its beauty alone made it the centerpiece of the room, though we'd had to utilize special equipment to place the six-foot, 1100-pound safe in its permanent resting spot. It was a deep, metallic purple, sporting a smoked chrome dial and spinning handle. Along the top, the name "Liberty Safe" was etched elegantly on either side of Lady Liberty's image.

I ran through the safe combination instructions in my mind, then on the dial. After I'd butchered the first seven attempts to open it, I finally succeeded. I pulled the door open and found a couple shotguns, a .44 magnum, and several papers. The diary lay resting on top. I took it in my hands but noticed the paper under the diary; an old mining rights plot map. I grabbed it for a closer look.

A plot map to an area by Currant Creek was located on one side of the paper and legal descriptions on the other. I read through it and mentally memorized it. Then I folded the paper, tucked it into the diary, and closed the safe.

I plopped onto the couch and started at the beginning. I was touched by the author's love for his wife and children and his deep testimony. It took quite a bit of time before I came upon the part about him finding the mine, but it was most interesting. Especially when I found that Wilton Rhoades was Grandpa's paternal grandfather and had built the home Grandpa eventually inherited as his own.

I flipped the page and read, "June 25, 1903. I made my way up Currant Creek the other day. Just after the narrows, I found a little trail off to the right. I stopped at a spring for Ginger to water up and saw a magnificent cliff. I climbed to the top and could see all around. It was then that I saw the clue to the mine that I'd been looking for."

BANG, BANG, BANG.

My reading stopped at the unfamiliar sound from upstairs. I listened for several moments more, and when it seemed to have stopped, I continued.

"It was a—"

BANG. BANG.

I tossed the plot map into the page I'd been reading and tucked the diary under my arm. I needed to discover the source of the sound, but I hesitated. I couldn't explain the uneasy feeling that was beginning to grow inside.

I moved slowly through the living room and flipped on each light on the way to the staircase. The floor creaked under my weight. I tiptoed barefoot up the stairs one at a time, until I reached the top. I crept toward Mom and Dad's room, and when I rounded the doorway, I found that not only was the window open but the door to the deck was slightly ajar.

I slammed it tight and set the diary down so I could do the same with the window. I cracked the blinds a bit and took a peek outside, but all I could see was the frightened look of my own reflection.

My eyes caught a movement. It was so quick I couldn't tell if it came from the darkness outside or if it'd been a reflection from something inside. My heart began to beat with such force it literally vibrated my shirt.

I replaced the blinds and turned around to head back downstairs, but I stopped. Cold, damp carpet squished between by bare toes. Rain must've blown in from the window.

CRACK! A clap of thunder erupted. I placed my hand over my heart and took a big breath. Quickly, I walked to the stairs and slipped and slid all the way down. Once I reached the living room, the lights flickered and went out. I stood in total darkness except for the occasional flash of lightning, which lit the house like midday. I checked the light switches. They were dead.

I felt my way to the kitchen between lightning flashes, where I found four small candles and some matches. I lit them and watched the flame-light dance along the ceiling and walls, grateful for the brightness they gave. I carried two of the candles into the living room and placed them on the coffee table, then curled up on the couch.

Another flash of lightning lit the entire living room. The shadow of a man outside was illuminated for a split second on the wall. Rain beat heavily on the roof, but I could still hear the unmistakable pounding on the door. I held my breath.

The door handle jiggled, and I was never so grateful that I'd taken the time to lock it earlier. The knocks grew into bangs. A man's voice yelled through the door. It mumbled at first then grew louder and more insistent. "Lex, are you in there? Open the door."

"Brad?" I ran to the door, flung it open, and nearly tackled him when I threw my arms around his neck.

He patted my back with one hand. "What's going on? Your mom's been trying to get a hold of you."

"Is that why you came?" I pulled away from his rain-drenched shirt, which clung to his body. His muscles could've been etched from stone.

"She called me when she couldn't get your neighbors, but yes. I'm here to check on you. What's going on?"

"Come in and I'll tell you." I ushered him into the darkened living room and bolted the door after us. "Do you want a dry shirt? You can use one of my brother's."

He ran his hands along his arms. "Do you think he'd mind?"

"Nah, he's on his mission, he won't even know. You can change in his room."

He chuckled. "Now I know what happened to all my stuff." He took a candle and walked to the main level bedroom.

When he returned, changed and dry, we took a seat on the couch.

"Is the power out at your place?" I asked.

"No, I think it's just this area." He looked my direction. "I'm sorry to hear about your dad. Is he going to be all right?"

"He'll be fine after some time and observation in the hospital."

He studied my face. "Have the police looked into his 'accident'?"

"You don't think it was?"

"No, I don't. Your grandpa, your tires, the Price Museum, the strange people you've seen, getting shot at, and now your dad. I'm worried that Chet Strong is still after that map, and I'm worried about . . ."

"What?"

His sea-blue eyes looked over my features. "About you."

My face shifted to look at the candlelight dancing on the table. "You don't need to worry about me; the police didn't find anything suspicious, and no one else believes anything different than what they've said."

"And do you believe them?"

The uneasy feeling I'd had before started to swell again. "No." A loud crack of thunder jolted me, and my hand flew to my heart.

Brad tried to suppress a smile. "How've you been? I haven't talked to you in awhile."

"I've noticed." *Why did I just say that?*

"I'm sorry. I've been busy lately." He ran a hand through his damp hair.

"With Li Shan?"

His mouth opened and the tiniest hint of a smile twitched at the corners of his lips. "Yes, she's never been to America before."

"Oh," I said.

"So, why didn't you answer the phone? I tried calling before I left, and there was no answer."

"I never heard the phone ring."

"I even tried your cell," he said.

"Dad still has it."

"Let's go check your phone line." Brad rose from the

couch, and I followed him into the kitchen where he picked up the phone.

"Well?" I asked.

"It's dead. The phone lines must've been struck by lightning." He replaced the receiver in its spot. "I have my cell phone with me if you want to call your mom and let her know you're alright."

"Good idea." I took the phone from his hand and dialed Dad's room number. Mom answered, and I explained what had happened. She updated me on Dad's condition and said she'd be home as soon as she could.

"Thank you." I handed the phone back to Brad.

"No problem."

"You think Chet Strong is still looking for Grandpa's piece of the map?"

His eyes told his answer before his lips. "I do."

"You're right, you know. The piece of map was taken from Maxwell Rhoades in Tabiona."

His jaw dropped. "I didn't know. When?"

I rubbed my brows. "A couple of years ago. Chet was put behind bars afterward but was released early for good behavior."

"I'm almost certain he didn't find the map at your grandpa's or he wouldn't be messing with you and your family. If he got his information from that book we read, then he knows your grandpa got the location of the mine from the diary and that he also had a map that he tore into thirds."

"He could be looking for the diary *and* the piece of the map," I said.

"Right, but we read through the diary and there's nothing of importance in it."

My eyes widened. "Wait. I've read through almost the whole diary and found a section where he tells of the mine's location."

"Really, where?"

"It's . . ." I held out my arms and tried to remember. "Oh, I left it in my parents' bedroom."

Brad's cell phone rang. He checked the ID and answered it. "This is Brad."

I grabbed a candle and climbed the stairs to my parents' room. A cold draft caused a chill in the air when I walked near their door, and goose bumps crawled up my arms. I held up my candle and peeked around the corner. The door I had closed earlier stood wide open.

My candle went out. The smell of wet clothing and skin slapped my senses. I took a step back and bumped into someone right behind me. Dampness from his wet shirt seeped into mine. I opened my mouth to yell, but a gloved hand covered my mouth and another held me tight. I screamed through the dense fingers that muted most of my voice. My legs and free arm flung about, until my nails found the perpetrator, and I gouged as much flesh from his upper back as I could.

He grunted and dropped me to the floor. A candle flickered somewhere in my subconscious, and the silhouette of the man bolted through the open door and into the night.

"Are you all right?" Brad asked. His breath was heavy. He held a candle in one hand and helped me to my feet with the other.

"Did you see him?" I asked, struggling for breath.

"Just a shadow."

I searched the dresser where I'd placed the diary, but it was gone. "He took the diary."

★   ★   ★   ★

After the police did a thorough check of the house and surrounding areas, the best any police force could do in the dark, I was about to collapse. I closed the door behind Officer Reynolds and leaned against it. The diary was gone, and had Brad not been there. . . . I couldn't think of the consequences.

Brad checked his watch and said, "I really should be going back now."

I heard his voice, but his candle-lit features were blurred through my tears. A sob erupted from my throat. I held onto my face, and he gently took me in his arms. I had reached an emotional boiling point; the man's gloved hand over my mouth, the missing diary, and now Brad, my only source of comfort and safety, wanted to leave.

I didn't know how long my tears fell, but when there were no more, I felt much better. It was then that I noticed his arms had tightened affectionately around me. He buried his smooth face in my hair and ran his fingers through the ringlets. Then he tipped my chin and stroked the outline of my face.

Why did he hug me so? Not that I was complaining. There was a comfort in his arms I couldn't explain. Was he feeling sorry that he hadn't talked with me all week? Was he over-come with the knowledge that we'd just come out of a scary situation mostly unscathed?

He placed a kiss on my forehead and another on my temple. All tears and frightening images were forgotten. The tempo of my heart stepped up a bit. *It's just Brad, it's just Brad.*

His lips worked their way to my cheek for a soft kiss and then hovered over my own. A single spark of electricity ignited within me, and it frightened me more than the gloved intruder. The power flickered back on, and he stepped back.

"I . . . I should be going," he said.

The garage door hummed, and Mom pulled in. I knew he was right.

★   ★   ★   ★

The next couple of days flew by at work. Kirsten had come down with the flu and had taken time off work. Unfortunately, her absence meant more effort for the rest of us, and my feet throbbed by the time I returned home mid-week.

I gave a slight wave to the officer permanently parked

in front of my house and pulled into the driveway. When I reached the front door, I fumbled around with the new deadbolt and walked into the house. In the kitchen, another note from Mom lay on the counter saying that she'd gone to the hospital to visit Dad again. I knew she felt guilty for leaving me so much, but I was a woman now, and Dad needed her more than I did.

I stretched out on the living room couch and rubbed the ache from each toe, ball, and heal of my feet. When I finished, I lay back my head and closed my eyes. The exhaustion I felt was so complete, I knew I could fall asleep in less than two minutes, if I had the chance.

Just when I had drifted off, the phone rang. I didn't want to move, but since I was expecting Mom's call, I peeled myself off the couch and answered the phone.

"Hello?" I asked.

The gruff voice on the other line caught me off guard. "Your dad wasn't supposed to live."

My hands and voice trembled. "You're insane! What do you want from me? You have the diary."

"You know what I want." The receiver went dead.

I felt sick all over, but I remembered the undercover officer outside. I ran out to his car and pounded on the window.

He unrolled it and spoke smoothly. "We've been monitoring your phone lines and have traced the location of the call. Officers are on him right now." With that, he rolled the window back up, turned on his sirens, and sped out of the cul-de-sac.

I ran back into the house and called Dad's room number. Mom answered, and I explained what'd just happened. She said she'd leave within a few minutes to come home.

I tried to relax on the couch but it was useless. I paced back and forth across the living room, the hall, and the family room for nearly an hour. What was taking her so long, and why hadn't I heard anything from the police?

I peeked out the front window and noticed Mom had pulled halfway into the driveway, but she'd gotten out and was talking with the officer who'd just arrived out front. I dashed outside to meet her.

"Lexi!" She waved me closer.

"What is it?"

"Chet Strong is dead!"

"Dead? What happened?" I couldn't breathe.

The officer, fully decked out in police attire, towered above us both. "We traced his call to a place in Park City. When we reached his place, he was dead. He'd been shot. Two of his men took off in a vehicle and were followed over Guardsman's Pass. But they were going so fast around one of the bends they lost control and drove into the ravine. No one survived."

My knees nearly buckled. The nightmare was all finally over.

CHAPTER 9
★ ★ ★ ★ ★

It was a beautiful Saturday morning that I drove to my sister's place anticipating the Fourth of July celebration with Derek later that day. For the first time in weeks, I felt completely refreshed and peaceful. The sun was shining, there wasn't a cloud in the sky, and Dad was doing well and would soon be home. Most important, Derek, the guy I'd admired since I could walk, seemed to like me.

Dark green trees and colorful foliage lined each street on the way to my sister's home in Springville. I unrolled the window a bit, just to get a whiff of the delicious floral fragrance that drifted in the air. When I stepped out of the car, I stretched, retrieved my luggage from the trunk, and carried my things up the steps to the front porch.

I rang the bell and was nearly bowled over by my nieces three seconds later. "How're my favorite girls?" I asked. I gave them all a hug.

Kate tipped her head up and smiled. "I'm good. Are you going to sleep in my bed?"

"I don't know where your mom wants me to sleep," I said.

"I'll go get my mom," Britt, the oldest of the girls, said with a bright smile. She turned and climbed the stairs.

Little Beth took me by the hand and led me inside. Vaulted

ceilings soared above a large curved staircase that led to the upper bedrooms and an iron-railed balcony. A cozy living room sat off to the side. The knotty Alder kitchen was hidden from view, but I could smell something marvelous cooking.

Lydia came down the stairs with a baby on her hip and greeted me with her unoccupied arm. Her blond hair was pulled up from her face in a haphazard bun. "It's so good to see you."

"You, too. I've missed you and your kids." I pinched baby Brook's cheek, and she gave me a toothless grin. "I can't believe she's almost twice the size as when I saw her at Grandpa's funeral."

She laughed. "It seems like she gains a pound a week."

"Thanks again for letting me stay with you," I said. "I hope it's not too much of a problem."

"It's no problem at all. You can stay in the guest room. The sheets are clean, and you get full reign of the bathroom down here."

"Good, maybe I'll even soak in the jetted tub for awhile."

"Be my guest. That's what it's there for. . . . Oh, by the way, you mentioned on the phone something about family history on the Rhoades side. What did you want to talk with me about?"

I looked at my watch. I still had a couple hours before Derek would arrive. "I'll go put my bag down, and then we can talk."

When I returned, Lydia sat on one of the deep-set couches, holding a very sleepy baby in her arms. She motioned me over, and we talked quietly.

"Where're the girls?" I asked when I noticed the emptiness in the room.

"They're playing games with Aaron in the den. They should be content for awhile. So what did you want to talk about?"

I thought a moment before I began. "Well, you know

about our ancestor Thomas Rhoades and how he knew the location of several mines in the Uintahs." She nodded and I continued. "Grandpa had a map, too."

I didn't think her eyes could get any bigger. "Are you serious?"

I nodded and told her of the missing map piece, the diary, and Chet Strong. Then I mentioned the mystery surrounding Enoch Rhoades's death and the date discrepancy.

"I have a couple of books you can look at." She handed me her sleeping baby and walked to the den. She returned with a scrapbook and her own copy of the book I wasn't able to check out from the library.

I reread the story that'd brought tears to my eyes once before and noticed another story for the first time. According to one woman's account, Enoch invited friends and family to his place in Price to witness him taming a wild horse. This event took place shortly after the wedding of one of Enoch's half brothers in the spring of 1884 or 1885.

Enoch fell off the horse several times before his half-brother Caleb told him he'd had enough and decided to tame the horse himself. He used some of the skills he'd learned from his father and soon broke the horse. However, when Enoch threw out his hand to congratulate him, it spooked the horse so badly that it rebelled and fell on and crushed Caleb's leg.

Caleb had planned to collect some gold from one of the mines to help fund an addition to a church but was unable to do so with a severely broken leg.

I was certain Enoch wanted to go not just for a chance to have adventure in gold hunting, but because he felt responsible for what had happened and wanted to make things right. Caleb must have told Enoch where to find the mine in the Currant Creek area and sent him off. But Enoch would never return.

Excitement shot through me when I realized I had a

huge clue on the page before me. If I could find out when Enoch's half brother was married, I'd know the year he died. I asked Lydia for permission to log on to the Internet with her computer and pushed the power button. I clicked the Internet icon and tapped my fingers while it connected. Soon, I heard a familiar voice say, "Welcome. You've got mail."

Email? I realized I hadn't checked mine in at least a month. I clicked the mailbox icon and found myself looking at two hundred unread messages; ninety-eight percent of which were SPAM. I started deleting and was surprised to find an email from Brad. I opened it and read,

> **Lex,**
> I take it you are either not reading your email messages, or you are deliberately not responding to what I've sent. Please respond.
>
> **Brad**

Had he written others? I scanned down and found another message from him that was dated a few days earlier.

> **Lex,**
> Sorry to hear about your dad. I'm glad you're okay. And about the other night, I need to apologize for my behavior.
>
> **Brad**

What behavior was he referring to? My curiosity grew as I waded through spam to get to his next email.

> **Lex,**
> I've had so much fun with you the past couple of times we've been together.
> Well, except for being shot at, but other than that . . .
> I couldn't sleep last night, thinking of all the "ifs." I'm glad you're okay.
> I need to talk with you about something, and I don't know

exactly how to mention it.
Please email me and I'll try to explain. Gotta go. Be careful!

Brad

There were no more messages from him. I felt so awful. I clicked the reply icon and typed,

Brad,
I owe you an apology. I haven't checked my email in nearly a month and was surprised to find your messages. Please know it was not deliberate.
By the way, what did you need to talk with me about?

Lexi

I sent the mail but still felt sick inside. Was that the reason he'd seemed a little distant at first the other night? I checked my watch and realized I needed to log on to the website if I was going to get it done before Derek showed up. When I found the website, I searched for the two names given in the book.

Several matches popped up, and I clicked on the first one. I giggled out loud. I knew it was a matter of minutes before I'd find that I was right. Certainly a twenty-three-year-old man wouldn't write the wrong year on his letter.

"What?" I said aloud when I read that they had married in 1884. I refused to believe Enoch died in 1884 and yet here was another clue to show that he did. Was the wedding date wrong? Or was it possible the woman who'd related the story was wrong? How could I find out?

"What time did you say Derek was coming to get you?" My sister's voice startled me.

"Three, why?"

"I think he's here."

I jumped from the office chair, smoothed my clothes and hair, and answered the door.

"This is a nice home." Derek's eyes followed the details of

the vaulted ceiling, grand staircase, and skylight.

"So where're you two headed?" Lydia asked.

Derek cleared his throat. "We're going to catch a movie, go out to eat, and then go to the fireworks show."

Her eyes bounced between Derek and I. "Well, I'll let you two kids get going. Have fun, and don't get back too late. . . . But don't come back too soon either." She winked at me, but it was Derek who blushed.

$\star$ $\star$ $\star$ $\star$

It was dark, and Derek and I had finally made it back to my sister's place after being in traffic for over an hour. Visions of fireworks played over in my mind, and the faint echo of their explosions remained in my ears.

We'd spent an enjoyable day together eating out and watching a movie at the mall. He'd held my hand for the first time, something I thought he wouldn't attempt again after I'd mistaken the tickle of his fingers for a bug and shaken it off.

Derek's voice broke through my thoughts. "Are you going to get out of the car?" He stood outside with my door wide open, drumming his fingers on the hood.

"Oh, sorry," I said. I took his outstretched hand and climbed out of the car.

The moonlight filtered through trees and fell on his handsome face. "You know, I've always wondered about you," he said.

I raised an eyebrow. "Wondered about me?"

He kept my hand in his, and we began our stroll to the door. "When you were younger, I always wondered what you'd be like."

"You knew I existed back then?"

"How could I not notice my kid sister's cute friend that was always at our house? And at the Strawberry campouts each summer; the way you'd gut fish, hike, and keep up with the guys. You don't know how many times I told myself, 'I'll have to keep my eye out for her in a few years when I'm back from my mission.' And now . . ."

I stopped. I couldn't believe that the man of my dreams was telling me words I'd wanted to hear for such a long time.

His muscular arms wrapped around me and pulled me close. He shut his eyes, and his lips moved nearer to mine. Fireworks exploded in the background.

Our lips met. Mine were hesitant, and his were hungry; so hungry, in fact, that I was nearly devoured. Was this the kiss I'd waited so many years to receive? I turned my head.

"Is something wrong?" he whispered.

I shook my head. "I . . . I don't know."

He started for my lips again.

"Wait," I said.

He pulled back a bit. "Did I get too carried away?"

"A little, yeah."

"I'm sorry. It's just that I'm falling in love with you."

My eyes widened. "You are?"

He cupped my neck and kissed my cheek. "Mmmm. You sound surprised. How about I try again?"

I looked at his moonlit features and nodded.

He moved in close and placed a tender kiss on my lips. It couldn't have been more perfect, but where was the electric spark I'd anticipated? When he pulled back, we embraced for a time. Finally, he said, "See you tomorrow." He walked down the walkway and disappeared into his car.

I stepped in the front door and found my sister sitting in the dim light, rocking her baby. She whispered, "How was it? Did he kiss you?"

I brushed my fingers over my lips. "Yes, but . . ."

"But?" she asked.

"It was just different from what I expected. I guess I pictured a magical, romantic kiss that'd sweep me off my feet. But it was just a kiss."

"Why's that?"

I plopped down on the couch beside her. "I don't know."

"Is there someone else you like?"

I shook my head.

"Not even Brad?"

My mouth dropped open. "Brad? He's just my friend."

A smile formed on her lips. "A friend who adores you and who happens to be gorgeous."

I gasped. "Lydia, you're married."

"I'm married, but I'm not blind. Don't pretend you haven't noticed how handsome he is."

Warmth settled into my cheeks. "Okay, so I've noticed, but that doesn't change anything."

"Really? Not even your kiss with Derek?"

I sighed. I almost wondered if my thoughts and feelings were clearly printed on my forehead where everyone could see them but me. "Brad always knew I liked Derek, and I could tell he wasn't happy about that . . . But now that he has that Li Shan woman, I've hardly seen him."

She rubbed her baby's back. "And that bothers you, doesn't it?"

I nodded.

"Are you in love with him?"

"No, certainly not." A warm memory of Brad holding me flashed before my eyes. "But you're asking the wrong person. How do I know what real love is?"

"That's something you'll have to figure out on your own. When I met Aaron I thought a lot of him. I loved being with him, I loved the way he treated me, and I knew he was a good and decent man."

I twisted a ringlet around my finger. "So is that real love?"

She smiled. "I thought it was, but the real love came after we were married."

"After?"

She nodded. "I was so young and only had a small idea

of what marriage would be like. But each day, I felt our love grow. In fact, it still does."

"How did you know he was the right one?"

She smoothed a wrinkle in her baby's pajamas. "Heavenly Father knows all of his children, and He knows Aaron a lot better than I do. So, before we married, I prayed to know if he was a suitable companion, and I received such a strong answer that he was. A lot of people may not have that same experience, but I'll tell you that it's been a wonderful blessing to know that the Lord is pleased with our union . . . but enough about me. What are you going to do?"

"I don't know. I guess I have a lot of questions to answer, and a lot of thinking and praying to do."

"Good thing it's fast Sunday tomorrow."

"You're right. Thanks so much for your help."

"Hey," she said, brushing a golden ringlet from my face. "What are sisters for?"

★   ★   ★   ★

The next morning, I sat on the hastily-made guest bed and slipped on one sandal. I glanced at the clock; Derek would be here any minute to pick me up for church. The doorbell rang just at that moment. I grabbed my other sandal, shoved it onto my foot, and attempted to fasten it while I hopped to the door. Luckily I was successful, and when I opened it there was no sign of my unusual trek—other than the bead of sweat that had developed on my forehead.

"Wow," Derek said, stepping back to take a look at me. "You look really nice."

"Thank you." I couldn't help but blush.

He escorted me to his air-conditioned car, and we drove to his meetinghouse.

It had been several weeks since I had attended a singles ward, and I'd nearly forgotten what testimony meetings could be like. The second the bishop had borne his testimony, a dozen ward members filled the seats on the stand and eagerly waited their turn. I was impressed with what was said and with the spirit that was present.

I was a little anxious about attending Relief Society with a bunch of strangers, but a beautiful young woman, blessed with amazing dark silky hair with tan highlights and sea-green eyes, sat next to me. "Hi, I'm Rebecca Sterling. Are you new in the ward or are you visiting?" she asked with an adorable smile.

"I'm visiting."

"What's your name?"

"Lexi Rhoades," I whispered when I noticed the meeting was about to start.

"Well, it's nice to meet you." She held up a hymnbook for us to share, and I listened to her angelic voice while we sang. I had a feeling she wouldn't be in a singles ward for very long.

Throughout the lesson we exchanged smiles. When the meeting came to a close and there were a few minutes left for testimony sharing, Rebecca stood and bore a simple, yet beautiful, testimony of the Savior and the restored gospel. But what struck me with force was her testimony of our Father in Heaven's personal interest in our lives, and that we can receive personal instruction through prayer and fasting. Warmth filled my heart, and I knew the words she spoke were true.

After the closing prayer, I turned to her and said, "I really enjoyed your testimony. I needed to hear what you said today."

"Thank you. I'm glad you enjoyed it. Will you be visiting us again or is this a one time thing?"

"I'm not exactly sure," I said.

"Are you here with someone?"

"Yes, Derek Manning."

"Are you his friend or something?"

I was caught off guard by her question. "We're dating."

I didn't have to be a rocket scientist to see the sudden hurt on her face. "Oh . . . well, I better go. It was nice meeting you." She jumped from her chair and lost herself in the crowd before I could respond.

I met Derek outside the Relief Society room but was still puzzled about Rebecca. He lent me his arm, and we walked through the parking lot to his car. As he helped me into his shining silver BMW, I noticed a streak of dark hair with tan highlights running towards a red car parked near Derek's. I recognized the distinguishable hair as Rebecca's, but what should've been beautiful sea-green eyes were instead red and tear-filled.

Most of the trip back to my sister's place, I said nothing. I couldn't stop thinking of Rebecca and her sweet testimony. I said a silent prayer that I'd be able to figure out my future.

I thought again of Rebecca's tears, and when we approached my sister's home I asked, "Do you know Rebecca Sterling?"

"Why?" His honey-brown eyes searched me.

I shrugged. "She just seems nice."

I studied his facial expression, but it revealed nothing. Then again, I wasn't very talented at the face-reading thing. When he didn't answer, I continued. "She has long, shiny dark hair, beautiful sea-green eyes, a nice smile, about five foot five, an olive complexion, super nice—"

"Are you sure you just met her? Sounds like you've known her for a lifetime." His hands tightened around the steering wheel until I thought he'd break it. He looked over at my stunned face and said, "I'm sorry. It's just that she's uh . . . she's my ex-fiancée."

My jaw almost fell right into my lap. "No wonder she seemed more than a little disappointed to see us together at church today," I said. I hoped I didn't sound like a jealous girl-friend. That wasn't my intention at all.

"Well, she'll just have to get used to the idea." He sat in the driveway for a full minute before he finally shut off the engine.

After we walked to the front door in silence, he turned to

me and said, "I'd like to spend more time with you today, but I have some church duties I'd already planned before I knew you were coming."

"That's all right. I understand," I said.

"Are you going on the Strawberry Campout this week?"

"Yes, why?"

"I know everyone is heading up Wednesday night, but I have a seven-hundred bag order due Thursday, so I won't be there until Thursday evening."

"That's understandable. At least you'll be able to go."

He smiled and said, "Yeah, it should be fun." He pulled me close, gave me a sweet kiss, and then held me against his thumping heart. "I'll see you Thursday."

★   ★   ★   ★

Wednesday morning, I received a phone call at work. All week my thoughts had been preoccupied with Derek's kiss. Why had I turned away, was I crazy? Why hadn't I felt any chemistry? The more I thought of the matter, the more I realized that though he was the epitome of tall, dark, and handsome, we really lacked the friendship that I enjoyed so much with Brad.

"Hello?" I asked when I reached the phone behind the counter.

"Lexi, its Barbara Manning. When do you need us to pick you up?"

I pictured the slightly graying, dark-haired mother of Brad and Derek on the other line before I said, "I don't want you to worry about picking me up. I'll just meet you at your place. What time are you planning to leave?"

"Around 6:30. We want to get up there with plenty of time to set up the tents and get situated before dark. But it's really no problem for us to pick you up. We'd love to."

It was a tempting offer; I was already time-crunched as it was, but my conscience wouldn't hear of it. "Thanks for the offer, but you have enough to worry about just getting your own family ready. I'll be at your house by 6:30. And thanks again for letting me ride with you."

We exchanged good-byes then hung up.

After a glitch at work, I dashed home and nearly knocked Mom over with the front door. I sprinted to my room where I changed into a simple white T-shirt, my holes-in-the-knees jeans, thick socks, and hiking boots. I knew it could get cool in the evenings, so I grabbed a couple of sweatshirts to wear under my hooded, rainproof jacket if needed.

I pulled my long hair into a ponytail and looked over everything that I'd packed. I had my sleeping bag, jacket, toiletries, scriptures, a change of clothes, my flashlight and lantern, and a first aid kit. My cooler was in the kitchen, already packed with enough food to sustain me for my trip, plus a little extra.

I looked around the room and spotted the Uintah Atlas on my dresser. I shoved it on top of my camping bag and headed out of my room. I still needed my fishing pole and tackle, so I skied down the stairs, ran to the garage, and gathered what I needed. I then hauled all my camping supplies out to the car and then ran back into the house to say bye to Mom.

"Good-bye, sweetheart," she said when I entered the house again. "Have a good time, and try to forget about Ron."

Ron? I hadn't thought of him in ages. "I'm sure I will. Say bye to Dad for me when you see him, and tell him I can't wait 'til he comes home. Oh, I forgot." I ran to the closet and grabbed my backpack. "I was going to pack some snacks." I flew to the kitchen and grabbed some fruit, a box of granola bars, and a couple bottles of spring water, crammed them into the backpack, and waved to Mom as I headed out the door.

I tried not to speed on the way to the Manning's, but it was a challenge. When I finally pulled up to their home and was met with the serenity of their yard, my nerves began to ease up.

I parked alongside the fence made of tree limbs, climbed out of the car, and half jogged up the stone path that led to the front door. An unexpected jolt of nervousness rushed though my body.

I wiped the moisture from my palms and rapped on the door. Soft steps sounded on the marble entry inside. The knob twisted, and the door crept open, but I was totally unprepared for what I found on the other side.

The most delicate and perfectly created piece of artwork from the orient stood before me. She stood a little over five feet on a tiny, well-formed frame and had tanned, baby-smooth skin and large molasses eyes. Sheets of black satin hair draped down her back and full lips parted in a pleasant smile.

"You . . . must be Li Shan." I extended a hand but was afraid I'd break hers if I shook it too hard.

"Yes, and you are?" Only the slightest of pauses was left between each accented word.

"Lexi."

"Oh, Lexi." Her smile broadened. "Brad say I get to stay in your tent."

I noticed for the first time the duffle bag she wore on her shoulder. Of course the Mannings wouldn't just leave her behind to fend for herself in an unfamiliar country. My heart fell onto the floor where I was sure it would get stepped on.

"I get Brad," she said. Her ebony satin locks flipped when she turned to call him. Foreign words poured eloquently from her mouth in a beautiful singsong nature.

Brad bounded down the stairs, responding to her in Mandarin. When he reached the door, he said to me, "I see you've met Li Shan. I hope you don't mind her staying in the tent with you and Morgan. Oh, did you already load your bags in the Suburban?"

"Uh . . . no. I haven't yet." It took me a moment to pry my eyes from Li Shan before I turned from the porch and began to walk the path back to my car. I was surprised when I heard Brad behind me.

"Let me help you with your things." He jogged up to meet me then turned around to Li Shan and spoke more Mandarin.

She smiled and said, "Sye sye," then disappeared into the house.

"Bu sye," he replied a little too late.

I looked at his smile. "What did you just say?"

"I told her that if she put her bags on the porch I'd load them into the truck. She said 'thanks' and I said, 'no thanks,' meaning no thanks needed, or 'you're welcome.' "

"Oh, cool." I unlocked my trunk, and he piled all my camping supplies on his shoulders and arms. I carried my car keys. "Can I take something?" I asked.

"No, I've got it."

"Well, sye sye," I said.

His eyes studied me for a second. "Bu sye."

"Did you get my email?" I asked, looking over my shoulder toward the front door.

"I did. Don't feel bad."

"What did you need to talk to me about?"

His eyes shot toward the door and then back to me. Li Shan walked out with several large bags and plopped them on the porch. "Uh, nothing. It's not that important," he said.

We walked to the suburban parked in the driveway, and he began to load my belongings. I felt guilty that he was loading all my stuff, so I grabbed my camp bag and stacked it atop all the other bags. I also removed the atlas.

Brad watched me. "I was wondering if you were planning to look for treasure."

Before I could reply, Morgan came out of the house and met us at the truck. "Lexi, I'm so glad you decided to come with us. Do you want to sit in the back with me?"

"Sure, I can do that."

After all was loaded and everyone was buckled in, we offered a prayer and began our journey to Strawberry Reservoir. I sat in the back seat next to Morgan, which gave me a close view of Li Shan's long, liquid hair that spilled over the back of her seat. I could tell I was in for the camping trip of my life.

Partway to our destination, I pondered Uncle Enoch's letter. I had studied his unique cursive handwriting and his numbers on the date. There was no way it could be mistaken for a four. It was most definitely a five. After I'd read the letter all the way to the bottom, I realized for the first time he had written the date again, July 7, 1885. But upon closer examination, what I had thought to be a seven, looked more like an open nine, July 9, 1885. So he'd begun his letter in one location on July 7, and ended it in another on July 9. That made sense to me, but what didn't make sense was for him to write the wrong year twice, on two separate days.

I pulled out the atlas and was about to look for the Currant Creek area when Morgan asked why I'd brought it. I explained to her all the events of the past couple of months, and she couldn't hear enough of what I had to say. It was nice to have a fresh audience.

After awhile, my throat grew dry from talking so much. I asked her a question but when she didn't answer, I turned and saw her sound asleep. I wondered how long I'd been talking to no one. My own eyelids became heavy. Li Shan had rested her head against Brad's shoulder, and Brad was doing the head-bob thing. There must've been an exhaust leak I didn't know about.

My eyes began to cross, and when the street signs began to move and dance with each other, I knew I was already in dream world. I lay back my head and succumbed to slumber, interrupted only by an occasional snort. I hoped it hadn't come from me.

My bottom lip flapped up and down and smacked against

the top lip, making a soft noise that eventually awoke me. My eyes popped open, and I found Brad's outstretched finger strumming my full lips like a bass guitar string.

"Thought that'd wake you," he said. "Look at this." He handed me the atlas, which he'd obviously taken from my lap while I was unconscious, and pointed to a small portion on it. "It's Currant Creek."

"What is?" I tried to air the fog from my mind.

"This, right here." He touched his finger to the atlas. "And this is where we'll be camping." His finger slid to the large lake just an inch away."

"Are you serious?" I whispered so I wouldn't wake Li Shan and Morgan. "They're so close you could walk."

"Well, not quite, but we could certainly drive. You have enough info on just what you read in the diary and the plot map to have a general idea where the mine might be. We can leave first thing in the morning."

"Okay. There's no way I'd miss it." My answer was so naïve.

CHAPTER 10

★ ★ ★ ★ ★

"There, tent's up." I brushed my hands while Morgan and I stood back and admired our handiwork. It'd only taken us twenty minutes to set up, stakes and all, and with no help.

I spun in a slow circle, absorbing all the details of our beautiful campsite. Tall pines and aspens grew in thick bunches, which nearly encircled us. The rushing echo of a river in the distance, coupled with a light smell of the fresh outdoors and the scent of surrounding campfires, filled my senses.

Our group of campers was smaller than normal this year—just the Mannings, the Whitmans, and of course Bugzy. I was the only representative from my family. We were camped at the top of a horseshoe-shaped dirt road. Luckily, the aromatic restroom facilities were far enough away they weren't a bother, yet close enough they could be reached in an emergency.

★ ★ ★ ★

That night, when I sat next to the roaring campfire, I was glad I'd brought a sweatshirt. Even in July, the mountain air could cool off significantly after the setting of the sun, leaving a chill in its wake. I tried to flatten the goose bumps along my arms by rubbing them. My eyes absently followed Bugzy, who sniffed around the leftover dinner plates, sneaking a bite or a lick wherever he could.

Morgan, who was seated next to me on the log bench, looked at me and asked, "Are you cold?"

"Yes, I think I must have cold blood running through my veins."

She laughed. "I'm cold too. Here comes Dad with some hot apple cider. Maybe it's for us."

"Do you want some?" Brother Manning handed me a steaming cup. He must've noticed the way I hovered close to the fire, trying to absorb as much of its heat as possible.

"Thanks." I took the steaming cup and wrapped my frigid hands around it. The warm, sweet liquid slid down my throat.

"What about me, Dad?" Morgan asked. "Isn't that other cup for me?"

"No, this one's for me. You have to get your own."

"Dad! You get Lexi one but not me? That's rude."

He chuckled. "Okay, here you go. I only took a few sips."

"Are you serious?" She pulled a face. "Did you really drink out of it?"

"No, I brought it over for you."

"Oh, thanks. You're the best."

"I know," he said with a wink, and then handed her the drink.

Soon, the entire group of families gathered around the campfire for ghost stories. Across the fire, Li Shan's eyes lit up with new experiences. On second thought, her eyes could've been lit with the excitement of being unnecessarily close to Brad.

Brother Whitman stood and gave an introduction to the traditional telling of ghost stories. His tall shadow danced among the surrounding aspens and pines. "Years ago, when Park City was known for its silver mining, there was a terrible rain storm and a young child was lost. His loving father searched around the city and surrounding mountains for many hours but had no luck. As it grew dark and it began to storm more heavily, he returned home for his yellow slicker and lantern and set out to look again. He searched and searched, calling the child's name but didn't even know if his voice could be heard over all the thunder. He gripped a lantern in his trembling hands, squinted in the torrents of rain, and desperately hoped to find his beloved child.

"The man trudged along the railroad tracks that ran through Park City in order to keep out of the mud that was so thick and deep; it was a great deterrent to his mobility. Incredible thunder and lightning blinded his ears and eyes as he walked along the tracks. Unfortunately, it prevented him from hearing the whistle of the train speeding toward him. Not until the train was right behind him did he notice the whistle . . . but it was too late. He was struck and killed instantly."

He paused for gasps and sympathetic comments from those who hadn't heard this story before. "Since that time, there've been many sightings of this poor man—or at least his apparition, walking where the railroad tracks once were, wearing a yellow slicker with a lantern in his hand, and calling for his child."

Brother Whitman remained silent and looked into the eyes of each person sitting around the campfire. I had to smile. His version of "The Man in the Yellow Slicker" was certainly different than the one-sentenced version I'd heard a few times before.

Sister Whitman then shared a story of a ghost that haunts Park City's Washington School Inn. When she was done, I rubbed the chill from my arms and noticed that Li Shan clung to Brad with pale knuckles.

A movement in the trees caught my eye and two men emerged. One of them spoke. "Sorry to bother you, folks. I'm Carl, and this is my friend, Wes. We're camped just right over there." The campfire's light danced on his dark hair and tan skin. He only reached the shoulder of his large friend and looked to be half the weight. "We thought we saw a bear in the area and wanted to let you know."

"A bear?" Brother Manning sounded as shocked as I felt.

Carl eyed the group. His eyes rested on me a little longer than was comfortable. "Yes, it didn't seem aggressive or anything. But we just wanted to let you know about it, just to be extra cautious."

"Thank you," Brother Manning said. "That must've given you quite a start."

Carl placed his hand over his chest. "It sure did, especially being my first time camping. I'm from California. I'm not exactly used to the wilds of the Utah mountains."

"You're from California?" Sister Manning asked. "What brings you to the Uintahs?"

"Well, we like to fish and we heard there's some good fishing up here. And Wes is an avid skier. He's been to Utah several times for the ski season."

"Have you ever been to Park City?" Sister Whitman asked. Her hazel eyes danced with interest.

Wes spoke for the first time in a deep yet quiet voice. His height was matched with bulk. "I've skied Park City, Deer Valley, Sundance, and Brighton. I'm looking to move here, maybe someplace in Park City."

"We're from Park City," Sister Whitman said.

"Really?" Carl scanned the group again. His eyes stopped on me and absorbed every detail of what he saw. I squirmed in my seat. Guys had checked me out before, but hardly ever like that. The stranger's eyes seemed to say, "Yeah, I'm looking at you, babe, and there ain't nothing you can do about it." Shivers crept up my back, and I pulled my jacket closer around me.

Brother Manning stood and shook their hands. "We're telling ghost stories and having some hot apple cider, if you two boys would like to join us."

Wes and Carl looked at each other and then at the group. Carl winked and flashed a dimpled smile in my direction. His piercing, dark eyes bounced around Morgan for a bit before they finally locked onto me. "We'd love to join you."

I was never so glad that the tiny log bench Morgan and I shared was just that—tiny. Had it been a few inches larger, I may have found the dark and handsome stranger by my side. Thankfully, they found a seat on the log bench next to the Manning's.

For the next half hour we shared stories. Some I'd heard before, some I hadn't. After a few stories, there was silence for several minutes. I wondered if storytime was over, but Brad suddenly shifted and said, "A lot of people have lost their lives in search of the gold in these mountains. It's said that the ghosts of those killed, as well as the ones who mourn their deaths, can be heard weeping and wailing in the wind, even to this day . . .

"But that's nothing compared to the story I have to share with you tonight. Well over a hundred years ago, there was a young man named Enoch Rhoades." As he related the story I could feel his eyes on mine through the smoke.

"He was killed in these mountains while getting gold," Brad said, "but the story doesn't end there. More than one person has said that Enoch's ghost haunts these mountains."

I couldn't move or even blink.

"About five years ago, a couple of guys came up here to see if they could find any of the lost gold mines that dot the Uintahs. Not too far from where Enoch had supposedly been killed, these two men were walking along an old path just after a rainstorm. The rain had washed the dust from a small nugget of gold. One of the men bent down to get it when he heard a voice whisper, 'Leave it.' The man turned to his friend, thinking it was him who had spoken. But his friend denied it. The man again reached for the gold, but he felt the presence of someone beside him and heard another whisper to leave it.

"Well, this spooked them since they'd both heard the voice and felt the presence of something or someone. They ran from the old trail and headed back to their camp. Soon, a bullet, shot from a very real gun, flew past them and lodged in a nearby tree. They packed up what they could in three and a half seconds, and jumped in their truck and left. They didn't know if the bullet had come from an Indian, still protecting the gold, or from other gold hunters who were trying to scare them away. But they're fairly certain that it was Enoch's ghost they heard, trying to keep them from taking gold that didn't belong to them."

I wasn't the only one left speechless. No one said a word until I finally asked, "Did you make that up?"

A smile spread across Brad's handsome face. "Maybe I did, maybe I didn't," he said.

There were times when I loved to be teased, and there were times when I didn't. Right now wasn't the time. "Do people really say that Enoch's ghost haunts these mountains?"

He was silent for what seemed like an eternity before he said, "Yes."

"I don't know about you," Carl said, "but doesn't the story of this Enoch guy's death seem a little suspicious? I mean, they say his body was never found. How do you know he didn't fake his own death and run off with the mother lode?"

Through all the thought and work I'd spent trying to find more information about Uncle Enoch, I had grown to love him, and this stranger was insulting him!

I stood with clenched fists. "That's absurd! He never found the 'mother lode.' He was killed trying to get well enough to go home after he was shot with an arrow. He loved his brothers, and even if he did find a lot of gold, he wouldn't have just left them. Plus, he wasn't going to mine again after he returned from the mountains."

I heard crickets and a pop from the fire but nothing else.

"How do you know?" Carl studied me with dark, narrow eyes.

"Because, he's my great-great-great-uncle, and I have a letter that he wrote to his brother before he was killed. He mentioned something along those lines." I relaxed my fists.

His narrowed eyes softened until he finally looked away.

After my little outburst, the mood for ghost stories was gone. I left the campfire and found another cup of apple cider at the picnic table. It wasn't very warm but at least it got my mind off Carl. Others stood and began to wander around the campsite. A moment later, I felt a tap on my shoulder. I turned around and looked into Carl's eyes.

"I'm sorry," he said. "I didn't know he was your uncle. How about we start over? I'm Carl, and you are?" He extended his hand.

My hand dangled at my side. I was torn between never wanting to speak to him again and being a little embarrassed I'd acted so defensively. I reluctantly shook his outstretched hand. "Lexi."

"I really am sorry. Maybe I'll see you around."

"Maybe."

"Well, it's nice meeting you." He flashed another dimpled smile, which somehow seemed hollow, and turned to find his friend.

I spun toward the blackness of the nighttime camp, and cool air hit my face in the absence of the flames. I stumbled through darkness to my tent, where I retrieved my toothbrush, toothpaste, and flashlight from my bag, then headed down the little dirt road to the restroom facilities. I would've taken someone with me, but when I left, Li Shan was still sitting too close to Brad by the campfire, and Morgan was thoroughly enjoying the attention she was receiving from Wes and Carl.

While I walked down the road immersed in thought, I heard a sound in the road behind me. Someone else was headed to the bathroom as well, and by the pace of the step, I'd say they had to go pretty bad. I glanced behind me to see who the poor guy was but could see no one. Maybe my mind was playing tricks. Ghost stories sometimes had that effect on me.

I quickened my pace and was a little disheartened when the pace behind me quickened as well. I walked even faster, more like a combination between a walk and a jog, but the steps behind me grew closer.

My legs carried me in a full-out sprint the rest of the way to the restrooms, and I slammed and locked the door behind me. I stood with my back against the door and listened to the footsteps pacing around outside for a couple seconds before I remembered the reason I'd come in the first place.

After I used the restroom and washed up in the little metal sink, I heard a knock at the door. At first I didn't dare answer, but then I decided it could be someone legitimate. "Who is it?"

"Lexi, are you in there?" Morgan's voice was muffled through the door.

"Yes!" I fumbled with the lock, pulled her inside then slammed it. "Did you see anyone or anything outside when you came?"

"Just Bugzy, poor little thing couldn't keep up with you. But I was actually trying to find you. Wes and Carl have invited us to go on a hike with them tomorrow!"

"What?"

"They want us to go hiking with them first thing in the morning."

"And what did you tell them?"

"Of course, I said we would. Have you noticed how cute they are?"

I couldn't believe it. I'd be perfectly content never seeing Carl for the rest of my life, and now I was supposed to go hiking with him?

"What's the matter? Don't you want to go?" Her eyes sobered.

I shook my head.

She studied a little beetle that walked across the floor of the bathroom; the smile and excitement present just moments before had completely drained from her.

I felt guilty for bringing the mood on her, and yet . . . "It's just that Derek will be coming tomorrow and—"

"Oh no! I forgot you were his girlfriend. He wouldn't like that one bit." She bit her lip in thought, and I was glad she was starting to realize the predicament this had placed me in. She twisted her face, and just when I thought she'd be forced to back out of the hike, she said, "What if we invite Brad and Li Shan to go with us! It wouldn't be so much like pairing off, and you can tell Carl that you're practically engaged. Then if Derek is upset at all, I'll talk to him about the whole thing and tell him I begged you to do this. Because, in fact, that's exactly what I'm doing. I'm begging you. Please come, I can't go alone, and I really want to get to know Wes better. Please, please?"

She studied me while I contemplated my options then added, "I know you probably don't like Carl much after what he said about your Uncle Enoch, but he feels really bad. When I was talking to him and Wes a few minutes ago, he kept saying over and over how he wished he could go back in time and take back what he said. He doesn't want you to hate him for the rest of your life, so that's part of the reason they wanted to go hiking tomorrow, so you could get a chance to see that he's really a nice guy. . . . I hope you let him have a chance to make things right."

It was hard arguing with her. Every time I thought I had good ammo against going, she would shoot it down with missiles. I also knew she wouldn't let me sleep at all until I gave in. "Fine," I said. "I'll go, but only if Brad goes."

She jumped up and down and squealed. "I'll go ask him now!" She ran out of the bathroom, leaving me to brush my teeth and walk back to camp alone.

I slipped into the lonely tent and changed into my night sweats. Then I offered my prayers, read my scriptures by flashlight, and climbed into my sleeping bag. I was only subconsciously aware of Morgan and Li Shan's quiet whisperings when they finally retired for the evening.

Sometime later, I became aware of a soft growling sound just outside the tent. My eyes popped open but saw nothing.

I could hardly even see my hand in front of my face, let alone anything else. Blood raced through my veins. The growls were so close, I knew I could reach out and touch them if the tent's wall didn't separate us.

I didn't know what was worse—my fear for whatever-it-was outside the tent or my need for using the restroom. Apparently, I should have skipped the second cup of apple cider. I felt for my self-lighting watch and pushed the button. It was 2:00 AM. There was no way that I could hold it until morning, but I wondered if I'd even be around in the morning if I tried to make it to the restroom now. I tried to scoot my sleeping bag closer to the center of the tent, but I was already there.

The growls grew louder and with more intensity until they erupted into Bugzy's yap. My muscles released their tension. I felt for my flashlight and slowly unzipped the tent; his wet tongue met my face the moment I climbed out.

I grabbed my shoes then stood up and flicked on my flashlight. Bugzy stuck to my heels all the way to the bathroom and patiently waited for me outside. On our way back to camp, he startled me when he stopped and turned toward the black trees; his stubby tail and ears were thrown high in the air.

My flashlight shined into the trees, but I saw nothing. I moved the light back and forth slowly for several seconds until it illuminated a pair of glowing eyes. My heart nearly stopped. I sprinted back to the tent and hid beneath the covers of my thick sleeping bag. I felt safer just knowing that I slept in the middle of Li Shan and Morgan. If the wild beast's razor-sharp claws would slice anyone through the thin tent walls, it wouldn't be me.

Moments later, Bugzy returned to his vigil outside my tent. Through the remainder of the night, I was subconsciously aware of his intermittent growls and occasional yaps, but I didn't mind. Though he probably couldn't do much to defend me, he was still capable of warning everyone if something was wrong. I was never so grateful to have him as my friend.

CHAPTER 11
★ ★ ★ ★ ★

I gladly welcomed the morning light, though it was dimmed with dark clouds. I studied the condensation on the inside of the tent in an effort to keep me from staring at the black pool of Li Shan's hair that lay about her perfectly formed, sleeping face. She was not only beautiful, but she had such a delicate, sweet nature about her that most everyone at the camp desired to take her under wing and protect her. I should've felt happy for Brad, but instead I was struggling to ditch the uncomfortable feelings that crept into my heart every time I thought of them together.

My thoughts were interrupted by a low growl, different than Bugzy's. It circled around the tent and grew loud enough to wake both Morgan and a wide-eyed Li Shan. The three of us sat straight up in our sleeping bags, and I was sure I reflected the same panicked look I saw on their faces.

"What is it?" Li Shan whispered.

"I don't know. Maybe it's the bear!" Morgan answered. She jumped back when it clawed at the tent. It made such an awful noise that I was sure it was going to tear a hole in the wall and devour the three of us in five seconds flat.

We screamed, though Li Shan's voice wasn't very loud since it was muted by her sleeping bag.

"Help, bear!" we yelled. Where was everyone? Surely

we'd awoken everyone within a two-mile radius and should be hearing the sound of a shotgun by now.

The growls and scraping stopped. Our hysterical screams were all that could be heard before we finally calmed down enough to hear Brad's laughter just outside the tent.

It took no time at all for me to realize that we'd fallen prey to another one of his practical jokes. "Bradley James Manning! Was that you?" I asked.

I was answered with hysterical laughter. "Ah!" More laughter. "You should've heard yourselves scream. 'Aahh Aahh. Help us, bear!' "

I took that as a yes. "We did hear ourselves scream; my ears are still ringing," I said. "And by the way, that was not funny!" I grabbed my jeans, T-shirt, and hiking boots and threw them on. I planned to beat him up. Morgan looked like she was going to do the same, and Li Shan popped out of the safety of her sleeping bag with a confused look on her face.

Brad still roared with laughter outside the tent. "Did I scare your bajeebies?" he asked. At least he was having fun, even if it was at the expense of my sanity. I could picture him wiping the tears from his eyes. "Just so you know, there're a couple of guys out here pacing a hole in the road. Come on. It's 8:30 already."

I unzipped the tent and noticed his hand lowered to help me out. I nearly didn't take it, but then decided I probably should. It was impossible to stay mad at the guy for more than a few minutes.

He kept my hand in his and used it to pull me close. He pushed his nose through my hair to my ear, and whispered, "Looks like we won't be doing any treasure hunting just yet . . . but be careful around that guy. From the look on his face you'd think he spent the last five years trapped in these mountains with not a woman in sight. Especially one who's as nice to look at as you."

He lingered a bit, letting his words of caution soak into

my mind. His nearness and the warmth of his breath on my ear sparked unforeseen pleasantness through my whole body. I didn't realize how gelatinous my knees were until he stepped back and offered his hand to Morgan.

She stood, reeled back her balled-up fist, and slugged him in the gut with all her might. Fortunately for Brad, but unfortunately for her, his six-pack was so hard, her hand bounced right off, and she whimpered away.

After I ate some fruit and a couple of granola bars for breakfast, I returned to the tent and traded the sweatshirt I'd been wearing for my jacket. Morgan was sitting on her sleeping bag and had just finished the last stroke of the mascara wand. She pulled out her brush and combed through her thick hair again.

"Are you ready?" I asked.

"Yup." She threw her brush onto her bag and climbed backward out of the tent to face me. "I'm so excited! Wes is so nice. . . . Oh, you were asleep last night when I went to bed, so I didn't have a chance to tell you that I talked to Brad, and he said he'd love to go with us today. In fact, he said he wouldn't dream of missing it."

"Yes, he and Li Shan are waiting for us with Wes and Carl by the breakfast table."

She peeked over my shoulder. "Oh, I didn't know they were waiting, I just wanted to look nice. It's a depressing fact that it's hard for people to tell me from a boy with long hair when I'm not wearing any makeup."

"You're funny," I said. "Wes obviously doesn't think you look anything like a boy from the way he keeps looking over here."

"Thanks." She blushed and then turned to zip up the tent before we headed to join the group.

It was hard not to notice Carl's crisp, white shirt that clung to him in such a way that I wondered if it had just been painted on him. His dark eyes took several seconds to thoroughly study me.

I zipped my jacket and hid. Thankfully, Brother Manning joined our little group and said, "So, where're you kids headed, and when should we expect you back?"

Carl spoke to Brother Manning, though his eyes never left me. "Well, there's a little trail nearby with some amazing views, and we should be back before lunch."

"All right, we'll be expecting you." He patted Carl on the back with such force, it sent him forward a couple of steps. He lowered his voice but not enough that I couldn't hear. "And take good care of the ladies. Remember," his eyes shot between Wes and Carl, "I brought my shotgun . . . and I'm looking for a couple of moving targets."

Wes swallowed hard, but Carl didn't flinch.

We headed to the trail in silence. I was glad the sun finally decided to show its face from behind the clouds. Temperamental weather was one situation I'd learned to expect in the mountains.

"You ladies are looking mighty fine this morning," Carl said when we'd just left camp.

I fidgeted under his penetrating eyes. The last thing on this earth I wanted to do was to go on a hike with a walking hormone. I could tell this was going to be a long morning.

We walked the dirt road by camp a little ways before a couple of scantily clad young ladies walked around the bend in the road. They must've been freezing.

Carl whistled and hollered so loudly my ears rang. Then he flipped around and walked backward just to keep them in view a little longer. The two young ladies turned and smiled. But the disgusting look on Carl's face made me sick.

"Give it a rest, will you?" Brad said aloud, looking straight ahead.

"What's the matter with you, man?" Carl said. "Don't you like women?"

Brad whipped his handsome head around and looked right at Carl. "Of course I do. I just think that modest is hottest, and cat-calling isn't any way to treat a lady."

"Whatever, man."

Soon we were lead to a tiny path that broke its way through tall grasses, hills, and scattered groves of trees. Carl and I led the way, followed by Wes and Morgan. Brad and Li Shan brought up the rear.

We walked awhile in awkward silence before Carl said, "So, do you still hate me after what I said last night?"

"No." I didn't hate him. I just didn't want him to have any reason to think that I was one of the chicks that seemed to flock around him.

"Good. I was so mad at myself for thinking I'd already blown my chances with you before I even knew your name."

"Your chances with me?"

"You know, to get to know you a little better."

His explanation didn't help. We marched in silence again. I didn't want to "get to know him better." At least, not in the way I thought he was referring to.

"So you're related to Thomas Rhoades?" he asked.

"Yeah."

"I remember hearing something about the Lost Rhoades Mines awhile ago. Do you know where any of them are? Being related and all."

"No, I don't. I think that's why they're called the *Lost* Rhoades Mines."

"So what do you do for a living?" he asked.

"I work at the Tanger Outlet Center in Park City, but it isn't what I want to do permanently."

"Really? I thought you would've said you were a model."

"Not hardly."

"You know, girl, I'm surprised you have enough energy to go on a hike this morning."

"Why's that?"

" 'Cause you were runnin' through my mind all night."

I gasped and picked up my speed. I concentrated on the

small hill ahead, but I could still feel the weight of his eyes on my back.

"You're going pretty fast, girl. Why don't you slow down?"

"I need the exercise, and my name is Lexi." I increased my speed a bit more and began to feel the burn in my legs and glutes.

"Wait, I need to catch my breath."

I stopped. The brisk hike had left me with beads of perspiration along my forehead. The sun was bright, and it was definitely too warm for a jacket. I removed it, tied it around my waist, and tried to swallow the cotton in my throat. I felt for my water bottle but realized I'd left it at camp.

Carl pulled a canteen from his waist, twisted off the cap, and took a long swig. "Do you want some?" he asked.

I was desperate. "Sure."

He handed me the canteen, and I wiped its mouth with my shirt before taking a drink. I didn't want to take a chance that conceited letch was contagious.

"Has anyone ever told you what amazing eyes you have?"

I nearly spat the water from my mouth but managed to choke it down. "Just my boyfriend." I thrust the canteen into his hands and continued up the hill.

He followed right behind. "You have a boyfriend? Who is he?"

I didn't really consider Derek my boyfriend, but . . . "His name is Derek. He'll be here tonight, and he's very protective." I knew it wasn't exactly true, but I also knew that he'd put a stop to Carl's comments if needed.

"You're in great shape," he said.

Was he referring to my athletic stamina or my figure? I stopped and spun around. "Is there anything else you can talk about besides how very obvious it is you like females?"

"Hey, girl, don't flatter yourself. I'm just having a hard

time keeping up with you. Plus, you may be hot, but it's not enough to melt your icy attitude."

"My icy attitude?"

"Look, I told you earlier I was sorry. I'm trying to make conversation with you, and I've even complimented you a few times. The least you can do is act a little more Christian."

My jaw dropped. "I . . . I'm sorry. I didn't realize I was being so rude. But I really would like to talk about something more intellectual."

"I can do that."

We started up the hill again and before long we reached the top. I started down the other side with Carl right behind me. He was silent for a long time, and I wondered if it was because he was panting so hard. When we'd gone down the hill a few steps, he said, "So, you're from Park City, huh? You must be a pretty good skier."

I grinned. "Yeah, if you consider bowling down some unsuspecting seven-year-old after wiping out on the kiddy run good."

He laughed for the first time since I had met him the night before but quickly grew silent again.

"So, do you . . . like granola?" he said a minute later.

"Granola?" I didn't mention I'd had two granola bars for breakfast. Did that count?

"I just thought I heard that you Park City people are really into healthy things, like granola, and yogurt, and stuff."

"Actually, I guess you could say that's true, generally speaking of course. And as long as you're talking about unsweetened yogurt with live active cultures, for good digestive health, and naturally sweetened granola without hydrogenated oils and preservatives . . ." I stopped when there was no response, and I could picture a blank expression on his face.

"You're not one of those chicks that have fur growing in their armpits, are you?"

My jaw dropped so far it nearly touched the ground. "No,

I shave. Not that it's any of your business." A small boulder flicked into my boot. I stopped abruptly, and he crashed into the back of me. The momentum almost knocked me over.

"Sorry." The word barely escaped his mouth between pants.

"I have a rock in my boot. I need to stop for a minute." I hopped on one foot to loosen the lace but longed for a spot to sit; the bur bushes that surrounded the narrow trail weren't very inviting.

Off to the left a few feet, tall trees shaded a large rock. "I'll be right back," I said, then made my way through the tiny burs and other foliage to the rock.

I had just sat down when Carl approached and took a seat next to me. "I need to sit, too."

I bent over to untie my boot and noticed the lack of chatter. "Where're the others?" I tried to sound casual. I slipped off my boot, shook out the surprisingly tiny rock, and looked toward the trail.

Carl offered me another swig of water from his canteen. "You ditched them." His dark eyes searched the hill we'd just descended and then me.

Suddenly, the implications of what I'd done in my haste down the hill hit me. I shoved my boot over my foot and began to lace it. I messed up several times in my attempt to tie it faster than lightning, but eventually succeeded. "I'm going to go wait for the others by the trail." I stood to leave.

He jumped ahead of me and rested an arm on one of the trees, purposely blocking my exit. "Don't you want to wait here for them? It's nice and shady . . . and private."

"You can stay here if you'd like, but I'm going to the trail." I tried to move around him, but he shifted and blocked my way.

"Come on, girl, why don't you stay here with me? You can't tell me it's just a coincidence that you ditched everyone and led me over here."

I gasped and stepped back but bumped up against a tree. He closed in on me and scanned me from head to toe. I felt sick. But the look quickly changed to greed when his eyes rested on my locket. "El aguila guarda su jerarquia," he whispered. He reached for the locket, but I ducked out of the way and maneuvered through the trees. Just when I thought I had made an escape, he grabbed my arm and spun me into a tight embrace.

"Let go!" I yelled.

"Come on, girl, quit squirming around. I'm not going to hurt you."

"You jerk! Let me go!" Panic welled inside me. I screamed for help and landed my boot on his shin. He dropped me to the ground and muttered a couple of words I wouldn't repeat.

I scurried off the ground and began to run but didn't get five steps before I crashed into Brad.

He took me by the shoulders and looked me over. "What happened?"

I knew if I spoke, my throat would squeeze off any words, so I just looked in Carl's direction.

I watched the concern in his eyes turn to anger. His fists flexed by his sides. He faced Carl, who sat on the rock holding his shin. "Lex, will you go tell everyone to go back to camp? I'll meet you there in a few minutes."

Part of me didn't want to leave his side, but the other wanted to hightail it back to Brother Manning and his shotgun. Brad sensed my hesitation in leaving him. He turned his head back to face me and settled his calming, aquamarine eyes on mine. "It's okay. I just need to have a chat with Carl. Go on."

I waded through the growth between the trees then worked my way to the trail where I found the others.

"What's going on?" Morgan asked with wide eyes. "We heard you scream. Did you see a snake or something?"

"Yeah, actually, I did, and his name is Carl. Brad is having a little chat with him right now, and we're supposed to go back to camp."

Her face fell, and she studied a motionless pebble in the trail. "Sorry."

We turned around and headed back up the hill to where poor Li Shan had just finished struggling to the top. She looked like she'd had more than enough physical exertion for one day. Then I noticed she looked very frightened as well.

"Is something wrong?" I asked. Was she scared to have Brad out of her sight?

"Yin di an ren! Yin di an ren!" she said. Her voice shook.

"What?" I repeated her words the best I could. "I don't understand."

She pointed into the trees by the road. "Over there. I cannot say English. Yin di an ren." She shifted her frightened eyes to me. "Brad is where?"

"He's down the hill talking to Carl. He wants us to go back to camp."

She looked into the trees and then back down the hill. Finally, she whirled around—her black satin hair reminded me of a shampoo commercial—and began to descend the hill as fast as I'd ever seen her delicate legs carry her. What had she seen in the trees?

Wes and Morgan were deeply engaged in conversation and strolled down the hill behind us. Though I didn't mean to, I couldn't help but overhear the part of their conversation that sounded an awful lot like a missionary discussion. I observed their voices for several minutes more and noticed that though Wes seemed to be a little quiet with the group, he talked quite easily with Morgan.

When we finally reached the road that lead to camp, I stopped and looked behind me. I could see Wes and Morgan, but Brad was nowhere in sight, and Li Shan looked like she was about to collapse. We walked into camp, and after we had gotten drinks, she climbed into the tent and zipped it closed.

I decided to freshen up in the bathrooms. When I emerged, Brad and Carl were walking in the road, though not together. I couldn't help but notice two angry twist marks on Carl's "used to be" crisp white shirt, and a couple of dark red spots that hadn't been there before.

He eyed me and then dabbed at his lip with the back of his hand. "Are you sure he's not your boyfriend?" He nodded toward Brad and revealed the scarlet gash on his lower lip. His icy stare in my direction was enough to give me shivers.

CHAPTER 12

★ ★ ★ ★ ★

After lunch, camp was virtually deserted. Morgan and Li Shan had crashed in the tent, Brad was quietly finishing his meal, and the Whitman's were getting Bugzy and their fishing things together for a trip to the reservoir.

I lay in a hammock and listened to the sounds of nature around me. Cool clouds covered the sun and were a welcome reprieve from the heat. The morning's hike had left me a bit weary, so I closed my eyes.

Just at the point when I began to drift off, an annoying little bug tickled my face until I became conscious enough to shoo it away. For a moment, I enjoyed its absence, but the joy was short-lived.

Again and again I shooed it from me, until I finally raised my eyelids in determination to kill the pesky little thing. Instead of finding a bug, however, I found a long piece of grass attached to a hand. I didn't even have to guess it was Brad's. I smiled pleasantly and looked into the handsome face that suddenly appeared over me.

"Hey, Sleeping Beauty, did that hike do you in?"

"A little." I reminisced about my speed hike and the chills I had felt when Carl touched my locket. My hand shot to my neck. "My locket!"

Brad took a step back. "What about it?"

"It's gone." I sat up so abruptly that the hammock was thrown off balance, and it dumped me. Brad grabbed me mid-air before I hit the ground.

My feet remained in the twisted hammock, and my hands were sprawled out on the dirt by his feet. He hung on to my up-side-down shoulders and was the only thing preventing me from doing a face plant in the ground.

He carefully lifted me upright and untangled my feet. "I always wished you'd fall for me, but that wasn't what I had in mind."

"Thanks," I said with a beet-red face. "You're quick."

He smiled and gave me playful punch on the arm. "I have to be when I'm around you. . . . So your locket's missing?"

"Yes, Carl reached for it when I ducked away from him. It must've been yanked off." I brought a hand to my neck and felt the small tender spot.

His brow furrowed. "Well, he shouldn't be bothering you anymore. If he even thinks about it, it will be the last thing he ever does."

"I have to go look for it."

He looked at the dark clouds above. "Now?"

"Yes. If I don't, I may never find it."

"Let me grab my jacket. I'm going with you."

We made our way to the road, passed the bathrooms, and then found the little trail off to the side. We walked for a ways in silence, but my subconscious mind kept bugging the conscious one.

"What was I going to ask you?" I said. I wasn't giving him a line.

"I don't know. Were you going to ask me why I'm so wonderful?"

I laughed. "No, I'm more interested to know why you're so humble. But that's not it. I'll let you know when I remember."

The trail seemed endless. I was anxious to find my locket,

but first I had to find the rock. Finding it again wouldn't be as easy as I had thought.

"Did we pass it?" I asked when the surroundings off the trail began to look unfamiliar.

"I don't know. I wasn't paying attention to the trail when I heard you scream this morning."

"Let's go back."

We turned around and headed back the way we came. We looked carefully to the side for the rock that had been shaded by trees but had no luck. Then my eyes met with freshly matted-down growth.

"There it is!" I led us off the trail and followed the previous path that led to the rock. We searched for the locket for what seemed like hours, rummaging through the grass and dirt.

A drop of rain smacked into my forehead.

"We better get back to camp," Brad said.

More rain fell from the sky. I untied the jacket from my waist and slipped it on. "Wait, just let me look a little longer. It's got to be here somewhere." I ran my hand through the grass and looked around the rock again. Fat raindrops pelted us in a downpour, and it was getting hard to see anything. I kept feeling around in the grass and mud. Just when I was about to give up, a glint of light caught my attention, and I saw the locket at the base of one of the trees. I grabbed it and shoved it into my pocket, though the chain was gone.

"Come on, let's get out of here." Brad led the way, but instead of going back the way we'd come, he turned the other direction and led us deeper into the woods.

"Where are you going?" I asked.

"I saw a deserted cabin just over the next hill. We can take shelter in there until the rain stops."

The hill was a little steeper than the one we'd hiked earlier, and I began to wonder if I had the stamina to go farther. Fortunately, my desire for dry shelter pulled me up, and before I knew it, we'd reached the top.

A large meadow surrounded by enormous trees lay at the base of the hill. A small stream dotted with raindrops, trickled nearby.

He pointed and said, "There it is."

"Where?" My eyes followed his finger to a tiny cabin at the base of the hill.

"Come on. I'll race you." He took off before I could even reply.

I did my best to catch up to him, but he was far ahead of me. When I reached the bottom, he paced the ground outside the cabin, only slightly out of breath. "What kept you so long?"

I laughed. "You took off before I was ready."

"Come on, let's go inside." He stepped into the doorway.

I looked at the aged cabin. It was hardly bigger than an averaged sized bedroom, and it leaned to one side.

I hesitated. "It doesn't look very safe."

He pushed the doorframe, and it only moved a little. "It's sturdy enough, and at least it's somewhat dry. Come on."

I took a breath and followed close behind. There was no furniture in the one-room cabin, save an old cot that had only two legs and had crashed to the dusty floor.

A rusted pan lay on the floor across the room. Brad took careful steps across the wooden floor to the other side. "Look at this pan. Miners used these to sift the gold from dirt and other things."

I shook the water from my jacket and shivered, then walked to him and studied the dirty pan with only my eyes.

He set it down and sat in a dry corner of the shack, leaning carefully against the wall. "Speaking of gold mining, we should go to Currant Creek tomorrow after we go fishing," he said.

"I know. I can't even imagine how absolutely thrilling it would be to walk the same ground as Uncle Enoch." I sat next to him and wrapped my jacket tight around me.

"What about the treasure?" he asked.

"It'd be fun to search for gold just because I find the whole mystery of these mountains intriguing, but to be honest I wouldn't want it."

He put a hand to my forehead. "You don't have a fever, so you must be insane."

"No, I really feel that the gold is there for a purpose other than for exploitation. Look at all the people who've been killed looking for it. Not to mention, in his later years, Caleb Rhoades planned to use the gold of one of the Spanish mines for personal use. He even promised the government a portion large enough to pay off the national debt if they would alter the boundaries of the Indian Reservation in order to allow him legal access to the wealth. And look what happened to him."

"What did happen?"

I looked into his eyes. "He died of an illness three months before the boundary changes became official."

"But the mine we're looking for isn't sacred gold. It's just a mine that's supposed to be worth that of the sacred mine."

"Just like the one Caleb died before he could legally mine, and just like the one Enoch was killed getting to."

CRACK! Thunder shook the cabin at the same time the lightning lit it up. I grabbed onto Brad's jacket.

Another flash lit the little cabin. Rain pounded over the cabin, and water dripped through a couple of holes in the roof. The rain and the thunder were so loud I could hardly hear anything else.

He looked at my white knuckles clenching onto his jacket and smiled. "Are you scared of thunder?"

I let go. "Only when it startles me nearly to death." My teeth chattered. I rubbed my hands over my arms, but even though I was wearing a jacket, my shirt was soaked to my skin.

Brad patted the floor beside him. "Why don't you scoot closer to me? I'll try to keep you warm."

I searched his eyes for any sign of a joke, but there was none. I slid close enough that we nearly touched, and he closed the gap so we actually did. My shivers vanished.

"So do we have a way to get to Currant Creek?" I asked, just to get my mind off of being so close to him.

"Huh? Oh . . . yes, don't worry about that," he said.

I'd forgotten about my locket. I pulled it from my pocket and examined the intricate carving of the eagle, then flipped it open to the pictures of my ancestors. My jaw dropped, and new chills formed along my spine.

"What is it?" His voice was concerned.

"I remember something Carl said when he saw my locket. It was in Spanish, but it was something about an eagle." I squeezed my eyes shut and rubbed my temples. "The eagle . . . the eagle guards his nest."

His eyes grew large. "Do you think it has anything to do with the gold?"

"I don't know."

"Let me look at it." He took the locket from my outstretched hand and felt the etchings in the cover. He popped it open to the pictures inside and fumbled around with them. Next, he took out his pocketknife and poked at one of the pictures.

"What are you doing? Those are my ancestors." I reached for the locket, but before I had a chance, he popped the pictures out and pulled something from behind one of them. "What is it?" I asked.

It looked like a deep yellow rectangle. Brad carefully unfolded it to reveal a tiny, torn piece of paper.

"The map piece," we said simultaneously. Squiggly lines and mounds were drawn with faded ink on one side. On the other was an "x" with several river-like lines all about and a cluster of pines sketched at the bottom. The two sides had been torn off.

"There's no way to tell where this map leads without the

other pieces," he said, and then handed the map piece and locket back to me. I studied the map for quite some time before I folded it back up, stuck it behind the picture of the woman, and snapped it back in place.

"Not unless you've happened to read the diary and know it's in the Currant Creek area." I rolled the locket between my fingers. "The chain's gone," I said.

Brad searched his pocket and pulled out a small first aid kit. In it was a long leather string. He measured around my neck and cut it with his pocketknife, then took the locket and threaded it on the string. "Here, try this."

I brought it up to my neck and struggled to tie it in the back.

"Let me try," he said.

I turned my back to him and lifted the hair off my neck. He quickly knotted the string and laid it against my skin. Tingles filtered through me at his touch.

"There, it's a Boy Scout knot and will never come undone." He smoothed it with his fingers and carefully replaced my hair so that it hung in damp ringlets down my back.

I slipped the locket under my shirt and shivered when the cold metal touched my bare skin. "Thank you, but how will I get it off?" I asked.

"You can cut it off, or use your teeth if you have a spare hour."

I was about to turn back around, when his fingers combed through the ends of my hair. I closed my eyes and couldn't move.

Too soon, he cleared his throat and said, "Sorry."

"Why?"

"For messing with your hair."

"You don't need to be sorry." I turned to face him and found his lips just inches from mine.

"Really?"

"Yes," I said. It was only a whisper. His aquamarine eyes

penetrated mine, something that had always caused me discomfort. But now, a jolt of electricity surged through me. His lips moved closer to mine, or were mine moving closer to his?

No, I can't do this. I turned my head and jumped to my feet. "It stopped raining. We better go back now. The others are probably worried about us."

His face seemed a little flushed. "You're right."

When we walked the long, wet trail toward camp, out of nowhere, I remembered what I'd been meaning to ask. "Did Li Shan tell you what she saw this morning?"

"No, why?"

"What does 'Yin di an ren' mean?"

The look on his profile wasn't pleasant. "Where was she when she said it?"

"Down the road a little ways. Why? What does it mean?"

He searched the surrounding area with concerned eyes. "It means . . . American Indian."

"Do you think it was?" I tightened my jacket around me.

"I don't know. But whoever it was, I don't like the thoughts of someone creeping around up here."

We finally reached the road and had rounded the bend when I saw the bathrooms. One look was all I needed to realize it had been quite awhile since I'd last used them.

"I need to make a pit stop," I said.

"I was thinking the same thing."

When I had finished and exited the restroom facility, Brad was nowhere in sight. I hadn't even had a chance to tell him how much fun I'd had today. I tried my best not to feel discouraged, but it was near impossible.

I studied the mud-pocketed road, trying to devise the best route through the maze of mud and water puddles. Suddenly, I felt an arm around my middle, and my feet were whisked right out from under me. The intake of air into my lungs nearly depleted our surroundings of precious oxygen.

Brad cradled me in his arms and chuckled.

"What are you doing?" I asked. I couldn't help my open smile.

"I'm carrying you, so your feet won't get all muddy."

"I didn't think they could get any worse." I wrapped my arms around his neck. "What about your shoes? They'll be covered in mud."

"I know, but I brought others to change into. Besides, you can pay me back later by cleaning them."

I laughed.

He turned his head to me. "You know, you're awfully vulnerable right now."

"Why's that?"

"Because, if I wanted to, I could drop you in the mud," he said. The smile on his face widened. "Like this." He leaned over and held me just inches from a huge mud puddle.

I squealed and tightened my hold around his neck.

He laughed and dipped even lower, then finally stood upright and continued down the road.

I noticed with disappointment how close we were to the tree-lined trail that led to our camp. Brad pretended to trip like he was about to spill me onto the ground right into another mud puddle.

I yelped. "Don't even think of it."

"Think of what?"

"You know, accidentally tripping and dropping me into a mud puddle."

"I wouldn't do that, you know me." He immediately pretended to trip again.

"One of these times you really will trip, and we'll both end up in the mud." My lips were stuck on dry teeth.

My side view saw a form stop directly in front of us. I pried my eyes from Brad's incredible profile, and then my smile vanished. "Derek!" I said.

Brad dropped my feet to the ground like they were two hot coals, which splashed muddy water over everything within a six-foot radius.

My mouth went dry. "We were just . . ."

"I didn't want her feet to get muddy, so I was carrying her," Brad answered.

Derek's questioning eyes bounced between Brad, me, and my mud-soaked boots. "Everyone's waiting for you so we can start dinner," he said.

No one moved or said anything for the longest time. Finally, Brad left my side and returned to camp, leaving Derek and me in sober silence.

CHAPTER 13
★ ★ ★ ★ ★

I poked at my boots with a stick, though I knew they were as clean as they could get. I wanted to ignore the pangs of hunger I felt and spend the rest of the evening in the tent, but I knew dinner was waiting and so was Derek.

Finally, I tossed the stick, zipped my jacket, and sauntered to the campfire. I didn't see him, but I wasn't exactly looking that hard either.

For several minutes, I warmed my hands and boots by the fire, mesmerized by the dancing flames. I felt a tap on my shoulder. Derek stood behind me with a full plate and a wan smile.

"I got you something to eat," he said. "Where're you going to sit?"

My mouth opened. "Somewhere close to the fire. I'm a little cold." I found a seat on top of a not-so-comfy log bench, and he handed me the plate. It smelled very appetizing. I was starving, so I didn't hesitate before I dived in.

Minutes later, Derek wrapped a thick blanket around my shoulders with one hand, while balancing his own dinner in the other. He then had a seat next to me. *Why is he being so nice?*

I could see Brad and his five-foot shadow take a seat just across the campfire from us. I concentrated on my dinner and hoped my eyelashes were long enough to block them from my peripheral vision, but when Li Shan laughed aloud, I couldn't help but look.

She cupped her mouth with her hand and laid her head against Brad's arm. He laughed softly, his head dropped to face her. I knew I shouldn't stare, but it was hard not to; they made such a handsome couple.

He looked up and our eyes met. I watched his laugh turn to a mere awkward smile and then disappear completely when his eyes moved to his brother beside me.

Derek cleared his throat. "I'm glad your boots came clean," he said to me.

I whirled to face him. His smile was gone.

"Yeah, me too." I loosened the blanket around my shoulders. I was beginning to feel a little warm.

Derek didn't say a word or even look in my direction. I made designs in my potatoes. I knew I was hungry, but I could feel my appetite inching away from me. I took a chunk of roll and slowly began to chew.

He pushed steaming beans with his plastic fork and unexpectedly met my eyes. "I think I may be getting a new sister-in-law," he said.

My face must've asked the question my mouth couldn't ask.

He nodded toward Li Shan. "I overheard her telling Morgan while Brad was helping you divert mud puddles."

I couldn't swallow and began to choke on my roll.

"Do you need a drink?"

I nodded; it was all I could do. He handed me a cup, and I took careful sips while he patted my back until I could breathe again. I opened my mouth to speak but never had the chance.

Morgan joined us. "Are you guys ready for the devotional?"

Derek nodded and turned to me. "If you're finished eating, I can take your plate."

I glanced at my half-eaten dinner and handed it to him. I had no desire to finish it.

He stacked my plate atop his and carried it to the trash. Morgan had a seat on the adjoining log bench.

Just then, Wes and Carl showed. I wasn't a bit surprised. Wes scanned the group, and the moment his eyes met Morgan's, a boyish grin lit his face. He immediately walked over and sat beside her, leaving his friend behind.

Carl's dejected face lightened significantly when he noticed the vacancy by my side. He ran a hand through his hair and smoothed his shirt, all without removing his dark eyes from me. He nodded to Brad and ambled toward my direction. I pulled the blanket tight around my arms, but I knew the chill in the air wasn't the cause of the shivers that suddenly sprinted through my body.

When he reached me, he ran his other hand through his hair, flexing his muscles as he did so. "Hey, about this morning. I acted like a jerk."

Before I had a chance to reply, he sat next to me.

"That seat's taken," I said, but it did little good.

Brad looked up. "She said that seat was taken." His voice was stern.

Carl's eyes narrowed. "Really?"

"Yes, really," Derek said. He had just returned. "I was sitting there. You can sit on that stump by your friend."

Carl stood and looked up into Derek's face. His eyes narrowed, but then he turned to me and said, "Is this the boyfriend you were telling me about?"

I looked at Brad, Derek, and Carl, each wearing anxious faces. I swallowed. "Yes."

Carl shifted then took a seat on the stump.

Brother Manning stood and addressed the crowd. "Tonight, we're grateful to have Wes and Carl join us. Camping is an annual tradition for our families, and we feel that these devotionals are a good way for us to express our thanks to God." We opened the devotional with a song and a word of prayer, followed by a spiritual message given by Brother Manning. The time was then open for sharing testimonies. Barbara went first, followed by Brother Whitman, and then a couple of others.

Morgan spoke in a quiet voice but with such a spirit, there was not one dry eye that I could see, except Carl's. The reverence had touched even Wes, and I wondered if he genuinely liked being around us. I loved how strong the Spirit could be among a small group in the mountains, and I didn't hesitate to share my own testimony.

Then Brad began with a simple, yet powerful testimony of the Savior, Joseph Smith, and the Restoration of the gospel. He paused a moment, looked down at Li Shan and added, "I'm grateful for Li Shan. She's helped me through difficult times, and I appreciate it. I know it was very hard for her leave her family and friends to move to America, but I hope she'll feel at home with my family."

She smiled up at him. Her molasses eyes danced with admiration. When Brad finished, she squeezed his hand and didn't let go for the rest of the night. Neither did he.

I tore my eyes from their clasped hands, but I couldn't take them from my mind. Only the looks I received from Carl through the campfire diverted my attention.

When the devotional was over, Derek walked me to the restroom where I could brush my teeth and clean my face. When I was done, we strolled down the muddy road that led back to camp, in silence. The moon was full and bright, accenting the features I found attractive in Derek.

Just before we got into view of camp, he stopped and turned to me. He gazed at me for a minute before he said, "These past few days have been so long. I've been doing a lot of thinking, and . . ."

I shivered. I didn't know if I wanted to hear what he was trying to tell me. Luckily, I didn't have to. Brad and Li Shan rounded the corner arm in arm, heading to the restrooms.

Derek glanced at them then at me. "Well, it's getting late. I'll see you in the morning." He spun around and returned to camp.

I tried to move, but I couldn't. I just stood in the road and watched Derek walk back to camp. He'd been noticeably subdued since he'd seen me with Brad. But the heaviness of my heart occurred mostly when my mind envisioned Brad and Li Shan's hands clinging to each other.

I shuffled all the way back to my tent, quickly changed into my nightclothes, and took the opportunity to pray. If anyone could help me wade through the mud I was in, it was my Father in Heaven.

When I finished, I climbed into my warm sleeping bag and pulled it up tight over my head. But just as I laid down, Morgan and Li Shan entered the tent, giggling.

"What are you two so giddy about?" I asked, though I had no desire to hear the answer.

Morgan's face beamed, and it wasn't from the flashlight directed toward her. "Wes just asked me to go fishing tomorrow. I'm so—"

"Brad give me English name," Li Shan cut in. Her smile outshone the moon.

I sat up on one elbow. "What is it?" My surroundings started to take on a green hue.

"Lisha. It sound like Li Shan. You like?"

"I think it's cute," Morgan said.

"Uh, yeah. It fits you." My mouth said the words, but I ached so much that it scared me. "So, *Lisha*, did Brad ever tell you that he gave me a Chinese name?" The words spilled from my lips before I could stop them.

Her smile vanished. "Brad give you Chinese name?"

"Yes, it's Mae Jin." I didn't even try to hide my joy.

She was quiet. I wondered if I had deeply hurt her. Feelings of guilt began to emerge from me, but they weren't necessary. She cupped her hand over her mouth and began to giggle.

Giggle? "What's so funny?" I asked.

"Your name."

"Oh, did I use the wrong tones? 'Mae' means beautiful, and 'Jin' means gold, because of my golden hair." I twisted a ringlet on my finger.

Her giggle erupted into laughter. "Yes, I know."

"Then what's so funny?"

"Brad need to tell you."

"Tell me what?" I tried to get an answer from her, but she couldn't stop laughing enough to even breathe, let alone speak. Finally, I turned over in my sleeping bag and closed my eyes. Silent tears wet my pillow for at least an hour before I finally drifted into a fitful sleep.

★   ★   ★   ★

My eyes sprung open. I couldn't remember what had awoken me; all I knew was that I was wide-awake. Modest light filtered through the canvas walls of the tent, whether from the first inklings of dawn or from the full moon outside, I couldn't tell.

Crunch. Crunch.

I jumped. Steps emerged from the trees by the tent. I held my breath and counted each one, until I heard it move right outside the tent. My heart nearly leapt out of my chest.

I pulled the sleeping bag tight over my head, hoping it would mute the noise, but I could still hear it brush against the tent. What was it?

There was nothing but silence for a brief period. I stuck my face out of the sleeping bag and filled my lungs with fresh air. But I couldn't exhale. The faint shadow of someone crouched beside the door stood motionless on the tent wall.

I sat up. Morgan and Li Shan breathed deeply on either side of me.

"Who's there?" I said in a bold voice.

The shadow stayed motionless.

"If you don't leave, I'll scream," I commanded. "There's more than one man in this camp with a shot gun and plenty of will to use it." My heart beat so loud I could hear nothing else.

The shadow stayed put and then finally elongated and faded away.

I waited until the footsteps had completely vanished before I decided I should probably go tell someone what'd just happened.

I quickly dressed then pulled at the zipped door, but it didn't budge. I tried again to unzip the tent, but it was futile. The vertical and horizontal zippers were attached to each other. I worked at them for several minutes before I was able to slip my fingers through to the other side.

I found a very long string, knotted about one hundred times and pulled it through the opening. There was a note attached.

Girls, hope you had a good sleep. We are going fishing before the sun comes up. We'll be back for breakfast and to pick you up for a day of fishing. Good luck in your feeble attempts to escape the confines of your tent. We know you'll eventually be successful and be rearing to go when we return.
— Brad & Derek

I looked at my watch. It was nearly six. I couldn't believe I'd let myself be duped again. Brad must be laughing right now, thinking of the panic in my voice.

I slipped off my jeans and lay back down in my sleeping bag. I knew I couldn't sleep, so instead I ran the thoughts through my mind that had kept me awake for the better part of the night. Brad had always been a dear friend, nothing more. But yesterday in the cabin, there was no mistake—I felt something exciting stir within me when I anticipated his kiss. *No, it's wrong, it's all wrong. He's my friend; he has Li Shan, and Derek's in love with me.*

Sleep was far from me, so I decided to get re-dressed and undo the heavily knotted string. With any luck, I could have us free from the tent before the call of nature became unbearable. I began to remove the knots, one by one, grateful for my long fingernails.

When I managed to remove the string and unzip the door, I decided to freshen up. A good sponge bath and shampoo did wonders on the third day of camp. I grabbed my toiletry items and my jacket and headed for the bathrooms.

Awhile later, I entered camp feeling refreshed and clean, though there wasn't much I could do about the circles under my bloodshot eyes.

Sister Manning rummaged through an opened cooler. "Good morning, Lexi. Did you sleep well?" She hardly glanced in my direction.

"It was all right." I didn't mention anything else. "How about you?"

"Oh, I slept fine, but I couldn't go back to sleep after the boys left this morning. So I finally decided to get ready for the day and get an early start on breakfast. They'll be back in about an hour. How do hot pancakes and eggs sound?"

"Great. Do you need some help?"

"Sure. You can mix up the pancake batter."

"Just let me put my things away." I ran to the tent and found Morgan and Li Shan still slumbering in La-La Land. I reached for my bag and noticed it was unzipped. I thought I had closed it before I left, but I shrugged. I must've been more tired than I thought. I positioned my stuff back into the bag, zipped it, and returned to help Barbara with breakfast.

My eyelids felt heavy while I flipped pancakes, but I did my best to keep them open.

"Are you sure you slept all right last night?" Barbara asked when she finally took a good look at me.

"Well actually, no."

"Did those boys wake you this morning? I told them to be quiet. No one wants to be awakened at five-thirty while camping. At least I don't."

My spatula froze mid flip. "Five-thirty?"

"Yes, that's when they left, but I won't have them leaving that early tomorrow if I have a say."

"Did they actually leave then, or was that when they got up?"

She looked up from the eggs and searched me. "They got up at five and left at five-thirty. Is something wrong?"

"Uh, no. I just thought I heard them at six. I guess I was wrong."

"It was probably just me banging pots and pans."

I nodded then flipped the pancake. I checked my watch. Could it be wrong? It seemed to be fine. So either Barbara was mistaken, or . . . Suddenly, I felt wide-awake.

When I'd flipped the last pancake, the Manning's Suburban drove into camp, and all the other campers emerged from their tents—perfect timing.

A few moments later, Barbara carried a stack of paper plates to the table but dropped them when she saw her boys. "What in the world?" she asked.

I looked up from the pancake griddle and nearly said the same thing. Brad and Derek sloshed into camp, sopping wet from head to toe. Water oozed from their boots with each step.

"We fell in," Derek said, but continued toward his tent.

Barbara stopped her husband when the boys had passed. "What happened?"

He rolled his eyes then handed her the fallen plates. "Those boys . . . I don't know what to do about them."

"What's going on?" she asked.

His eyes shifted to me and then back to his wife. "Let's just say we'll have to work a little harder on Mosiah 4:14 and 15 with a couple of our children." He gave her a quick kiss on the cheek, rolled his eyes again and then headed for his tent.

I dished up my breakfast and pondered what had just happened with every bite. *Mosiah 4:14–15?*

I could feel my appetite fade, but I forced myself to eat anyway. When I had finished, Derek joined me. His lips smiled, but his eyes didn't.

"Are you okay?" I asked.

He just shrugged. "You ready to go fishing?"

"I'll go get my fishing stuff together while you eat. I'll be right back." I left before he could say anything.

Luckily, I didn't have a lot of fishing stuff. My disassembled fishing pole was neatly contained in a small plastic cylinder. I glanced at my backpack. It was so big and awkward, I decided to leave it behind, but I retrieved a granola bar and an apple, just in case. I placed them in the big outside pockets of my jacket, grabbed the fishing pole canister, and backed out of the tent. I bumped into Morgan on the way out.

"Sorry, I didn't know you were there."

"It's all right." Her smile was wide. She had just arrived from what looked like a shower with her damp, neatly combed hair. Puddles formed on her jacket.

"How come you're so chipper this morning? Does it have anything to do with Wes?"

She blushed and momentarily diverted her eyes. "He's coming fishing with us today. . . . Oh Lexi, he's so nice; we can talk about anything. He's so cool. I think he likes me. Oh, and he wanted me to apologize to you for Carl's behavior."

"Really?" Wes did seem rather nice. It was hard to believe that he and Carl found anything in common to establish a friendship. I tried to feel happy for her, but I had too many things on my mind. "Is Carl coming?" I asked.

"No, Wes says he doesn't feel very well today."

That was a relief.

"Oh, I almost forgot," she said. "Brad is looking for you."

"Really?"

She nodded. "He said he needs to talk to you about something."

Talk to me? About what? "Do you know where he is?"

"He's waiting for Lisha to get done with the bathroom."

"Thanks." I set down my pole and then dipped into the thick trees to the side of the tent for a shortcut to the bathrooms. It wasn't long before I found Brad pacing the dirt road in front of the bathrooms. Li Shan was nowhere in sight.

"Brad," I said in a mixture between a whisper and a yell.

He jumped, turned to me, and smiled. "What are you doing in the trees?"

"Morgan said you were looking for me."

The smile on his face faded. "Oh, I . . .uh really need to talk to you," he said.

"About what?" I asked. But before he could say anything, Li Shan emerged from the bathroom looking like a perfectly-crafted china doll.

His eyes searched mine. "It'll have to wait," he said, then turned around and walked to Li Shan.

What had he needed to talk to me about? Did it have anything to do with Li Shan or my Chinese name? My questions were left unanswered.

CHAPTER 14
★ ★ ★ ★ ★

I picked up my pillow, placed it back down on my sleeping bag, and checked my backpack once more. My water bottle was gone. I closed my eyes and tapped my forehead. *Where could it be?* Fresh footsteps outside the tent broke my concentration.

"Are you looking for this?" Morgan held out my water bottle. "I was filling mine and thought I'd fill yours while I was at it."

"Oh, thanks." I took the bottle from her outstretched hand.

She looked both ways outside the tent and climbed in. "Can I talk to you?" she said in a quiet voice.

"Sure. What's up?"

She took a big breath. "I, uh . . . I heard you and Brad talking about how close Currant Creek was on the way up here. You said there's a gold mine there, right?"

Her statement caught me off guard. "Yes. Why?"

"I was wondering if you'd had a chance to look around yet."

I sighed. "No, I haven't."

"Well, we can suggest to the guys that we go fishing there this morning. I'm sure they wouldn't mind. It's not that far from here."

"Do you think? I'd love to go."

"I'll go ask them." She spun around and climbed out of the tent.

I grabbed my bag again and dug through several belongings in an effort to retrieve my atlas. But before I found it, I heard footsteps outside the tent. "What did they say?" I turned, but instead of seeing Morgan, I found Li Shan, wearing a confused look.

"Sorry, I thought you were Morgan," I said.

She climbed inside the tent, sat down on her sleeping bag, and tucked a section of ebony hair behind her ear. "You like Brad?"

My mouth went dry. "Um, yeah. We're friends."

She looked to her hands then to me. "Yes, you are friends, but he love me. He bring me here to marry. It is hard for him to be your friend and marry me. He does not want you sad, so he does not say."

I stared into her large dark eyes but could only do so for a second. "You're engaged?"

She nodded, but the excitement on her face was hard to hide.

"Congratulations," I said. I could barely hear the word I had coerced from my lips.

"Thank you." She moved toward the door then stopped and said, "Derek is a good man. Do not put him in garbage. You will be alone." She smiled, then stood and left the tent. The sting of her words spread like venom through my body.

Morgan ran up to the tent. "We're going to Currant Creek! The boys are even packing a picnic for lunch. I'm so excited." She whirled around and left.

"Me too," I mumbled after she'd gone.

I rummaged through my bag, though I no longer had a recollection of what I'd been searching for. I remembered that I'd been looking for the atlas, when I awoke from my daze and found myself staring at it in my shaking hands. I stuck it in my back pocket, retrieved my pole and water bottle, and walked through mental fog to the dinner table.

I greeted Derek with a cordial nod, but neither of us said a word. We then headed to an old, used-to-be-white pickup truck.

"Is this yours?" I asked.

"Yup. It's a little beat up, but I like to keep it around for these kinds of trips."

"And the dirt bikes?" I motioned to the two motorcycles tied down in the back.

"One of them is mine, the other is Brad's. Have you ever been on one?"

I cringed. "Yes."

"I like to ride it in places a vehicle could never dream of going." He opened my door, and I climbed in.

"Do you know how to get to the creek?" I asked once Derek had settled into the driver's seat.

"No, I don't. But Wes said we could follow him." He turned the ignition and plumes of gray smoke shot out of the tail pipe. I secretly hoped there was a spare engine in the back next to the spare tire.

I never imagined the dusty drive to the creek would be so torturously long. We drove so close behind Wes and Morgan, that I could see Li Shan resting her head on Brad's shoulder in the back seat. The sight left me at a complete loss for words, and the squeak of my chair was the only sound over the roar of the engine.

I looked at Derek. His dark hair fell onto his forehead and almost reached his brows. He was so attractive. I thought of the kisses we had shared, kisses that seemed almost empty compared to the excitement I had felt with Brad in the cabin. I shook the thought from my mind. *Derek is a great guy. What's wrong with me?*

My chair squeaked again and made me conscious of the lack of conversation. The tension in the air was so thick I could taste it. Then again, it could've been the truck's major exhaust leak and the fact that we were eating Wes' dust.

Finally, I mustered the courage to at least speak. "So, you left at five-thirty this morning?"

He kept his eyes on the road. "Yeah, why?"

"Well, someone was outside my tent this morning around six. I thought it might be you, but . . ."

"Bugzy was sleeping by your tent when we left. Maybe it was Brother Whitman getting him."

"Oh, I didn't think of that." A small weight lifted from my shoulders, but it was quickly replaced with a heavier one, and its name was Derek. I had a feeling he was upset about seeing Brad and I together last night, only there were no words I could offer to comfort him.

We drove along the road next to Currant Creek, and I let my eyes soak in every detail. The rich-colored earth and vegetation ascended from either side of the water, gradually in some places, and sharper in others.

This is where Uncle Enoch walked. He was here! I tried to picture him riding his horse with his pack mule in tow through the reddened narrows of this very canyon, unknowingly living out the last of his days. My heart leapt inside me, and I felt I was riding through sacred ground.

We stopped just short of the narrows and staggered out of the truck. I grabbed my fishing gear and followed Derek up the creek until we came to a comfortable spot.

I found a large, mostly dry stone to sit on, and Derek sat on another just beside it. I set up my fishing gear, removed the lid from the worm container, and pulled out a wiggly, little worm. After I'd attached it to my hook, I cast my line into the crystal clear water and hoped for a bite.

A movement caught my eye. I scanned the creek down a ways and could see someone walking through the surrounding trees. Seconds later, Brad and Li Shan worked their way to an area just beside the creek with Bugzy at their feet. The sun glistened like diamonds off the water, and green foliage waved slightly in the breeze. It was a beautiful spot for fishing; romantic too.

The familiar irritation I experienced whenever I saw them together was increasing in strength. I closed my eyes. *No, I'm happy for him. They're a great couple. They need each other.*

"Are you praying?"

Derek's voice startled me, and my eyes popped open. "No, I was just . . . thinking."

He sighed. "I've been thinking too. I'm sorry I haven't been myself. It's just that work's been really stressful lately. I try not to let it affect me, but sometimes it does."

"Oh, well, that's understandable. Finals have that affect on me."

He smiled. "I've had other things on my mind too." His eyes searched my face and hair. "There's . . . there's something I need to talk to you about."

"What?"

He didn't answer me. He only studied the details of my face with such intensity I couldn't meet his eyes anymore. I glanced on the bank where Brad and Li Shan were fishing. He gently held her hands on the pole and helped cast her line. Did he really need to do that? Couldn't he just chuck her the fishing pole and say, "Here, push that button and throw?"

"Are you going to reel in that fish?" Derek's voice broke my concentration. "It's been struggling on the end of your line for quit awhile."

I glanced down at my jerking line, and my face grew warm. I stood, slowly reeled it in, and grabbed the net. I was about to scoop up the slippery, squirming little guy, when it made one last wild attempt at freedom. He plopped back down into the cold water and swam away.

Derek's eyes moved between the bank where Brad and Li Shan fished and me, but he said nothing. "So," he finally said. "What do you do to get your mind off finals?"

I shrugged. "I don't know, sometimes I go for a jog or a hike. What about you?"

"I ride my motorcycle." He looked into my eyes. "Do you want to go for a ride?"

My throat grew dry. "Now?"

"Yeah, we can ride up the road a bit, have a picnic, go on a hike . . ." his eyes shot to Brad and Li Shan down the river, "and we can talk without distraction."

I glanced at them on the bank, sitting beside each other. Brad had obviously moved on with his life, and I needed to let him. "All right, let's go."

We packed up our fishing things and followed the path down the creek. When we reached the truck, Derek hopped into the back of it and started untying his motorcycle. I searched for the cooler with all the picnic supplies, but it wasn't in the back of Wes's truck anymore.

"Derek," I said. "Do you know where the picnic cooler is?"

His fingers fumbled with a tight knot in the rope. "Uh, I think I saw Brad with it. Li Shan has some things in there she needs to keep cool."

I scoped the winding dirt path toward Brad and Li Shan. "I'll be right back," I said. I started off on a jog to the secluded trees that hid them. A few minutes later, Brad and Li Shan's voices drifted on the air from their spot in the trees, and I slowed my pace. I glanced in their direction and spotted the cooler sitting in the shade.

When I grew close enough to see them clearly, I stopped. They spoke Mandarin, side by side, on a fallen log. She placed her tiny hand on his cheek, closed her eyes, and pulled him close.

I squeezed my eyes shut. The sudden pain in my heart was unbearable, and I couldn't handle what I was about to see. I took one silent step back, then another. Just when I began to feel confident that I could slip away unnoticed, I stepped on Bugzy, and he yelped like I'd never heard before.

My eyes sprang open, and I gasped. Brad and Li Shan stared at me with stunned faces. I snatched Bugzy into my arms and hid behind his bushy fur.

"What's going on?" Brad asked.

"I uh, just needed the cooler."

Brad looked shocked, almost dazed. "What's wrong?" he asked me.

"Nothing."

He stood and walked to me. "You look sick. Maybe I should take you back to camp."

"No, I'm fine, really. I just need to get lunch out of the cooler."

He shook his head. "I know you too well. Something's bothering you. What is it?"

I looked toward Li Shan, then Brad.

He turned and spoke Mandarin to her. She seemed to protest, but he led me far enough from the bank that we could have a semi-private conversation.

"What is it?" he asked. His eyes moved from me to Li Shan who was struggling with the fishing pole at the bank.

I shoved my trembling hands into my pockets and took a big breath. I thought about making light of the situation, but somehow I knew he'd see right through me. "I was just surprised to see you two together just now."

"Why?"

I shook my head. "Never mind, I should be going." I started to move past him, but he stopped me with a hand on my arm.

"Are you jealous?"

"No!" The word shot from my mouth, but I knew it wasn't true.

Li Shan shouted toward Brad. She held a worm with the edges of her nails and wore a disgusted look on her face. He answered her over his shoulder and turned to me. "Then why are you so upset?"

Butterflies fluttered around in my stomach. "I—"

"Brad!" Li Shan called, and then finished her sentence with words I couldn't understand.

He turned to face her, and though the words he used were unfamiliar, the agitation in his voice was obvious. Her lips curled in a pout, and she fumbled with the casting button on the pole.

Brad faced me again. His eyes searched mine. "What is it? You can tell me."

The swarm of butterflies burst out of my mouth. "How can I tell you when I don't even know the answer?"

He stood with an expression on his face I couldn't read. Before he could reply, a wayward worm attached to a hook and line sailed through the air and caught the hood of his jacket.

Li Shan ran toward us. "Dwei bu chi! Excuse me, I am so sorry!"

Brad had barely peeled the jacket from his arms before she grabbed it from him, apologizing over and over. Her hands worked to remove the hook, but her eyes narrowed when she looked at me. "You need to tell her what Mae Jin mean." She gave a satisfied smile in my direction and waited for Brad's words.

I'd nearly forgotten the hurtful fact that she'd laughed for a half hour after I told her my Chinese name, and the reminder filled me with frustration. I looked into his face and asked, "What does it mean?"

He shook his head. "Now's not a good time."

"He play joke on you," Li Shan said.

"A joke?" My voice was tight, and pain stabbed my heart.

He shot a look to her and rubbed his face. "It's true that Mae Jin means beautiful and gold but not in the way you think. 'Mae,' or beautiful, is the Chinese word for America, and gold is its money. So your name basically means American money. I'm sorry, Lex. I'm so sorry."

Li Shan slipped an arm around Brad's waist.

"Oh, I see," I said. "I'm the one who's sorry. I've got to go." I tried to blink away the tears welling in my eyes, but they threatened to spill down my cheeks, anyway.

Bugzy stiffened and jumped from my arms. He ran up a little hillside into a gathering of trees and virtually disappeared. I was tempted to run after him, but I remembered Derek was waiting for me. I shoved past Brad on my way to the cooler, pulled out a couple sack lunches and bottled waters, and started marching back to the truck. I needed to ditch these emotions I didn't fully understand.

"Wait," Brad called from my heels, but I didn't stop. "I didn't mean for it to turn out this way. It just came out. It's what we did to new missionaries all the time in Taiwan."

I swiped at the burning tears rolling down my cheeks. "Do you see a name tag on me that says 'Sister Rhoades'?"

"No."

"I didn't think so." I continued down the road without a glance behind me.

"Come on, Lex, wait. Let's talk about this."

"There's nothing to talk about. Besides, Derek is waiting for me."

He pulled me to a stop and turned me to face him. Li Shan was nowhere in sight. "He can wait, but this can't. I need to talk to you." His voice wasn't soft but not harsh either. "I'm sorry I gave you that name. I was in a weird mood that night. I was going to tell you it was just a joke. But you looked like a girl on Christmas Day, and I didn't want to spoil it."

"Why didn't you tell me before I made a fool of myself?"

"I tried to, and besides, I didn't know you were going to tell her." His eyes widened, and he looked straight through me. "Wait a minute—you are jealous, aren't you?"

I bit my lip. My mind struggled for words, but my heart knew exactly what to say. "Yes, I'm jealous, I'm jealous that you spend more time with her than with me. I'm jealous that she's your friend . . . and I'm not."

"You're jealous of our *friendship?*"

I nodded.

His shoulders slumped then he held me by both arms. "You are my friend. I care about you. But I can't be just a friend to you anymore, Lex; it's too painful." His voice softened to a whisper, and he looked right into my eyes. "Whenever we're together, it's all I can do to keep myself from showing you just how much I care for you."

"But you're engaged to Li Shan."

His mouth dropped open. "Where did you hear that?"

"She told me this morning."

He rubbed his forehead and groaned. "Before she came to the U.S., I told her we could see how things would work out between us, but I never proposed to her, nor do I plan to. There're just too many things I found out about her that I don't like, and manipulation is one of them."

"Manipulation?"

"Exactly. She knows how I feel about you and she's really upset. I think she was hoping that by getting you out of the picture it'd change things, but it doesn't. Nothing can change the way I feel about you."

"Then what were you doing with her by the river a couple minutes ago?"

He shook his head and smiled. "What you saw was a desperate Li Shan trying to bust a move on me. What you didn't see, apparently, was me ducking out of the way."

"You ducked?"

"Of course. How could I even think of kissing another woman when I'm in love with you?"

I stared at him with an open mouth. The feelings consuming me were indescribable. I was too stunned to speak.

When I said nothing, he continued. "I'm crazy about you, and it rips my heart out to see you in my brother's arms." His voice broke, and he turned his head. "I know you like him, Lex, but is he your best friend? Can you talk to him about anything? Does he make you laugh? If you can tell me right here and now that you're in love with him and you feel nothing for me, and never will, then I have no choice but to move on with my life. But if there's even the tiniest doubt as to how you feel about my brother, or a hint of interest in me, I'll never leave your side, never."

He slipped a hand around the back of my neck, looked into my eyes, and whispered, "Please tell me I mean something to you. Please tell me there was meaning behind the excitement I saw in your eyes at the cabin. Tell me the reason you're jealous of Li Shan is because you're as much in love with me as I am with you."

I couldn't speak, I couldn't even breathe. I just nodded my head. The lunch bags and water I'd been carrying dropped to the ground unnoticed.

His fingers ran along my jaw and tipped my chin to meet his face. Then he cupped my face and leaned in close. His warm lips brushed against mine initially, but became more and more determined with each passing moment.

I returned his kiss with emotions I didn't know were possible. Nothing could've felt closer to heaven than this kiss that filled me with such profound electricity.

Moments later, we pulled apart and held each other.

"I love you," I whispered.

He tightened his arms around me and buried his face in my hair. "You don't know how long I've prayed to hear you say those words." His lips pressed against my cheek, and then moved to caress my lips a second time. I thought my heart would leap right out of my chest.

"Brad?" Li Shan's tiny voice sounded somewhere deep in my mind, like an annoying alarm telling me it was time to wake up from a wonderful dream. I shoved it from my thoughts, and Brad shooed at it with a hand he reluctantly tore from my waist.

"Brad!" she yelled. This time our lips parted, and we

whirled around to face her. I expected that her eyes would be red and puffy, but instead it was her face. She spat out words in a language I couldn't understand, then picked up a small stone and chucked it at Brad with all her might. Luckily, her might wasn't much, and the stone merely grazed the pants around his shin. Her eyes narrowed, and then she spun around and left the way she'd come.

A gnat nearly made its home in my opened mouth before I finally closed it. But if her reaction was shocking, there wasn't a word to describe Derek's. He stood in the middle of the road with tight fists and clenched jaws, glaring at Brad.

"What are you doing?" Derek asked, but he didn't wait for an answer before he lunged at Brad.

CHAPTER 15

★ ★ ★ ★ ★

"Do we have the picnic supplies?" Brad sat atop his dusty, red Honda 650 motorcycle and warmed up the motor with a twist of the handle.

"Check," I answered.

"Map piece?"

"Check."

"Your cute smile?"

I giggled. "Check."

"Then hop on and hang on tight."

I zipped up Brad's backpack and threw it over my shoulders. I took his hand to help me climb aboard and wrapped my arms snuggly around his waist. It had been awhile since my last ride on a motorcycle, but the memory was as fresh as if it'd happened last week; it wasn't pleasant.

Brad revved the engine once more and took off. I squeezed my eyes shut and uttered a silent prayer for our safety. The wind caught my hair and slapped it into my cheeks. I'd hoped to absorb every detail of the narrows of Currant Creek as we passed through them, but I didn't dare open my eyes for more than a few seconds at a time.

We slowed a bit and turned off the main road. Brad leaned to the right with the bike, but I did my best to stay put. "Try to lean into the turn," he yelled over the bike's motor.

"I can't. I'll fall off," I said. My eyes were still closed.

"You won't fall off. You're holding onto me so tightly I can't breathe."

"I'm just following orders." I did my best to lean into the turn, but I wouldn't loosen my grip around his waist. He would just have to deal with a lower intake of oxygen until my feet were safely planted on solid ground.

We rode for awhile more before I found myself leaning forward to fight gravity up a steep and winding road. My hold around Brad's waist tightened even more until I heard his labored breathing. I took a peek out of my clamped lids. A steep drop off on one side left no room for mistake on the narrow dirt road. My mouth went dry, and my legs began to tremble. A silent prayer for our safety played over and over in my heart. Eventually, we descended the hill, slowed, and came to a stop. I opened my eyes only after Brad had killed the engine, and I knew we were stopped for good.

"What do you think?" he asked.

I took a look at our surroundings: dirt, rocks, thick green trees, and mountains. Not too different from the scenery we had just left. But off to the left of the trail the earth sagged, and in its very center was a small amount of water. "Is that the spring my ancestor wrote about?" I asked.

"It might be. What else did the diary say?"

I squeezed my eyes shut. "There was a cliff or a mountain or something that he climbed."

"Like that one?"

I followed his pointed finger to the hill and ledge to our right. I couldn't explain the chills that crept up my back. "I think so." I jumped from the bike and hoped my knees would hold me.

Brad dismounted and took his backpack from my trembling hands. "Have you ever been on a motorcycle before?"

"Yes, and I swore I'd never do it again."

"And now?"

"I'm never getting on one of those things, again."

He laughed. "It's not that bad once you get used to it."

"I'm sure you're right. But doesn't that imply that I'd actually have to get on one to get used to it?"

"How else are you going to get back to camp?"

I grinned. "You can carry me."

He gave me a quick peck. "Let's find a spot for lunch. I'm starving."

We hiked up the hill though shady trees, until we came to a beautiful spot where a sunny ledge overlooked the valley below. My jacket had long been tied around my waist. We set up our little picnic in the shade of the trees and enjoyed the view.

Our lunch wasn't a grand feast; just a couple of sandwiches, some veggies, fruit, and chips, but it did the trick. My eyes wandered to Brad. The day's growth of stubble on his chin added to the rugged look of his jeans, hiking boots, and T-shirt. I still couldn't get over the fact this handsome hunk loved me, nor that I loved him. I couldn't stop giggling inside.

"Do you feel guilty about ditching everyone to come over here?" I asked.

"No, not in the least. We can't waste a trip up here and not look around for the mine."

"I hope Li Shan will be okay." I couldn't get her red, angry face from my mind.

He was thoughtful a moment, then replied, "She'll be fine after she gets her medication."

"Are you serious?" I didn't know whether or not to laugh.

"Totally. There're a lot of things about her that aren't readily apparent."

My eyes shifted to the crack on his lower lip. "I'm sorry about Derek."

He brought a hand to his wound. "Well, I can't blame him for being upset, especially when it's you he's lost. He thinks he's in love with you, you know."

"I know." My heart ached. "Do you think he'll be okay?"

"He'll be fine after a good motorcycle ride cools him down." His eyes moved across my face. "You have a little bit of sandwich in the corner of your mouth."

I picked up my napkin, but before I brought it to my lips I stopped. "I'm not falling for that one again."

He smiled. "No, I'm serious. It's right there." He pointed to the corner of my mouth.

I didn't budge. I was pretty sure he was teasing me, but . . . if there really was a big crumb on my face, I didn't want to let it sit there.

He sensed my inner dilemma and shifted closer to me. "Here, let me get it for you."

I expected him to grab a napkin and begin wiping my face, but instead he brought up a finger, traced my lips, leaned in, and gave me a kiss. "There, I got it," he said after he pulled back and examined me.

"Did I really have a crumb?"

"No, I just wanted to kiss you." He wiped a bead of sweat from his brow, picked up his water bottle, and took a long drink. "So, are you ready to go treasure hunting?"

"Of course."

He turned his head and raised an eyebrow. "Did you hear that?"

"What?"

"I thought I heard something over there." He pointed into the trees. "I'm going to go check it out. I'll be right back." He stood and started to leave but stopped. "Oh, I almost forgot." He picked up his backpack and unzipped the outer pocket. "You can use this to look around." He chucked binoculars into my lap and went deeper into the trees behind me. I listened to his footsteps fade, and then gathered up all the garbage from lunch and shoved it into the backpack.

I stood and walked as close to the ledge as my fear of

heights would allow. I shielded my eyes from the sun and took in all I could of the landscape. I could see for miles from my point of view. I brought the binoculars to my eyes and moved it over the valley. Nothing jumped out at me at first, but then I saw something that made me gasp.

Brad stepped up behind me and slipped his arms around my shoulders. "It was just a squirrel. Find anything interesting?"

"I think so." I moved the binoculars along the sharp descent of the ledge on which we stood, to the small valley and stream below. "There, on that rocky hill." I handed him the binoculars and pointed.

He moved the binoculars around for a bit, trying to steady them. "Is that a statue of an eagle?"

"I think so. It looks just like the one on my locket, except its wing and beak are chipped off."

He let out a whistle. "The eagle guards his nest."

"But if the nest is the treasure, where would it be? Would he be sitting on it, or watching it from somewhere else?"

"I don't know. Maybe your map-piece can give us a clue."

I pulled the locket from the inside of my shirt, popped it open, and used my fingernail to release the picture. I searched the map, flipping it to several different angles. I stopped on one. "Look at this. I think this mark might be the mountain with the eagle on it, but you can see here that this line, which I think is the trail to the treasure, leads off the map."

"So the eagle is watching the nest." He put the binoculars to his eyes and moved them around. "His beak is pointed toward that hill over there."

I looked at the hill. Yellow and gray rugged rocks jutted out of the ground surrounded by thick, green trees. I tugged on his shirt. "Let's go."

Brad grabbed the backpack and threw it over his shoulders.

We jogged down the hill to the bike, but as soon as we reached it, my stomach churned.

"What's wrong," he asked when he noticed the look on my face.

"Are you sure we can't just walk?"

"Not if you want to reach the mine before sunset." He placed a sympathetic hand on my shoulder and said, "Come on. I'll drive slow and safe. You know I wouldn't ever let anything happen to you."

I shook a dusty memory of a motorcycle wipeout from my mind and took his hand. He helped me up, and once again, I wrapped my arms around him and squeezed my eyes closed. If I didn't look, I wouldn't witness the potential wreck that would play over and over in my mind.

The second ride was worse than the first. There was no road. We drove up and down hills, bumped over weeds and brush, and weaved between trees. Some may have found the experience exhilarating, much like an amusement park ride. But I nearly lost my lunch.

Brad killed the engine when we finally made it to the base of the rocky, tree-covered hill. "What exactly are we looking for anyway?" he asked.

I opened my eyes and was taken aback with the enormity of the jagged mountainside before us. "A cave or a mine or something," I said. "Let's just look around." An unexplained feeling came over me, and I grabbed onto Brad's shirt. "This is it," I said in a whisper.

He turned his head to study my face. "How do you know?"

"I don't know. I can just feel it."

We jumped off the bike and walked around the base a bit, but quickly decided that the best way to explore the shadows that dotted the side of the hill was to hike. Our first destination was a deep shadow between two large rocks partway up the mountainside.

164

The closer we got, however, the lighter the shadow became until it was very obvious that it was not an opening, merely a crevice. We repeated this process with every shadow we encountered until we spotted another close to the top.

I couldn't take my eyes from the deep crevice, hidden behind thick trees and a large rock.

"We've got to keep going," I said. My legs ached, but I forced them up the mountain's side.

When we'd reached the deep shadow I was encouraged. It seemed to go quite a ways into the mountainside, but its looks were deceiving. It was merely a deep crevice, shaded by the afternoon sun. "I need to catch my breath," I said and found a spot to sit by some tall bushes.

Brad tossed me his backpack. "There's more water in there."

I unzipped the bag, grabbed the water bottle and gulped it down. Brad did the same. Water poured from the bottle and squeezed between the cracks of his lips, down his chin and neck where they added to the wetness of his shirt. "Are you ready to give up and go back, or do you still want to look around?" he asked.

Before I could answer, he focused on something behind me. I turned to see what he looked at and brought a hand to my mouth. In the makeshift cave, etched in stone, were the words, "E.R.—1885"

My hand reached out and felt the etch marks in the cold stone. "Enoch Rhoades. He was here in *1885!*"

A little warning sounded in my heart, and I wondered if we should go back. I should've listened to it but instead found myself saying, "Let's keep going. We've come too far to give up now. We're so close, I can feel it."

He looked at the ledge above us. "We're almost to the top. Come on, I'll race you."

I slipped the backpack over my shoulders and followed close behind him, grabbing onto rocks to help me up. I focused on my destination. To look behind me would have stopped me with a fear of the altitude.

Brad wiped at his brow when we reached the top moments later. "Wow, look at the view," he said. He propped one leg on a rugged boulder and looked over the rolling hills of green and brown that stretched as far as the eye could see. The scene looked like an ad from an outdoorsman magazine.

I tossed him the binoculars from the backpack, and he brought them to his eyes and focused. "The eagle is staring right at us."

A shiver slid through my body. "But I haven't seen anything that looks like a cave or a mine."

"Let's take a look at the map again."

I popped open the locket and retrieved the map piece. I looked at the front, and then flipped it over to the back. The "x" with the maze of branches intrigued me. What did they lead to? I held out the map for Brad to take. He leaned down to grab it, but it slipped from his fingers and drifted off the ledge on an air currant.

My hand flew to my mouth. "Oh, no!"

"Don't worry, I'll get it." He jumped to the ledge and leaned over.

"Don't scare me like that. You're going to fall over."

"Like this?" He made preparation to leap but stopped and flashed a handsome smile before he gave me an actual heart attack. But then his smile faded, and he said, "It's gone with the wind."

"Are you serious?"

"I'm afraid so, sorry."

I sighed. "Oh, well. We should probably go back, anyway."

"Maybe we just haven't looked everywhere yet." He got on his knees and leaned his head over. "There's another ledge down below." He turned around and let his feet hang over the edge.

The warning sensation I'd been suppressing finally erupted like a volcano. "We need to leave right now!" The words just poured from my mouth, and my heart burned with their truthfulness.

Brad's expression turned to surprise, but he took me seriously and started to climb off the ledge.

"Wait," I said. A couple four-wheelers kicking up dust below us caught my attention. "Who's that?"

He shrugged. "Probably just a couple of guys out for a joy ride. Why?"

"They've stopped, and they're looking right at us."

Brad put the binoculars to his eyes. "I can't tell who they are, but . . ."

"But what?" I could see the men getting off their ATV's, but they were too small to make out any details. My clammy hands added to the anxiety in the pit of my stomach.

"They've got guns."

My blood ran cold. Part of me rationalized that they were just exploring and brought guns along for protection. But for reasons I couldn't explain, I knew that wasn't the case.

Instinctively, I hugged the ground and crawled to Brad at the ledge.

"We've got to go down there," he said. "It's the only way." He looked back at the men who were now bounding up the hill on foot. "Come on, quick. I'll help you down."

"I can't." My hands clammed up, and my heart raced when I noticed the drop on the other side of the ledge.

"Lex, I'll lower you down. Just grab onto me!" He held onto me tight and led me over the edge. My feet slipped but he gripped my arms until my aching feet reached the lip of rock below.

"All right, I made it." I wiped my palms and glanced up at Brad. Only his hands and worried face were visible from the lip where I stood. Then I noticed cool air radiating from a hollowed section in the hillside right next to me, hidden behind a large tree. Goose bumps prickled my arms and legs. "The cave!" I shouted.

A shot rang out and kicked up dust on the ledge above. Brad let out a soft moan and disappeared from my view.

"Brad!" I yelled but wasn't answered. Frantically, I searched for a way back up but it was impossible without a rope. "Brad!" Tears burned my eyes and cheeks. My breathing was quick and shallow.

The steep, heavily wooded hill below was the only way back to the other side of the mountain. I started down the hill. A shot from the ledge shattered a section of rock beside me. Another caught my calf. I dropped to the ground in pain. "Brad!" There was no answer to my calls. Another bullet flew past me. I scrambled to the cave where I could find cover from the shower of bullets and check my wound.

Once I reached the cave, I took a second to catch my breath. My heart pounded in my chest and in my leg. But any physical pain I experienced paled to the pain in my heart. *What happened to Brad?*

I peeled back my dusty jeans and was grateful to find the bullet had only grazed the skin. I grabbed the first aid kit out of the backpack along with some water. I was just about to rinse my wound and bandage it up when dust rained down and two unfamiliar legs lowered from the ledge above. I stuffed everything back into the pack and threw it over my shoulder. Then I stood and retreated deeper into the blackness behind me.

A man in silhouette entered the cave. The click of his pistol's hammer suspended over the firing pin made my heart stop. His flashlight flickered in my direction and nearly illuminated the friendly shadows that hid me.

I inched my way further into the blackness but could only go so far. A large boulder held rubble and blocked my way. Beneath it was a small black opening. The light came closer and the slow steps became louder. I got on my belly and eased through the opening, everything but my last foot. Bits of stone and dust sprinkled onto my head, and I prayed that I wouldn't cause a major disturbance.

The guy's hand grabbed my leg, and I screamed. I struggled to get free, but he began pulling me back through the opening. The ceiling groaned and dust rained down.

"Let go!" My voice revealed the panic I felt. "The whole thing is going to cave in!"

Instantly, my leg was freed, and I plummeted forward. The ground shook. Rocks and dirt dropped from the ceiling in every direction. I shot to my feet; my injury was completely forgotten. I felt along the walls for a way out with one arm, while shielding my head with the other.

Flickers from his beam bounced off the dust and walls in rapid jerks. I should've been grateful for the light but knew it meant he was chasing me. His heavy breathing closed in, though it was felt more than heard over the roar of the ceiling crumbling overhead.

The light illuminated a tunnel that branched off of the main one, and I changed my course. My pursuer approached me from behind and threw his body into mine, sending us both into the smaller tunnel. I braced for impact with the ground but found myself tumbling down a steep, narrow shaft.

Boulders and other debris from the collapsed tunnel above chased us down the shaft and into a small hollow cave. The flashlight's beam lasted only a second before a wave of dirt swallowed it. Tiny rocks bounced off me and echoed throughout the cave.

I slipped and struggled in the chocking black to get out of destruction's path. The sound and vibration of a large boulder preceded its actual presence. I threw my arms over my head and dove for cover, narrowly escaping its crush. But just when I thought I was safe, it rolled to a stop next to my foot, pinning it against another rock. An eerie silence and gritty, suffocating blackness surrounded me. It was then that I realized I had landed on something soft, warm, and moaning.

CHAPTER 16

★ ★ ★ ★ ★

Consciousness entered the body beneath me before I came to my senses. His muscular arms locked around mine. I clawed at them, but he only tightened his grip.

"What do you want from me?" I choked on the words with a mouthful of dust.

"I want the map, girl." Carl's voice and his hot breath in my ear brought waves of sickness almost to the surface.

"Let go!"

"I don't want to hurt you. Just give me the map."

I struggled to get away. "Let me go!"

His arms tightened around me even more, and his voice boomed. "Not until you hand it over!"

I wrestled to escape but realized that even if I could, my boot and pant leg were pinned between boulders. *If only I can get free.* "It's in my boot, but it's stuck. Help me get it off, and I'll help you."

He hesitated a moment before he said, "Do you have a flashlight?"

"I think so."

The intense pressure around my arms released, and I sat up. Brad's backpack still hung by one strap over my shoulder. I blindly searched its contents and felt the flashlight lying in the bottom. Its beam nearly blinded me when I pressed the button.

Carl kneeled beside me, snatched the flashlight from my hands, and shined it on my leg. A hefty boulder rammed my boot against a large rock. It looked painful, but my foot rested in a hollow pocket between the two.

He flashed the light in my face then dropped it to my neck. The sound of a switchblade being extracted from its cover, sliced through the fading rumble left in the cave. With one hand, he slid the cold, metal blade along my neckline until it met with the leather string holding the locket over my thumping heart. He cut right through the leather and clenched the locket in his hand. "Don't play games with me, girl. I saw where you put it."

He took several steps back and propped the flashlight on the backpack he'd ripped from my lap. The dim light illuminated his tousled, dark hair. His face was distorted with a scowl. He pulled open the locket, ripped out both photos, and swore. "Where is it?"

I didn't say a word.

He kneeled to my side, where I sat crumpled on the ground trying to free my pinned foot, and grabbed me by the shirt. "Where is it?" The veins in his forehead bulged until I thought they'd burst.

"I . . . it's gone," I said.

"What do you mean, it's gone. I watched you put it in the locket."

"I took it out, and it flew off the ledge."

He ripped the boulder from my foot in one swipe and started searching my boots, pockets, and every other place he thought I'd hidden it. I finally managed to push him hard enough to gain some freedom. "I don't have it. It's gone!" I yelled.

"You've ruined everything!" He yanked me off of the ground and threw me against the side of the cave.

My head smacked the lumpy wall. I shook away the spots forming before my eyes and rubbed at the pain in my head.

I have to get out of here. But where can I go? I forced my legs to move, but Carl lifted me and pressed me into the wall.

"Let me go!" My scream echoed in the small cave. Sharp rocks poked into my back.

His breathing was heavy, and though I could see nothing but the flashlight directed into my face, I could feel the heavy malice he carried for me. He dropped me to the ground, leaned against the wall, and slid down until he sat next to me.

My eyes roamed the dimly lit walls for another way out. Mineral formations hovered over our heads like colorful icicles. But the shaft we'd tumbled down was sealed off. There was no escape.

Carl shifted and pulled a couple of torn papers from his pocket, flipping them over absently with his fingers.

"Where did you get those?" I asked, staring at the other two pieces of Grandpa's map.

A twisted smile played across his lips. "From Chet."

"Did you kill him?"

His eyes narrowed as they focused on me, but he said nothing.

"Why do you need my piece of the map, anyway?" I asked. "We're already in the mine."

His dimpled smile returned. "One side of the map gets you to the mine. The other side leads to the treasure and gets you out." His eyes turned and wandered all over me. He reached out and slid his fingers down the side of my face.

I shoved his hand from my cheek. "Get away from me, you psychotic pervert!"

His eyes narrowed, and veins pulsed in his forehead. He ripped a handgun from the back of his pants and jammed it into my forehead.

I should've been terrified, but instead, a flaming inferno burst out of me. "If you kill me, you'll die a poor and lonely man in this cave. I've seen the map piece. I can put together what I've seen with what you have. I'm your only chance of getting what you want."

After what seemed like an eternity, he lowered the gun and said, "You're right, girl. Only you can give me everything I want." His eyes roamed over me with way too much liberty. "And I certainly won't be lonely if you're around." His tongue wet his lips while he looked at mine.

Every muscle in my body tensed up. What would be worse, having my life stolen from me, or my virtue? I prayed with all my energy that I wouldn't have to make that choice.

Without warning, he shoved the gun into the back of his pants, threw the backpack over his shoulder, and yanked me to a stand.

I took a moment to express silent gratitude for my life, and the fact that he was more interested in the gold than me. At least that was the only explanation I could think of for his abrupt change of focus. But I wasn't out of the woods yet. I wasn't even out of the cave.

Carl scanned our surroundings with the flashlight. Red-, yellow-, and rust-colored stalagmites jetted from the ground and nearly met the stalactites hanging from the ceiling. In the opposite end of the cave was a large column where the two had grown together. My eyes caught something between the column and the wall of the cave behind it. "Wait," I said. "Shine it over there again."

I walked to the column and felt around next to the wall, though I wasn't sure for what. Soon, a cool draft hit my hand through a crack between some rocks. I pulled one to the side, and Carl shined the light into our discovery—a tunnel. "Ladies first," he said, and shoved me into the opening.

Cobwebs caught in my hair, and I squelched a yelp when something scurried across my hand. The tunnel was tight, just large enough to crawl through, and I stifled the desire to kick at Carl behind me. Instead, something inside encouraged me to keep my cool and play along . . . at least for the time being.

The tunnel narrowed a bit, requiring that I slide on my belly in spots. I prayed with every movement that the path I was on would soon lead to freedom. But what would I do when we reached the end of the tunnel? *Should I keep playing along or make a run for it?*

Eventually, the narrow confines of the tunnel opened, and I breathed in musty air. I worked myself out and plopped onto the ground. Carl was struggling to get through the narrowest section behind me.

His light bounced off the walls just enough that I could see I was in a spacious hollow with stalagmites and stalactites forming on the opposite side. The rhythmic drip of liquid was audible over Carl's movements behind me.

There were entrances to another couple of tunnels branching from the hollow. I had no idea, which, if any, led to freedom. I only hoped my mind could piece together the map enough for me to find a way out.

My hand brushed against a large, smooth rock on the ground, and an idea formed in my mind. Carl was just about to join me in the hollow, and I needed to get away from him. How long would his lust for gold outweigh his lust for me? I didn't want to hang around long enough to find out, but I needed the light.

I scooped the rock in my hand and held it high. The seconds before he emerged out of the tunnel seemed to last forever. When his head came into view, I slammed into it with the rock. The flashlight dropped to the ground, but he didn't slump into unconsciousness like I'd expected. Instead, he lunged for me, cursing until my ears ached.

I jumped back and scrambled to the side of the hollow, feeling for a tunnel opening. I didn't care which one. My hands scraped against the rough, bumpy walls until I backed into another tunnel. Carl's fingers grabbed for me as I entered, but I jumped out of reach.

He backtracked to grab the light still lying on the ground,

and I took the opportunity to escape further into the tunnel. Confining blackness surrounded me until his light found the tunnel and illuminated the mineral crusted walls and me.

A bullet ricocheted off the rocky wall beside me. I stumbled forward through the dark, cold tunnel, using my hands as my eyes between the glimpses of light that grew closer behind me. The ground sloped a bit then leveled out. A noise to the side caught my attention. I could have sworn it was a voice, but there wasn't anyone there. A flash of light reflected off to the side, and I noticed a tunnel offshoot. I stumbled toward it and followed it until the light vanished.

Carl didn't see me take the tunnel offshoot and continued down the original path, calling after me. When the glimmer of his light was gone, I was left in thick, musty darkness. I took a second to catch my breath then remembered that my watch had a little light. I pressed the button. An eerie green glow illuminated the cold, rocky walls. It was difficult to tell whether the greenish hue to the walls was from the glow of my watch, or from the color of the mineral deposits.

I couldn't waste time leaning against the wall, so I decided to find where this offshoot led. I didn't want to take a chance that Carl would retrace his steps to look for me, which I was sure he would do unless, by some miracle, he found the treasure and the way out. Somehow, I didn't think he'd be so lucky.

I took off my watch and held it in front of me to light my way. The ground was rocky and uneven. Each step I made had to be carefully placed. My focus was on the ground before me, and I didn't notice the low-lying stalactite until I rammed into it with my head. I rubbed at the shooting pain with my hand and swallowed the solid lump in my throat.

Behind me was a sound. I whirled around and held out my light. It only illuminated two feet out tops, leaving the black void behind it a mystery. My heart thumped in my chest, and I could actually hear it with my ears. I stood still for several seconds, and when there was no more noise, I continued forward, praying that no one was lurking behind me.

Several minutes, actually hours later, my permanently indented thumb trembled from pressing the light. My legs ached, and the fingers on my free hand were raw from scraping along the walls.

How long had I been in the cave? It seemed like days. I was starving, thirsty, tired, and scared. Ironically, I found myself in a cave potentially filled with worldly riches, yet they were powerless to save me. I was even powerless to save myself. There was only one who could save me now, and I spent every moment beseeching Him for my life.

Father in Heaven, please guide me through this dark world and lead me to safety . . .

A measure of peace entered me, and somehow I knew that my humble plea had been heard.

A number of minutes later, I reached another hollow. This one had at least five different tunnels branching from it. Mineral formations dripped like petrified water down the walls. The light on my watch grew dim. I released the button and tried to rub away the sore indentation on my thumb. The moment I did, I was plunged into darkness.

My ears and hands became my second pair of eyes almost immediately. The roomy size of the hollow was evident just by the echo of my breathing and the sounds made from creatures scurrying about.

In that dark moment, an image of my piece of the map flashed in my mind, an "x" with a maze of river-like lines drawn around it. Now that I knew the map led to the inside of the mine and its tunnels, I could only assume the "x" was the treasure.

Another image of the map flashed through my mind, and I noticed something I hadn't before. A prominent line encountered the "x" and appeared to be a straight course to the sketched pine trees. My heart beat with new hope. If I found the treasure, I could likely find a direct route out of the mine! At least that was my expectation. Now, if I could just decide which tunnel to take.

I pressed the light again and held it up to the circular walls. I felt like I was in a good-sized igloo with several exits. I finally decided to take the tunnel just to my right and squeezed into the tall, narrow passageway. With the light button digging into my thumb, I inched down the tunnel, feeling along the cold, hard walls.

My steps slipped over rocks as they declined in altitude, yet I was grateful for a reprieve from some of the physical exertion I'd experienced earlier. After awhile, I almost smacked right into a column that blocked the tunnel. It wasn't so much that the column was vast, just that the narrowness of the tunnel was easy to fill. I tried to squeeze around it, but eventually relinquished any thought of continuing further down the path. I suppressed tears of frustration, turned around, and felt my way uphill through the tunnel.

Once I made it back to the hollow, I didn't even have time to catch my breath from the hike before flashlight beams bounced around the walls. I gasped and let off my light. Was it Carl? How could it be? We'd been going in different directions for hours. I slipped back into the tunnel. "Hey, girl," he called. "I know you're in here."

I held my breath and hugged the side of the cave. The beam of light shot across the tunnel where I hid, illuminating dirt and mineral crusted walls just inches from my protruding toes and chest. For several seconds, I stood motionless. I didn't even breathe. I just prayed and hoped that he'd go away.

His light shifted to another tunnel, and I let out my breath with a silent sigh. Then I waited until he headed down a different tunnel, and his light disappeared completely, before I tiptoed out of my hiding place.

I pressed the button of my watch's light, but it was dim and my thumb was so sore, I stuffed it back in my pocket. With raw hands, I felt along the chilly cave walls for another tunnel entrance.

My progress was slow down the tunnel, feeling above and below for stalactites and stalagmites that wanted to hurt me.

The pathway seemed to twist back and forth before the air opened up, and I sensed I was in another hollow pocket. The air was sticky and damp. A steady hissing sound rebounded from the walls close around me. I took a cautious step forward. The hairs on my arms stood tall.

My toe grazed the ground, but movement underfoot caused me to step back. Something slithered over my foot and brushed the skin around my ankle. I stood in a bed of snakes!

My better judgment begged me not to scream, but it was too late. The echoes of my screams burned in my ears. I fled in the opposite direction, tripping, falling, and stumbling in my haste. Mineral formations tore at my hair and clothing and bruised my knees.

When I reached the hollow, I was about to collapse. What other creatures would I find? What if all the tunnels were blocked? What if there was no other way out? My breathing became rapid, and I whispered another prayer. Peace filled me again, and I grasped at it in hopes it would stay. I had to have faith that everything would be okay even if I couldn't see visual proof at this moment.

I took a few minutes to catch my breath then found another tunnel. I crept along its walls like I had previously. Periodically, I'd retrieve my watch and direct its fading light toward the ground. I didn't want to find any more snakes. The path I was on seemed endless, and I prayed it wouldn't end in another blockage. Eventually, I rounded a sharp turn and felt my steps descend.

My legs suddenly felt heavy, and I stopped. A whisper sounded in my ear and seemed to swirl around me. I retrieved my watch and pressed the button, which dug into my trembling fingers. But the light had all but vanished. Shivers slid down my spine. My teeth chattered.

This is crazy! I shouldn't have been frightened of a tunnel, but I couldn't explain the dark and overwhelming feeling that threatened to swallow me. I forced one foot in front of the other for several more steps. I had to find out where the tunnel went.

The whispers grew louder and heaviness enveloped me. I was so tired, scared, and freezing. I slipped my long-forgotten jacket around my arms and hugged myself. It didn't do much for warmth. The frigid air seemed to penetrate to my very core. My feet stumbled a few steps further, but then I plopped onto the ground.

My head spun and ached all at the same time. Whispers, chanting, shivering darkness.

Leave, you're not wanted here. Go back, turn around.

No, don't leave. Join us.

The supernatural voices whispered in my ears with icy breath. Dread like I'd never experienced filled me from head to toe. I was on the wrong path. I flipped around. My arms helped carry me upward until my legs regained strength and could walk again. The cold faded; the whispers subsided.

Some time later, I stumbled back into the hollow, trembling and shaking. Fatigue hung over me like a heavy blanket, and I longed to rest.

I pressed the button again on my watch and nearly cried when it gave light. All around me were tunnels. I had no idea of which to try next, nor which ones I'd been down already. I slumped to the ground and sobbed. *Why haven't my prayers been answered? Why am I still here? Will I ever get out?*

I begged and pleaded with my Father in Heaven. Surely He wanted me to get out of the cave as much as I did. But when I opened my eyes again, there was nothing. No promptings, no green exit sign glowing above one of the tunnel entrances, nothing.

I was tempted to huddle in a ball, fall asleep, and never wake up. But finally, I made a decision to keep looking, to keep searching, to keep praying. I stumbled toward another tunnel, but I had scarcely taken ten steps when Carl's flashlight made it to the hollow along with his angry echoes. How long could I keep playing this deadly game of cat and mouse? I released the button on my watch and plummeted back into darkness.

I hoped he'd leave, but his light grew closer. I knew he was coming toward me. I moved forward, propelled with new momentum. After several quick steps, I slid down a narrow slope.

My tired feet leveled out, and my hands groped the walls. My fingertips met with a massive column, and I slipped between it and the wall. Relief came over me when he passed by.

I crawled into a hidden pocket behind the column, leaned against the hard, bumpy wall, and pressed my watch. It was nearly seven o'clock the next morning. No wonder my eyelids and every inch of my body felt like they were made of lead.

My mouth was swollen with dehydration, and I remembered the apple in my pocket. I pulled it out and bit into it, sucking all the juice I could from half and saving the rest for later. Then I peeled back the wrapper on the granola bar and took a couple bites.

I pulled my jacket closer around me, bowed my head, and began to pray.

The words to "A Child's Prayer," one of my favorite primary songs, came to recollection. Its peaceful tune played in my weary head.

Heavenly Father, are you really there?
And do you hear and answer ev'ry child's prayer?
Some say that heaven is far away,

But I feel it close around me as I pray.
Heavenly Father, I remember now
Something that Jesus told disciples long ago:
"Suffer the children to come to me."
Father, in prayer I'm coming now to thee.

"Are you really there, Father?" I whispered in words only I could hear. The answer came with the next verse, singing out in my mind.

Pray, he is there;
Speak, he is list'ning
You are his child;
His love now surrounds you.
He hears your prayer;
He loves the children.
Of such is the kingdom, the kingdom of Heav'n.

Tears slid down my cheeks, and I let them fall freely. "Heavenly Father, I thank thee for my life that has been preserved thus far. Please help me to make it out of this cave alive. Please help Brad, wherever he is. Watch over us and protect us. In Jesus' name, amen."

When I'd finished, I curled up on the ground and used my folded arm as a pillow. A measure of peace warmed me enough that I was able to drift into sleep, listening to nothing but an eerie silence.

My mind entered a dream state, and a dark hole formed before me, growing smaller, until I realized I'd been staring at the very center of an eagle's eye. It soared through the air, over mountains, rivers, and valleys. It landed gracefully on a high mountain perch.

Then I became the eagle and could see all that he could see. Spaniards fighting Indians. Men on horseback. Contention, greed, death. Women wailing, mourning the loss of husbands and fathers. Hungry children, crying in their mother's arms. I felt the sorrow of the eagle.

A tiny mouse scavenged for food in the brush below. The eagle swooped with graceful wings and clutched the squealing mouse in its talons. He wiggled and squeaked, fearing his future.

I awoke and screamed. A mouse had made its way into my pocket while I'd been asleep and was nibbling a hole in the granola bar. I grabbed it by the tail and sent it sailing across the tiny pocket where I sat. It landed with a smack against the wall and scampered away. A shiver trickled through my body, and it took several minutes for my heart and breathing to settle down enough for me to find sleep again.

I drifted off. All was dark except a tiny light in the far distance. Slowly, it grew until it lit everything around me. Such peace filled the light, and I longed to meet and embrace it. I shielded my eyes against the brightness and looked farther. Several people came toward me, their faces and features were in silhouette. One gentleman stood in the foreground of the others and spoke to me. "Sweet pea."

"Grandpa?" I asked. I tried running toward him, but I couldn't move. "Am I dead?"

He shook his head. "No, but I want to show you something." He motioned to the numerous people behind him.

Though most of their faces were in silhouette, I could still make out the genuine smiles they wore and could feel the love they carried.

"Who are they?" I asked, but the answer formed even before the words came out. These were some of my ancestors. Many of the faces I recognized, many I didn't. One tall young man donning pioneer attire stood out. He said nothing verbally, but I felt his gratitude.

"Enoch? Is that you?"

Grandpa turned to me. "We wanted you to see who's aware of you and helping you right now."

"Me?"

He nodded. "We love you, sweet pea. All of us. You're not alone."

I looked again at the crowd of people. Grandma was there, an aunt, the woman whose locket I'd worn, and literally hundreds of others. "But why me? What's so special about me?"

Grandpa seemed surprised at my question. "Because you're my granddaughter, and more important, you're a daughter of God. He's sent you to this earth and given you the Savior to help you find your way home. He's sent angels to help, too."

"Angels?" Tears trickled down my cheeks. Love burned in my heart, and I longed to join them in the light.

"I'm sorry," Grandpa said in answer to my thoughts, "but we need you on earth now. You have an important mission to fulfill. All of these spirits need the light you'll one day bring into their lives. Ancestors who'll be eternally grateful for your work and posterity, who can't live without you. He motioned to his side. Three beautiful young women, and a handsome young man with aquamarine-colored eyes and wavy golden hair stepped forward. Their faces glowed. I didn't need for them to speak. I knew they were my children. My eyes blurred with tears, but their faces remained unchanged.

Suddenly, the light began to dim, and they all started to fade.

"Wait! Don't go. Don't leave me alone!" I reached for them but they grew smaller.

Grandpa smiled down at me again and whispered, "You're never alone. We're right here. But it's time to wake up."

My eyes sprang open and I gasped. Dim light illuminated Carl's unblinking eyes staring right at me, just inches from my face.

CHAPTER 17

★ ★ ★ ★ ★

I brought a fist, hammer-style, to his face, but he caught it before it hit him. In his other hand he held out a water bottle, filled three-quarters of the way full.

"Here," he said. "I thought you might be thirsty." His tone and voice were soft, almost affectionate. The lustful look in his eyes had been replaced by fear.

My dry tongue ached, but I was still wary of drinking it. I swallowed hard and shook my head.

"You don't trust me? There's nothing wrong with it. See?" He took a swig, wiped moist remnants from his stubble, and handed it back to me.

My mind and body wrestled between fighting him and making a run for it, or taking the drink. But my body's thirst finally won. I took the water and gulped it down in one breath.

"Let's call a truce," he said, like we'd had a little spat or something. But this was hardly a little spat.

My eyes narrowed. "Why?" I asked.

"I'm tired of playing hide and seek, and I found the treasure." A smile spread across his lips.

Why is he telling me this? My eyes wandered to the exit from the pocket blocked by his body. I was so weary from the day before, I didn't know if I had it in me to try to escape and keep running.

When he realized I wasn't going to respond, he continued. "I found the treasure, but I can't find a way out. All the other tunnels either lead to a dead end, or circle back around. I need your help, and you need mine. I'll even share some of it with you if you help me get out." He took the two map pieces from his pocket and placed the flashlight on them.

I considered his words. If I played along, I could use his maps to help gain freedom. If I didn't, I'd likely end up dead, anyway. But what if I did find a way out? Would he actually give me some of the gold and send me on my way unscathed? Not hardly, but the plan could buy me some time, and at least I wouldn't be running and hiding anymore.

"Okay, I'll help you." I leaned over for a better look. Each piece had a smooth edge and one that had been torn. They almost looked like they could fit together, but the lines didn't match up. I took them in my hands and rearranged them to fit what my mind remembered of my piece of the map. But there wasn't anything new his pieces could tell me. I knew that we needed to get to the treasure in order to find a way out.

"What did the area around the treasure look like?" I asked.

Carl's face lit up then went dark. "It was huge. A massive cave, packed with stuff."

"I think that's where we need to go." I didn't dare say more. My life depended on his need for me.

He extended a hand to help me up and flashed his dimpled grin. Reluctantly, I took his hand, and then wiped my hand on the side of my pants. He led the way out of the pocket and back to the hollow. We walked in absolute silence. Only the crunch of our feet on the damp floor below and our breathing could be heard.

When we reached the hollow, we stopped for a brief break. His light bounced around the cold walls. Eerie symbols and etchings that I hadn't noticed before lined the walls. Some of them were covered with the turquoise and yellow mineral shawls that dripped down the cave's walls, but others seemed untouched. My mind scrambled for recognition, but they were too unfamiliar. A symbol etched above one tunnel entrance caused me to shiver involuntarily. It almost seemed like it was alive and wanted to tell me something. *Beware! Do not enter!*

I was dismayed when that was the exact tunnel Carl started down.

"Wait! I don't think we should go down here," I said. My heart beat faster with every step closer to the tunnel.

Carl's eyes turned on me. "This is where the treasure is and where you said we needed to go."

I knew he was right. We had to go down if there was any chance to escape the mine. It was the only other way out. Again we walked in silence, but there was a point when I wondered if the breathing I heard wasn't coming from either of us.

Goose bumps prickled the surface of my skin. I pulled my jacket tighter around me, but my teeth still chattered ferociously. Heaviness set in, and my steps became increasingly labored, though we were going downhill. "I can't go down here again," I said.

I started to turn around, but he spun me toward him. "You're going to get me out of this cave!"

The dread I felt fogged my senses. All the fight had drained from me. I continued to follow him into the heavy darkness.

Carl slowed a bit, but didn't seem to be struggling for steps like I was. Soon, the flashlight flickered and went out. He cursed aloud several words, then lowered his voice. "It did this before, but it came back on." He shook the light and it lit again, but it was very dim.

Heavy blackness swirled around us, and I could almost see the invisible hands that tugged on my arm, pulling me farther down the tunnel. Whispers echoed all around.

Come with us. We've been waiting for you.

No! I tried to speak and pull away, but I was paralyzed

with fear and the heaviness of my limbs. Slowly, I was dragged farther and farther down the tunnel until my body could no longer function.

Join us! We've been waiting.

No, you're not welcome here! Go away! Send them away!

Someone screamed through the heavy fog. I didn't know if it had been me or Carl, or something else. My legs numbly moved forward, obeying the pulling and pushing that led me deeper and deeper into the eerie darkness.

Save me, please! I couldn't speak the words, only think them. Seconds later, I dropped to the ground. Screams echoed in my ears. Where was Carl?

Heaviness seemed to press me into the ground. I tried to stand but could hardly get my shoulders off the ground, let alone my legs. I stretched one arm in front of the other. I had to get out. But where was I?

My hands landed against leather bags and smooth, cold, heavy bricks. Something in the back of my mind, the part that was alert, told me I didn't need light to see the treasure I'd found. Goose bumps trickled like electrified water from my head down to my toes.

Something scurried across my hand. My mouth opened to yell, but it was too numb to do so. Ghostly voices echoed on walls that I was sure soared above me. I searched blindly for the cave's wall, anything to give me a home base, but it wasn't there. A wave of icy cold air drifted past me, sending shivers through my whole body.

We've been waiting for you!

No, leave. Leave before they kill you!

The whispers reached my ears. My head sunk lower, my limbs grew heavier. I pushed one arm forward, then collapsed on a mound of leather bags. I willingly succumbed to the indescribable hopelessness. My teeth chattered violently, and my whole body shook to keep warm. But I didn't care anymore. Voices swirled around me, chanting, yelling, whispering, taunting.

Images drifted through my mind. Memories from my childhood. Running, talking, laughing, and hugging; all the things I loved to do in my physical body. Spending time with my sister, long chats with Mom, Dad's tenderness for his children, my first kiss with Brad. Would they miss me as much as I'd miss them? Was I prepared to meet my Maker?

Wake up, sweet pea. You've got to get out of here.

"I can't do it, Grandpa, I just can't. Take me with you."

You can do it. You're not alone.

I wanted someone to carry me, to lift me up and take me out of the living nightmare I'd found myself in. But no one came, and I finally realized that if I wanted to survive, I needed to keep trying. I couldn't give up.

Miraculously, the heaviness around me lifted to a degree, and I was able to resume my crawling. My mind began to work again, but with it came panic. All I felt around me were leather bags, coins, and bars of gold.

My breathing grew rapid and shallow. My palms were wet. I offered another prayer and began crawling in an uncertain direction. Shredded fabric over brittle bones cracked and crumbled under my weight. It took only two seconds for me to realize it was a human rib cage.

I let out a yelp and swallowed the sickness I felt growing inside. The echo of my voice seemed endless, but it also gave me an idea. I backed up and stuck my hand in cold, heavy coins. I picked one up and threw it. It landed a few seconds later with a soft plink what sounded like several feet away.

I picked up another and tossed it in a different direction. That one hit something hard a little closer. The third coin I tossed in yet a different direction and was ecstatic to hear it bounce off the wall of the cave. I scooped up several coins then one by one threw them until I could feel the wall's security with my own hands.

Another wave of cold air drifted past and enveloped me,

whispering words, some of which I couldn't understand, others, I could. Dizziness set in. I dropped to the ground and held my head.

Leave! You're not wanted here.

"No!" I yelled, "You leave. I just want to get out of here!"

A flicker of light nearly blinded me. It was Carl's flashlight heading my direction. He was calling for me. "What happened? Where did you go, girl? Find me a way out!" What was more frightening or potentially lethal—haunting whispers or Carl? I hugged the backside of a mound of leather bags and prayed he wouldn't notice me. If only I could find a way out, I'd be free of him and the cave!

No! Stay with us, we've been waiting for you!

I shook the whispers and fog from my mind. Carl's flashlight bounced off the soaring walls and mountainous treasure around me. My mouth gaped opened when I beheld with my own eyes the treasure I'd only imagined in my mind. Hundreds and hundreds of mounds of gold bars, coins, and other worldly riches filled the enormous cave from wall to wall. And if that wasn't enough, the walls themselves were made of gold. I'd have to literally search to find a vein of rock.

The light grew closer and closer. My heart pounded so hard I thought it would break right through me. He came nearer, and with every step sounded the jingle of the bagged coins he carried.

I crouched behind the mound and hid from the light's beam. I prayed that I'd blend into the deep shadows. Cold whispers continued through the cave along with an icy breeze. The beam of light stood motionless in Carl's hands. Black mist with dark, visible fingers swirled around the light's beam and swallowed what light it gave.

"Leave me alone! It's mine," he shouted at the darkness with a fear in his voice that matched what I felt inside. The whispers swirled around him in the dark cave.

But there was one voice I heard with my heart more than my ears. *Run! Now!*

I scrambled to my feet and used the wall to flee to the only place I knew was a certain exit from the treasure, the tunnel. Just before I reached it, light penetrated the cave of treasure once again.

Carl hollered again and the tunnel walls groaned. Dust sprinkled in my face. My determination to get out of the cave alive propelled me forward through the heavy darkness and invisible hands grabbing for me, until I reached the hollow. I leaned against the wall and took a second to catch my breath. There had to be another way out besides the treasure cave. There just had to be.

I plopped to the ground and whispered a prayer of thanks. I was alive. Now I needed a new plan. Carl said he had checked all the other tunnels, and they lead to nowhere. But what if he was wrong? I had to find out for myself.

Once I found the next tunnel, I groped along its cold walls for several steps. A faint light beamed in the distance. My heart pounded. Was it an exit? Adrenaline pushed me further.

Suddenly, my feet cascaded over a drop off, and the only thing that kept me from falling was a fragile rope I grasped in my trembling hands. I squelched the instinct to scream and settled on a small yelp. Small rocks dropped all around me, taking several seconds before they plinked on the ground below.

I pulled with all my might to lift at least one leg back up to the ledge and barely managed to do so.

"What do you want?" Carl's angry voice shouted in a distant part of the cave. "You can't have the gold!" I'd grown used to his yelling at the spirits.

"I don't want the gold, I want Lex! Where is she?" Brad's forceful words met Carl's with a determination I didn't know existed.

Brad! He's alive! *I thank Thee, Heavenly Father.*

A shot rang out, and my heart stopped. "No!" *Please let*

Brad be okay. Please. The unstable earth gave way under my weight, and my foot dropped back down. Moisture on my hands suppressed their friction. I began to slip. The rope's ancient fibers broke, one at a time, lowering me centimeter by centimeter. Echoes of my own screams pounded my ears.

Without warning, a dim light appeared above me, and a warm hand clasped my arm. "I've got you, Lex."

"Brad?" Tears of gratitude stung my eyes. Had my deliverer actually come? When he'd helped me up from the drop-off, I threw my arms around him and sobbed. "How did you find me? I thought you were dead."

His arms tightened around me, and he buried a kiss in my hair. "I've been looking all night and all day. I finally found another entrance. Then I just followed the voices." An ear-piercing screech bounced off the walls and pulled us apart in the same moment we had embraced.

"What was that?" I asked.

"I don't know. It sounded like an eagle," he said. "Follow me. We've got to get out of here."

When I let go of his shirt, my hand was moist and sticky. "Are you bleeding?" I asked in almost a whisper.

He didn't answer but instead turned around the way he'd come. "There's another tunnel that leads out." He led the way with a tiny flashlight.

Thoughts of the blood on Brad's shirt were pushed from my mind, and I focused on getting out of the cave. We worked our way back to the hollow and entered the tunnel directly across from us. Several feet into it, Brad shined his light onto the wall, and then up to the ceiling.

"Here, I'll help you up," he said, cupping his hands together.

"Up?"

Carl's voice echoed from the treasure cove. "Leave me alone!" he yelled. Suddenly, more gunshots rang out, and a low rumble vibrated the ground. Clumps of dirt sprinkled down on us.

I didn't know where Brad was leading me, but I trusted him. I stepped into his cupped hands and he hoisted me up the wall. At the top was a lip. I reached it and pulled myself up with Brad's help. But he didn't join me.

I peaked over the edge. "Are you coming?" I asked.

"I just need to catch my breath."

A flashlight bounced off the walls around us. Coins jingled, and I knew Carl was running toward us.

I stuck my hand down and helped Brad onto the lip. His little light illuminated a dark, narrow tunnel that was barely large enough to crawl through.

CRACK! A bullet broke a section of the tunnel's ceiling, and it crumbled before us, partially blocking our exit. I sped forward on hands and knees, climbing over boulders and rocks, ducking from others. My heart pounded, my lungs ached. When I reached the blockage, I hugged myself against the wall, slid through then continued to crawl with Brad right behind. A dim light appeared several feet ahead. I prayed it was the exit and that we'd make it before Carl caught up to us.

Faint light grew larger until we pushed through thick trees lining the exit, and fresh air filled my lungs. Heavy clouds hung so low to the mountain that they almost touched. I longed to quench my thirst with their moisture, but I couldn't even stop to catch my breath. Brad grabbed my hand and urged me into the thickest part of the trees on our way down the mountain's slope. The sound of Carl's jingling steps and pot shots at nearby trees, created a chilling visualization of the pursuer behind me.

When we reached the base of the hill, we ran to a thicket of trees and hid. But Carl paused only long enough to load the back of his four-wheeler at the base of the mountain with bags of gold and then bounded up the hill again.

Brad sank to the ground and leaned against one of the trees.

His eyes squeezed tight, his breathing was heavy, a trickle of black fluid oozed from his shirt.

"Brad!" I plopped to the ground beside him. "Are you all right?" A small bullet had torn a hole through his shoulder.

He didn't say anything, but the way his jaw muscles flexed I could tell he was in a lot of pain. I glanced around me. A light rain had settled in, but my eyes caught sight of a dirt road not far away.

"I'll go get some help," I said.

He blew me a kiss with a trembling hand and labored breathing.

I ran toward the dirt road and followed it west for a ways. The lonely road seemed endless, and I wondered if I should turn back. But then I saw a motor home concealed in the thick trees. Its whiteness gave away its location. I dashed through the little campground and pounded on the door. "Help! My boyfriend's been shot!"

No one answered. I rapped on the door again and repeated my plea. Again there was no answer. A look around the campground revealed a cold fire pit and crushed beer cans scattered about. Was there enough time to look for other help in this remote area?

I jiggled the door and it opened. Maybe they wouldn't mind if I borrowed a first aid kit or a cell phone—if it could get service. The motor home swayed under my weight as I climbed the steps and entered the musty-smelling kitchen area. I pulled open drawers and found a roll of paper towels that I tucked under my arm.

In the bathroom, I searched for a first-aid kit but found only a single band-aid and a pair of tweezers. Next, I fumbled around the sleeping area, feeling guilty that I was invading someone's personal living area, but also realizing I had no other options.

A small, attached dresser stood in the corner next to the bed. I clicked the overhead light and began opening the drawers. The top drawer held nothing of importance, except for a clean, white T-shirt. I balled it up and stuffed it into my jacket pockets next to the forgotten apple and granola bar.

When I pulled open the second drawer, I gasped. There sat the missing diary. The hairs on my arms and neck stood tall. My cold hands wrapped around the diary and pulled it from the drawer. The plot map was still tucked into its pages.

Lying in the bottom of the drawer were several papers, some were copies of the maps I'd seen at the library, and others were sketches of the Currant Creek area. I slammed the drawer shut, and for a moment I couldn't move.

A newspaper lay on the bed next to an empty bag of pork rinds. Large words read, "Chet Strong's death a hoax." My eyes widened as I scanned through the article.

To the side was a large black and white photo of the criminal. His head was shaven. His narrowed eyes were so dark they could've been black, his lips curled down in a scowl.

I recognized Chet's picture from the article Dad had read awhile ago. But there was something familiar about the guy. My mind placed a thick mane of dark hair on his head. His eyes made my skin crawl when they looked at me, and I could almost see his lips turning to a dimpled grin. My whole body trembled, and spots fashioned before my eyes. Carl and Chet were one and the same!

CHAPTER 18

★ ★ ★ ★ ★

The rumble of a four-wheeler startled me from my thoughts. I threw the article back onto the bed and shut off the overhead light. The motor stopped, and the sound of footsteps drifted from the campground outside. There was no time to exit the motor home, so I hid behind the door and hoped whoever-it-was would leave.

The door jiggled and burst open. "Who's in here?"

I gasped at the recognition of Carl's voice and prayed he hadn't heard me. The floor shifted under his weight as he entered the motor home. Lights clicked on in the kitchen.

"Come on, show yourself."

His shadow tiptoed toward the sleeping area where I hugged the wall. I held my breath and said a silent prayer. The 9 mm handgun, clenched in Carl's hand, came into view before he did. I smacked it out of his hand with the journal and made a run for the door. He caught me by the waist and slammed me against the wall.

"What are you doing in here?" he asked after he'd screamed a string of colorful words. His mouth, just inches from mine, reeked of recently consumed alcohol.

I heard his question, but there was only one thing on my mind. "You killed my grandpa!" I spat the words from my mouth while I struggled for freedom.

His fist pounded the wall behind me. The mistake of my words hit me when his cold, black eyes stared right through me, sending shivers down my spine.

"So that's where you get your feistiness from?" he said. He looked me up and down, creating waves of both nausea and panic.

I'd already escaped the psychotic maniac and a cave that was more like a living nightmare. Brad's life depended on me, and this guy killed my grandpa! With an explosion of adrenaline, I kneed him in the gut. He let out an involuntary grunt and shot backward then grabbed me and spun me around.

I rammed my elbows into his face and eyes, until he dropped me. He held his face and cursed. Blood dripped generously from his nose. I should've made a run for it right then and there, but I didn't want him well enough to hunt me down. Several more self-defense moves I'd learned were inflicted upon him before he regained his composure and pinned me against the wall.

"It's mine, you hear?" he screamed.

Just then, Derek crashed into the motor home, ripped Carl off me, and threw him against the kitchen cupboards. "Get your hands off of her!"

Carl ran at Derek and punched him in the gut. Derek stumbled backward then lunged at Carl, slamming him into the ground. Derek seized the gun from the floor and aimed it at Carl. "Let her go!" He motioned for me to exit the motor home, and I leaped from the open door. Derek hopped down right behind me. "To the trees, quick," he whispered.

We sprinted toward the trees and watched as Carl jumped on his four-wheeler and took off down the road.

Derek slid an arm around me and we embraced. A lump formed in my throat. "Thank you," I said. It was all that would come out.

He pulled back. Dark circles hung under his eyes, but I would've been blind not to notice the look of longing in them. "Where's Brad? We've been looking everywhere for you two."

"He's hiding in the trees at the base of the mountain. He's been hurt. Do you have your truck?"

He shook his head. "Just my motorcycle. Come on, let's go help him."

We ran through the trees to the dirt road where he'd hidden his motorcycle. He jumped on, started it, and pulled me up. I grabbed onto him. It was a good thing because the front tire lifted from the ground when we took off.

I squeezed my eyes closed. The light sprinkle turned into a downpour, and each raindrop stung my face. Derek started down the road toward the trees that hid Brad. But we'd scarcely done so when Carl's ATV came flying at us from a nearby hill. He landed on the road right behind us.

"Hang on tight!" Derek yelled. He gave it gas and we jetted down the road. "We need to lose him, or we'll lead him right to Brad."

The road was slick. We slid around each turn in the road, and even weaved in and out of trees off road. I checked behind me with one eye cracked open. Carl was so close I could reach out and touch him.

Derek rode up the side of a hill, and we literally flew in the air on the other side. We smacked into the ground, landing upright. Mud flicked up under the tire and caked my boots and pants. We slid for several seconds before we took off again. Carl was nowhere in sight.

"I think we ditched him," I said, but I said it too soon.

His ATV soared through the air right behind us. Derek swerved off the road and cut through a thicket of trees. Branches reached out and scratched my arms and legs. I buried my face into Derek's back for protection.

The motorcycle tipped back when we climbed a steep hill. I was sure we'd flip right over. I leaned forward. The back wheel spun and slid underneath. For a minute it seemed that we were going more vertical than horizontal. But finally, we hit a patch of brush, and it propelled us upward until we reached the top.

Derek paused a moment and looked back. Carl was struggling up the hill. "He's not going to make it," he said.

Carl only made it partway up the steep incline before his four-wheeler slid backward, out of control. Derek took off down the other side of the hill and led us to the dirt road. I squeezed my eyes again. Rain plastered my face, but thankfully, Carl wasn't behind us.

We drove around for several minutes before we found the base of the mountain that hid Brad.

"Is he in here?" Derek asked over the motor.

I cracked an eye open and scanned our surroundings. "Yes, he's just over there."

The motorcycle slowed and veered off the road. My eyes opened and searched for Brad. He was still lying at the base of the tree. I just hoped we could get him to safety before it was too late.

We pulled to a stop, and Derek helped me from the bike. His white T-shirt was sopping wet. I could almost see the goose bumps on his shoulders, but they weren't all I could see. Toward the top of his back, were four angry scratches. My mind flashed back to the stormy night and the gloved intruder in my home. The smell of wet clothes, strong, muscular arms squeezing the air out of me, bleeding flesh under my fingernails from his back. *No, this can't be real. Not Derek, no!*

My mind spun. My hands trembled. Spots materialized in my vision.

"Are you okay?" Derek asked when he looked at me.

"No, I'm sick." My eyes moved to the gun sticking out his back pocket, then to Brad, still propped against the tree several feet away. I had to warn him.

I looked back at Derek and watched his face turn from concern, to a look I'd never seen him wear. *He knows!*

I ran faster than I'd ever done before, but Derek was at my heels, grabbing for my shirt.

I stumbled toward Brad. "We need to leave, right now!"

His eyes fluttered open, and he looked behind me. "Oh, good, Derek's here."

I whirled around at the click of the gun pointed right at us. "Show me the treasure," Derek said.

"No!" I screamed. "He needs help, now!"

"And I need the money!" Derek's eyes moved from me to Brad. "That's all I want, then I'll help you."

"No, he'll die!"

"It's all right, Lex." Brad's voice was labored. "He won't shoot."

"I'm not playing around. I need the money." Derek's thumb pulled back on the hammer.

In an instant, Brad leaped to his feet and threw himself at Derek. The two fell to the ground, throwing punches, but Brad in his condition was no match for Derek. I jumped on top of Derek and pulled his hair. He whirled around, grabbed me, and held me against him; his gun was pressed into my throat. "Show me where it is." His voice broke with emotion.

Brad stared at his brother. Blood trickled freely from his shoulder and nose. "What's going on, bro? Whatever it is, we'll help you. You don't need a gun." He tried to get up, but he fell back to the ground.

"He's right, Derek," I said. "I'll show you where it is, just put the gun away."

Brad sat halfway up. "No, Lex, I'll do it."

My mouth gaped open. "No, I know where it is."

Derek gradually lowered the gun from my neck and stuffed it into his back pocket. My legs nearly buckled from the relief. "All right, where is it?" he asked.

I pointed toward the mountain that I never wanted to see again. I couldn't go back there, I just couldn't. Then my eyes shifted to Brad lying on the ground. My heart ached with a pain so intense I thought I'd faint. He needed me.

Derek nudged me in the ribs. "Let's go!"

The two of us sprinted to the base of the mountain. Carl's four-wheeler was parked at the bottom. I paused to catch my breath and to scan the side of the mountain. I hoped to find the opening to the cave but couldn't see a thing. I remembered pushing through thick trees, but thick trees covered the entire mountainside.

We started hiking. I glanced behind me and in front to look for matted growth. Partway up, I noticed a tight gathering of trees. Could they be the entrance back in?

At that moment, Carl bounded through the trees toward the four-wheeler with heavy bags in both hands. He stopped when he saw us.

Derek extracted the gun from his pocket and aimed it at Carl. "Part of it's mine," he said. "I helped you get here."

"And you will get some. Put the gun down."

Derek didn't move. He just stood there with a blank expression on his face, but this time I could see fear and uncertainty in his eyes.

Carl tossed a bag of gold toward Derek. He stooped to grab it, and Carl attacked him. The two men rolled on the ground, thumping each other with their fists. I bolted toward the bottom of the hill.

I sprinted down the road. A shot rang out, and seconds later, Carl was chasing me on his four-wheeler. The roar of his motor was as loud as if I were riding it. How could I outrun an ATV? I dove off the road and weaved in and out of thick trees, too tightly packed to allow his four-wheeler passage. He hugged the side of the road, waiting for me to cross.

Just then, another shot split the air. Carl careened off the road and slammed into a tree. A flash of black hair caught my peripheral vision from the hill to my side. I turned my head, but he was gone.

The rain had stopped, but the sun was on its way down behind the mountains. The air was cool. I hoped I could find Brad before it grew dark. For a moment, I thought I'd lost the grove that hid him until I saw him sprawled out facedown in the mud. My legs nearly gave out on me before I dropped to his side. He didn't move. I checked for a pulse and said a silent thank you when I found one. At least his skin was warm, maybe even too warm.

Behind him were marks he'd left in the ground from dragging his body. I swallowed the lump in my throat. This wasn't the time to get emotional. "Brad," I whispered. "Can you hear me?" I shook him gently and he groaned. "Can you move?"

Yelling in the distance caught my attention. It was Carl. His four-wheeler rumbled to life. I crouched as close to Brad and the ground as I could go. Luckily, the ATV's lights bounced to our side, and he continued down the road and out of sight.

Brad struggled to stand, but doubled over beside me. The moonlight illuminated the paleness of his face and his shirt spotted with thick, black fluid. My arms wrapped around him and helped him walk through dense trees toward the base of an adjoining hillside.

After a few minutes of walking, I stopped. "Did you hear that?" I asked. Trees rustling caused my heart to pound. I contemplated turning around but felt I needed to move forward. We continued for another couple of steps, but I stopped again when I heard more movement in the trees. "Someone's there," I whispered.

A figure emerged and headed toward us. We'd been found! My heart pounded, and adrenaline pumped through my body. I urged Brad to move, but he couldn't go any further. I cried aloud a plea toward heaven.

In no time, the man approached us, and I was both startled and relieved that it wasn't Carl or Derek. He was thick and sturdy. His long black hair, pulled back in a ponytail, hung down his back. Shadows from the moon formed under his high, prominent cheekbones and suntanned skin. "Do you need help?" he asked.

"Yes," I said. "Do you have a car? My friend's been shot. He needs to get to the hospital."

He shook his head. "I do not, but I can help him."

With hastened steps, the stranger supported Brad to a hollow in the mountainside surrounded by a thick hedge. A warm fire, invisible beyond the hedge, glowed in the tiny cave, and the man carefully sat Brad down beside it. He tore Brad's shirt from his shoulder and examined the wound, but surprised me when he lifted Brad's arm and looked at his side.

My hand flew to my mouth when I saw the gushing wound. "He's been shot twice?" I asked.

The man nodded. "One is fresh, the other looks to be several hours old," he said. "Do you know what happened to him?"

I shook my head. "I heard a shot before we were separated and another in the cave awhile ago, but I didn't see what happened." I pulled the band-aid, tweezers, and T-shirt out of my pocket. "Will these help?" I asked.

He raised an eyebrow and hesitantly took them from my hand. Silver strands I hadn't noticed before, streaked his hair. He placed white cloths over the wounds and said, "Hold these."

I ran to Brad's side and pressed the cloth to the wounds. His skin felt warm, and he was beginning to shake. The man pulled a blanket from further in the cave and wrapped it around Brad's shaking body, then crushed dried leaves in a bowl. Next, he poured hot water from a kettle into the bowl and stirred to make a paste. He crawled back to Brad and started to work.

"What are you going to do?" I asked. Whatever it was, I was determined to see it all.

"I will help you take out the bullet."

My eyes widened. "Me? But I don't know how," I said.

"You will learn."

"And what if that makes him bleed even more?"

His age-lined eyes looked into my naïve ones. "Trust me, and your friend will be fine," he said. "Now, take these." He handed me the tweezers, steaming from what looked like boiling water that had been poured on them.

I took them with trembling hands and pulled the cloth from Brad's wound. I felt sick. My eyes squeezed shut, and I turned my head to the side. "I can't do this," I said.

"Your friend needs your help. You can do it." The man's words were soft but gave me the encouragement I needed.

I moved the cloth back a bit and could see the bullet lodged not far from the surface. The next few minutes, while I extracted the bullet, Brad trembled and moaned in a way that frightened me. A whispered and continuous prayer in his behalf sounded from my lips.

Finally, the bullet was out. I pressed the cloth against the wound. "What about the one in his side?"

"It passed through him." The man pulled back the cloth he was holding a bit to show me two holes, an entrance and an exit wound. "Now," he handed me the bowl with the paste in it, "spread some of this on the wounds. It will burn a little, but it will also help stop the bleeding and kill infection."

Brad let out another moan and jolted from the shock when I applied it. When I was done, I set down the bowl, and the man opened a leather bag toward me. "Take some of this in your hands," the man said. "It will ease his pain and help heal."

I scooped the thick, clay-like stuff on my fingers, slipped them under the cloths, and applied it to the wounds.

"Very good," he said. He then grabbed the T-shirt I'd brought, tore it into strips, and handed them to me to cover the wounds and tie them in place. When I was done, I removed my jacket and wrapped it around Brad's shoulders, then pulled the blanket up around him.

"You did a good job," the man said when I finished. "Your friend will be fine."

"Thank you. Thank you for your help." I glanced at the bandaged wounds, expecting to see mounds of blood. Instead, only small, dark spots had seeped through the clean bandages. "What was that stuff?" I asked.

The gentleman moved to the fire and poured liquid from the kettle into a small bowl. His sun-dried lips blew steam from the top, and he inhaled the vapors. "Mother Earth provides all that is needed for illness and injury," he said while handing the bowl to me. "Help your friend drink this. It will help him sleep and allow his body to heal by building the blood."

My fingers wrapped around the hot bowl, and I brought it close. I blew on it and shook it until it seemed cool enough to drink. The bowl fit nicely under Brad's lips, and he was able to take slow sips. When he'd finished, his head slumped to one side and his eyes closed. His breathing was slow and steady.

"Are you hungry?" the man asked. Before I had a chance to answer, he handed me a large chunk of heavy, dark bread and a piece of jerky. I didn't realize how hungry I was until I felt myself gulping down the food.

The smile on his face was genuine. "I will get more."

After I'd eaten my fill and was refreshed with water, I tended to my wounded leg. The clay was amazing in its ability to relieve the annoying burn I'd been feeling for more than twenty-four hours. The man placed a blanket over me and my eyelids grew heavy.

"You know," the man whispered, and my eyes startled open. He reached for another blanket and wrapped it around himself. "I have no truck, but not far from here is a motorbike. I hid it in the trees, yesterday, to keep the others from taking it." His head nodded from the blanket, and I followed its direction.

My eyes widened. "Is it red?"

"Yes, does it belong to you?"

I nodded. "It's Brad's; my boyfriend's."

"What is your name?"

It seemed strange this man didn't even know my name. In a way it seemed like I'd known him forever. "Alexia is my real name, but people call me Lexi."

"Ah, nice name, Lexi."

"What about you?"

He smiled and formed words and sounds I'd never heard before. "It means 'the eagle who watches over his nest.' But my friends call me Ted."

My jaw dropped wide open, and I pulled the blanket tighter around me. "Was that you with the shotgun?"

He shook his head. "I have no gun."

An image flashed through my mind. Was he one of the silhouettes in my dream? No, it couldn't be. "I'm sorry about what happened, Ted. And I can't thank you enough for your help." My chin quivered despite my best efforts to keep it still. I was so very grateful to be alive and out of the cave, I couldn't even describe it.

"It is fine." A weathered smile played on his face. "Men often look for treasure that fades or can be taken. But real treasures cannot be taken from you; they do not fade. Wisdom, knowledge," his eyes looked at Brad and then me, "and love. Those are true treasures. You are lucky you have found them."

My heart burned with the knowledge of the truth he spoke. In the whole world, all I wanted was for us to make it out of these mountains alive and together. Nothing else mattered.

"Now, get some rest. You will need it for tomorrow."

I couldn't argue. I closed my eyes and fell into a deep sleep from complete exhaustion.

★　　★　　★　　★

Faint light broke through my eyelids. For a second I lay in the warmth of the jacket around me and basked in the comfort of being so near to Brad. The steady rhythm of his heart had kept me company throughout the night. My eyelids fluttered open, and I sat up.

The fire had long died. Brad was awake and checking his wounds. Ted and all his belongings were gone.

"How do you feel?" I asked.

"Much better." He tried to move his arm a bit and pulled a little face. "But still quite tender."

A rumble in Brad's stomach caught my attention. I remembered the granola bar and the half eaten apple in the jacket pockets and pulled them free. "Here," I said, handing them to Brad.

"No, you go ahead. I'm not that hungry." His stomach growled again, even louder. "Okay, maybe we can split them."

I broke off a small section of granola bar for myself and gave the rest to him, then did my best to split the apple. "Did you see him leave?" I asked.

"Who?"

"The man who helped us last night, Ted."

His face twisted as he chewed on a chunk of apple. "There wasn't anyone here last night."

My jaw dropped down. "Yes, there was. His name was Ted, and he helped me do everything."

He stopped chewing and swallowed. "I remember you taking care of my wounds, and I remember your prayers, but I saw no one else here."

I scanned the campground for any shred of evidence that I wasn't insane. My eyes caught sight of something in the bushes surrounding the cave. I reached for it and pulled out a large, brown-toned eagle feather. Goose bumps climbed my arms.

Our eyes met each other, but neither of us could verbalize our thoughts. Instead, we knelt together and offered a prayer of tremendous thanks for the guardian angel that had helped us the previous night. Then we asked for continued protection. When we'd finished, Brad pulled me close with his good arm and whispered, "You were amazing last night. You saved my life."

I pulled back enough to look into his face. "No, you saved mine. I'll be forever in your debt."

"Our prayers were answered."

My mind flashed back to the pleas I'd made while in the cave. "They really were."

His eyes looked into mine, and then he hung his head and wiped at his brows.

"What's wrong," I asked.

"Derek."

"I think he was shot; I'm so sorry."

His eyes were filled with pain. A crease formed in his forehead. "Is he dead?"

"I . . . I don't know."

"I need to find out. Where did it happen?"

I opened my mouth to protest, but I knew he'd never leave until he learned what had happened to Derek. "On the mountain in the trees."

"All right, let's go," he said.

"Now?"

His eyes looked past me and into the morning. "He's my brother."

★   ★   ★   ★

Bursts of sunlight kissed the tops of the mountains and provided a much-needed mental reprieve from the events of the night before. But a chill hung in the valley shadows where we walked through dew-covered wild grass and thick trees toward the mountain. Our conversation was mere whispers on the unusually quiet morning.

Before long, we came to the spot in the road where Carl's ATV had crashed into the tree. Other than a little broken glass in the area, there was no other sign of him. Then we found brown blood splattered around dried footprints in the mud.

They led to Derek's missing motorcycle. We tried to follow the motorcycle tracks for awhile but lost them in the brush.

"At least he's alive," Brad said.

We turned around and followed Ted's directions to Brad's motorcycle. Minutes later, a spot of red at the base of some trees near the road came into view. Our steps quickened in an effort to reach the bike and get back to those who were probably worried sick over our disappearance.

When we reached it, Brad smiled. "So, are you still planning to walk back to camp?"

"I thought you were supposed to carry me."

He looked at his shoulder and then at me. "Maybe in a few weeks."

The rumble of a motor startled us. I looked up to see the four-wheeler I'd grown to hate coming toward us. I didn't have to say a word. Brad jumped on the bike and kick-started the motor, but found himself in a predicament with only one arm to work with.

I looked at Carl racing toward us and then hopped on in front of Brad. My hands grasped the clutch and brake, and I revved the motor. Memories of being taught and driving motorcycles with Ron came clearly to mind. I just needed to focus on them instead of the memory of wiping out down that terrible hill. I trembled but heard Brad's encouragement behind me.

I eased off the clutch and gave it gas, a little wobbly at first. I planned to increase speed gradually, but the power of the bike was more than I'd ever driven before, and I was unprepared for the g-force it suddenly gave. We screamed right past Carl, who flipped around at the sight of us.

The hills, trees, weeds, and my caution at driving slowed us down until Brad notified me that Carl was gaining on us. I gave the bike more gas, and we went airborne off the next hill. My landing wasn't very stable, and we both stuck out our feet for balance. The ground was soft. The rear tire spun for a second, spraying sand and partially-dried mud, before pushing us off again.

Carl's machine flew over the hill and landed right behind us. My eyes searched for any sign of the road we'd come in on. Luckily, I noticed it several yards away. I throttled the gas and stood a bit to avoid the bumpiness of the rocks and foliage under our tires.

By the time we reached the road, Carl was in my peripheral vision. His four-wheeler careened into the bike and nearly tipped us over. We managed to keep our balance and continued up the path. Angels must've been watching over us.

The road increased in altitude, and we leaned forward for balance as we rode up a large hill. At least it provided us with the opportunity to gain a bit on Carl. When we'd reached the top, a drop off to the right caused my palms to sweat. I hugged the left side of the road so the cliff wouldn't distract me. I kept on the accelerator, feeling my hair slap against my cheeks.

A sharp bend in the road was just ahead. I slowed significantly. My heart nearly stopped its beating when the bend revealed the steep, descending and winding road before us. One slip could cause us to go over the edge of the road and tumble to certain deaths below.

The ATV grew closer behind us. I was horrified at the possibility of accidentally going off the road, but even more so at being forced off. My leg instinctively reached out around the bend, and when we'd made it safely around, I accelerated.

Carl flew to our side and nearly slammed into our bike. I swerved out of the way just in time, but Carl's machine was just inches shy of going over the edge. The next sharp bend caught me off guard. Thankfully, it was an inside turn, and I was able to ride the bike up the side of the hill and back down to the narrow, dirt road.

Without warning, Carl rammed his four-wheeler into the rear wheel of the bike. We spun almost completely around but somehow managed to correct ourselves. I focused on the sharp turn just ahead. Carl worked his way toward us, but I stayed as close to the hill as possible.

Suddenly, a black pick-up truck rounded the bend from the other direction. I leaned to the side and rode onto the hill, narrowly escaping a head on collision. Carl tried to veer out of the way, but the ATV's front end clipped the corner bumper of the truck and flipped over and over out of control. I skidded to a stop just in time to see the four-wheeler and its rider fly over the edge of the road. The truck didn't stop.

I killed the engine and Brad and I jumped off the bike. When we reached the mountain's edge, we looked in horror at the mangled pieces of four-wheeler lying at the bottom of the canyon below. Scattered gold coins reflected the sun, and Carl's twisted body lay crumpled over the earth, still and silent.

Stars and dots formed before my eyes. I tried to blink them away, but they were so stubborn. More and more came. Brad's voice carried through my thick, hollow ears. His strong arm tightened around me then everything went black.

CHAPTER 19

★ ★ ★ ★ ★

"I'm sorry about what happened, Lexi," Kirsten said when I rushed through the door to work.

"It's fine," I answered.

Her hands twisted by her sides. "No, I should've . . ."

"Please don't feel bad. What's done is done, and everything's fine now." I gave her a smile before I tossed my purse in the back room and dashed out to the floor.

It was a hectic first day back on the job. A steady stream of customers kept us busy the entire morning, but thoughts about the ordeal in the Uintahs still managed to slip into my mind. It'd happened nearly two weeks ago, and though my leg wound was just a scar, my mind was still dealing with the trauma I'd experienced. I hoped the knowledge of the gospel would eventually soften my heart and bring me the peace I prayed for daily.

Thankfully, Brad was doing well. Our love for each other had only magnified through our experience. So it made it all the more difficult to return to normal life; working and getting ready for a new school season. It'd only been two days since I'd last seen him, but every day we were apart seemed like a month.

After the lunch-hour-rush was over and things had settled down, Kirsten approached me. "So, how things are between you and Derek?" she asked.

Derek? The sound of his name sent chills down my spine. "He disappeared," I said.

Her mouth opened wide. "Why? What happened?"

"I don't really feel like talking about it."

"Oh, did you two breakup or something?" she said with an expression I couldn't read.

I stared at her for a full minute before I could answer. "Yeah, something."

The congenial smile on her face started to turn into a pout.

"I'm sorry. We did breakup, but that's not why he disappeared."

Her mouth opened wide. "You mean he's, like, gone?"

I nodded. "We don't know where he is."

The shocked look on her face said more than words ever could, but it quickly turned to a smile when Jessica arrived for her shift.

"Hey, Lexi," Jessica said. She walked toward me with a large bouquet of flowers in her hand. "Here, these are for you."

"Thank you. They're beautiful," I said.

Her eyes grew big. "Actually, they're not from me."

"Oh, then who?"

She shrugged her shoulders. "The delivery guy just handed them to me on my way in."

I lifted the flap on the envelope and took out the card. It read:

To Lexi,
All my love, forever.

It wasn't signed.

"Ahem," Jessica said. "I saw you on the news. Did you really spend the night in a cave with Chet Strong?"

I nodded and swallowed the sick feeling that his name created.

"Did you find any gold?"

"Yes, actually, I did." I didn't mention that the thought of it still gave me nightmares, nor the fact that I'd found one haunting gold coin in my pocket afterward.

Kirsten stepped a little closer. "Did you take any?"

"No, not on purpose. I just wanted to get out."

"Oh," Kirsten said, and quickly found other work to keep her busy.

A couple of dressing room doors stood open with clothes heaped on the floor inside. A glance at the clock showed I still had five minutes left until break. I smelled the flowers, set them in the back by my purse, then picked up the discarded items, all while trying to focus on the task rather than my thoughts. I was nearly done folding clothes in one of the stalls when I heard Jessica say, "Wow, who's that?"

I peeked out of the stall in time to see Kirsten straighten her shirt. "Ooh, I don't know, but I'm going to find out."

I slipped into the next stall and grabbed the T-shirt thrown in a heap on the floor. The front door jingled closed and Kirsten asked, "Is there something I can help you with, sir?"

"Actually, I'm looking for someone." Brad's voice startled me, and I almost dropped the clothes to the floor.

Kirsten cleared her throat. "Well, perhaps I can help you."

I glanced at myself in the dressing room mirror and smoothed my hair. My tanned skin, attractive shirt, and nice jeans were much more presentable than the horrid wreck I'd found in the mirror when I'd returned from the mountains. I sped out of the dressing room and chucked the clothes onto the nearest tabletop.

Brad's face lit up with a wide smile when he noticed me, and his eyes locked onto mine. "I'm looking for a woman with long, golden hair, amazing blue eyes, a sense of humor, and someone who can handle a motorcycle like a pro while being chased by a mad man."

He was dressed in slacks and a stunning casual shirt that

enhanced the breadth of his shoulders and sculpted muscles. He pulled me into his arms to steal a quick kiss when I reached him. "I'm kidnapping you for lunch, if that's all right," he said only to me.

A smile spread across my lips. "Absolutely! I've been dying to see you."

"It seems like it's been forever." His eyes searched my face and then focused on my lips. Time stood still in our own little world. He moved in closer but refrained himself from caressing my lips with his own when we realized Kirsten was speaking.

"Are you going to introduce me?" she asked.

I stepped back. "Sorry, Kirsten and Jessica, this is my boyfriend, Brad. Wait a minute. Don't you know him? You used to date Derek. This is his borther," I said to Kirsten.

"Well, yeah, but I never met his family. I wish I had, though." Her eyes wandered all over him.

I let them get better acquainted (but not too acquainted) while I grabbed my purse and flowers. I was back in less than ten seconds.

When I returned, he took my hand and said, "Nice flowers, where did you get them?"

"From you."

The smile on his lips faded. "I didn't send them, not that I didn't think about it."

"Are you serious? Then who are they from?" I showed him the card.

"Hmmm. Maybe they're from someone wishing you well from your adventures in the mountains."

I nodded absently. "Yeah, that must be it."

He took my hand and gave it a kiss. "Are you ready to eat?"

"Yes, I'm starving."

Ashley waved from behind the register. "See you tomorrow."

"I'm just going to lunch," I said over my shoulder.

"Oh, right. See you when you get back, then." Her face may have turned a little red, but it was hard to tell under her sun-kissed skin.

We were met with a lovely temperature outside. I shielded my eyes from the sun and looked for Brad's sports car in the parking lot, but it wasn't there. "Where's your car?" I asked.

"It's right here." He stopped in front of an older four-door sedan.

"Where's your other one?"

"I sold it."

My eyes widened. "You sold it?"

He opened my door and shrugged. "I needed some extra cash, and I got a killer deal on this one. It has a few miles on it, but it runs nice and gets good gas mileage. Do you like it?"

It certainly wasn't comparable in looks to his other car, but I'd ridden in them before, and I knew it was a good car. "I like the way they drive, and I hear they're reliable," I said.

He smiled. "Exactly."

After we'd left the crowded parking lot, I glanced at his shoulder and side. "How was the doctor's appointment?"

"It went really well. He was impressed with how nicely everything's healing."

I smiled, but it faded when I noticed the look of concentration on his face. "Is something wrong?" I asked.

He took a big breath, reached his hand across the seat, and took mine. "There's a little problem."

"What?" I wasn't convinced I wanted to hear the answer.

His eyes shifted between the road and my face. "A few weeks from now, I'll be going back to BYU, and you'll been going to Utah State. They aren't exactly in the same neighborhood, and I can't bear the thought of being so far away from you."

I gave his hand a squeeze. "I've been thinking the same thing myself. In fact, I've been toying with the idea of transferring my credits to either BYU or UVU. At least that way we can still see each other regularly."

"Could you do that? I mean, wouldn't that set you back in your schooling?"

"Not anymore than staying in Logan and failing all my classes because I miss you so much."

The worry lines in his face visibly disappeared. He placed my hand to his lips for a kiss and said, "I love you."

Moments later, we pulled into the driveway of his home. I hadn't even noticed where we were going until I saw the gorgeous view of Park City below us.

"I thought we'd have a little picnic in my yard," he said. He let me out of the car, and we strolled up the stone path to his home. Birds sang in the treetops. The light scent of flowers filled my senses. Brad loved me. Life was so beautiful; I shouldn't have been able to contain myself. But I felt weighed down emotionally.

When we reached the porch, Brad turned me to face him. "I, uh, went to Derek's apartment."

"And?"

"No one's seen or heard from him. I went to his business; he hasn't been there, either. But I did find that he was stealing money from the company."

I gasped. "Why would he do that?"

"I don't know. It just doesn't make sense. It wasn't like him at all." He tipped my chin and looked into my eyes. "Are you doing okay?" His voice was sincere and gentle.

My eyes shifted, and I just shrugged my shoulders. "I'm doing all right." Images of Currant Creek flashed through my mind. Derek, Carl/Chet, the cave, the voices, supporting Brad through the trees, Carl tumbling over the edge . . . I cupped my hands over my face trying to shove tears back, but Brad's embrace only opened the floodgates. I took a few minutes to let the poisonous tears drain, while his soft words comforted me.

I swiped at a tear rolling down my cheek. "I don't want to

forgive yet. How could I have ever dated Derek? I feel so used, and Carl killed my grandpa!"

He pulled back a bit and tilted my chin toward him. "Forgiveness was designed for all of us, not just because it's something we need to do, but because it brings happiness. If you decide never to forgive them, *you'll* be the one who suffers and the one filled with anger and hatred. Do you want those feelings eating you up every day, ruining your life?"

I shook my head.

He pulled my head into his chest and kissed my forehead. "One of the gifts of the Savior is that He's there to help you along the way. I know what kind of a person you are, and I know you'll be able to forgive completely, with time. So will I. But you also need to forgive yourself."

"Me?" When he said the words my eyes opened. *I* dated Derek, *I* hadn't heeded the warnings I'd felt to leave the mountain sooner, *I* nearly got Brad killed trying to save me. "How could Heavenly Father love someone as rebellious as me?" The words came from my lips but were spoken from my heart.

He was silent for a minute before he said, "We don't need to be perfect in order for Him to love us. He just does because He created us. Think of it. Would a loving parent not love a child who's learning to walk because they stumble and fall?"

I tilted my head back at his words. "No, of course not. They'd help and encourage their child through learning experiences."

"Exactly. You've gone through some pretty important learning experiences, and your Heavenly Parents have been encouraging you along the way. You may've stumbled a bit, but you also got right back up and are trying again. You are loved so much, by them and by me."

At that moment, I felt such a profound love fill me from head to toe that I couldn't speak. The angel standing in front of me had given the words and feelings of hope that I'd longed for since my return from the mountains. My Father in Heaven had forgiven me, and I would forgive others, myself included, with the Savior's help.

At that wonderful moment, the front door burst open. "Oh, there you are. Are you coming? We can't wait any longer." It was Sister Manning. She gave an excited smile and then shut the door.

"What was that about?" I asked.

"Nothing," he said.

"It didn't seem like nothing to me. What's going on?"

Brad looked away then back to me with a wide smile. "I'll tell you in awhile. It can wait."

"But . . ." was all I said before his lips cut off my sentence. At first I resisted, knowing the intent of his kiss was to quiet me. But I was just as determined to extract an answer from him. I tried to pull away, but he followed me with his soft lips and slipped his hand around my neck to hold me in place.

Whether or not he'd intended for me to lose my concentration, I didn't know. What I did know was that with each moment of our magical kiss, troubled thoughts dropped out of my mind and heart one by one, until all that remained was the moment we were sharing. When our lips finally parted, I couldn't even remember my own name.

"Did you do that on purpose?" I asked when I realized we were on his porch.

His smile was wide. "I fully intended to kiss you, if that's what you're asking. Shall we go inside?" he asked.

I nodded and took his hand. My eyes had to adjust when we walked into the house and spacious living room. When they did, I saw Morgan sitting on a colorful, fluffy sofa, reading a book.

"I'm going to set up the picnic. I'll see you in a few minutes." Brad left, and I took a seat next to Morgan.

I sat for a full minute with no acknowledgment of my presence from her. "So, how's Wes?" I finally asked.

She jumped and let out a yelp. "Sorry, I didn't know you were there," she said.

I smiled. "I didn't mean to scare you, I was just wondering about Wes."

"He's doing fine." She set the book on the couch to her side. "He saved us, you know. He took us back to camp and told everyone what was up. I just hope that now he'll find the happiness he's been searching for all his life."

"That's good to hear. Where's Li Shan?" I asked when I noticed she didn't seem to be around.

"She's at BYU, looking for housing."

"Was she really crushed?"

"Yes, she's been taking it pretty hard. But personally, I'd rather have you . . ." She stopped mid-sentence and smiled. "You're a good cook, aren't you?"

"Why?"

Sister Manning entered the living room and gave me a long hug. Her eyes were red when she pulled back. "So how're you recovering?" she asked.

My conversation with Brad on the porch came to mind. "A lot better, now. What about you?"

"I'm just glad you two made it out of those mountains alive." She wiped a tear from her cheek. "It's been a traumatic experience for us all . . ." Her eyes glanced up at the picture of Derek sitting on the mantle. She shook her head and forced a smile. "But next year I think we'll camp and fish by the pond in our yard where there isn't quite as much danger."

I smiled. I had to admit her idea was tempting.

"Here, this is for you." She flashed a smile and handed me a large manila envelope. A little white paper was stapled to its side.

"What's this?" I asked.

"Just read it. It's from Brad."

"Brad?" I scanned the note stapled to the envelope.

Lex,

    I know you must be feeling down because you didn't get much treasure. So I've devised a little treasure hunt where you'll find the greatest treasure of them all. ME! (And of course, lunch). Follow the clues and good luck.

Love,

Brad

P.S. I'm hungry, so the sooner you find me, the sooner we can eat.

I couldn't help but laugh, and from the looks on Morgan and Sister Manning's faces, they'd been expecting this. I opened the envelope and pulled out a perfect replica of a buckskin map. It was made of a crinkled, brown paper sack with its edges torn to give it an authentic look. A map was scrolled in black ink with an "x" drawn over what looked like a bunch of trees on a hill.

I looked to Sister Manning and Morgan for help. They just shrugged their shoulders, but at least they guided me to the back yard.

The mid-day sun warmed my shoulders the moment I stepped out of the shade from the back porch. I crossed the lawn to the base of the hill and studied the map. It appeared that the "x" was drawn somewhere near the aspens and rocks.

I searched the bark of each tree before finding another map tied to the branch of one of the aspens. On the map was a small, misshapen oval with a small "x" nearby. The shape of the oval looked suspiciously like the shape of the pond toward the top of the hill, so I began my climb through splotchy shade until I reached my destination.

Brilliant rays of light reflected off the ripples in the water. I searched the surroundings for another clue, but would've rather found Brad. I scanned the trees, columbines, and pansies that grew near the water's edge, but I couldn't see a thing. I was just about to give up and shout Brad's name, when I spotted a large "x" drawn into loose soil at the base of an aspen. A small, blue-handled shovel was buried partway into the earth.

I had the impression I was supposed to dig for something. I just hoped it wasn't our lunch.

I knelt down in the shade of the grove, grabbed the shovel, and began to dig. The soil was very soft and came up easily. In no time I reached a box; a small biscuit box from KFC. Somehow dirty biscuits didn't sound very appetizing, hungry as I was. I pulled it from the ground and brushed it off. Its weight was surprisingly light.

The top flap opened easily, and I peered inside. A small jewelry box lay in the bottom. Chills ran through me even in the warmth of the day. My fingers wrapped around the velvet box, and I slowly opened it with wide-eyes and mouth. Inside was a simple, yet elegantly designed diamond ring of white and yellow gold. Several smaller diamonds splashed about a lovely diamond placed in the center. Each caught different colors of the rainbow when sunlight filtered through the trees.

"Lex," Brad whispered from behind.

I whirled around to see him not standing, but kneeling beside me. He took the box from me then took my hand. "As you know, the only real treasures that we can take with us when our lives on earth are complete are knowledge that we've gained and eternal relationships formed through marriage between a man and a woman in the temple of the Lord. *You* are my treasure."

He took the ring from its box and held it gently between his thumb and forefinger. "This ring is a worldly treasure, one that can't be taken beyond the grave, but it symbolizes my love for you and our love for each other. The circle it makes is eternal, with no beginning and no end, like our relationship can be."

Brad separated the solitaire engagement ring from the diamond-accented wedding band then continued. "Separate, these two bands are unique and beautiful, but brought together, they are complete as one; strong, beautiful, and complementary, working together." He placed the two bands together, forming the complete set, and separated them again. "Like this band without the other, my life without you isn't complete." His eyes studied every detail of my face. Then he looked into my eyes and into my soul and said, "Will you complete me? Will you marry me?"

I knew the words were coming, yet hearing them filled me with emotions I didn't expect. My heart raced and filled with electricity at the thought of being this wonderful man's wife. "Yes," I whispered. "Yes, I'll marry you." I wasn't ashamed of the tears streaming down my face. I threw my arms around his neck and planted a kiss on his cheek.

He gently took my hand and slipped the engagement ring on my finger. I stared at it through tear-filled eyes before he put a finger under my chin and brought my lips to meet his.

By the time we were finished being congratulated by Brad's entire family, who had been peeking through the windows, I was starving. We enjoyed a lovely picnic in the shade by the pond, and I felt completely satisfied both physically and emotionally.

After we'd eaten, I glanced at my watch and let out a yelp. "I'm like two hours late for work!"

Brad just sat on the picnic blanket in the shade of the trees and smiled. "I forgot to tell you. I called your manager a few days ago and told her what was up. She said you could have the rest of the day off."

"Really? In that case, I'll just relax a bit." I lay my head down on the blanket and brought my hand to where I could admire my ring. "It's so beautiful."

"I'm glad you like it. I debated about whether or not to have you pick it out, but I wanted to surprise you."

"I love surprises." I tilted my hand in a section of sunlight and watched over and over the brilliant colors of the rainbow pop from the stones. "Mrs. Bradley James Manning. Lexi Manning. I like the sound of that."

"Me too." He played with a lock of my hair and asked, "If you could pick any temple in the world to get married, which one would you choose?" His words interrupted my daydreaming.

"The Salt Lake Temple. When I was growing up, my family always went to Temple Square at Christmas when all the lights were lit up, and I would think to myself, 'Someday, I'll get married in that temple.' What about you?"

"I like all the temples; each one is unique. But if you've always wanted to marry in the Salt Lake temple, then that's where it should be. How does October sound? That'll give us enough time to make—"

I cut off the remainder of his sentence with a kiss.

"What's that for? Not that I'm complaining."

"That's because we'll be married in the Salt Lake Temple. And this," I gave him another kiss, "is because I love you. And yes, October sounds great."

He chuckled. "Can you really transfer your credits? I mean, I could transfer mine to Utah State so you can finish your degree."

"No, it'd be easier for me to transfer, plus, Utah County is almost like a second home. My sister lives in Springville, and I love all the shopping the area offers."

"And if we live in Utah County, I can take over Derek's business."

"It's settled. I'll be the one—"

His lips stopped my words. "I love you," he said when he pulled back.

"And I love you." I couldn't help the grin on my face.

"Do you want to go apartment hunting?"

"Today?"

"Yes, today."

"Now?"

He laughed. "Well, we don't have to go right now. I'm not done playing with your hair yet. Plus, I could use a back rub. I was so nervous about asking you to marry me that my muscles are all tense."

"Are you serious?"

"About the back rub or being nervous?"

"Both," I replied.

"Yes, I'm serious, about both. But you don't have to give me a back rub right now. Are you ready to go?"

I smiled. "I'm not done admiring my ring, it's so beautiful. What if we actually find an apartment today? I have some money for first and last month's rent, but I don't know that I'd have enough for anything more than that."

"Don't worry, I have some cash. I've been saving throughout the summer, and I also have some money left after trading . . ."

"My ring? Did you trade your car to buy my ring?"

He was silent before he finally answered. "I'd much rather have you than a car. It was an easy choice to make. Plus, the sedan will make a good family car. So, you ready to go look for apartments?"

My mouth still gaped open. How could he be so casual about giving up his car?

When I didn't answer, he held out a hand and said, "Help me up."

I grabbed his hand and pulled, but he didn't budge. Instead, he pulled me toward him and kissed me soundly.

"Is that how you pulled Derek into the water?" I asked.

"How did you know it was me who pulled him in?"

"I just guessed. I had a fifty-fifty chance of being right."

He stole a quick kiss on the cheek. "Yes, that's what I did. Only I didn't kiss him afterward."

"Well, I'd hope not. At least not like that."

He laughed, and then jumped to his feet and pulled me to stand. "Let's go find our future home."

After what seemed like hours of searching through newspapers and making several phone calls, we set up a few appointments and toured a bunch of apartments. The moment we walked through the door of the fifth rental, I knew it was the right place. It was an older home in downtown Provo, but it was cute, and I loved the yard filled with private trees and a vegetable garden.

"Well, what do you think?" Brad took my hand, and we walked back into the living room.

"I love it. It has new plumbing, electrical work, paint, and carpet. And the floor doesn't even slope downhill when you walk into the kitchen."

"I think it'll last us for a couple of years while we finish school," he said, while pulling me close. "Plus, it has three bedrooms for when we decide to start our family."

Warm blood began to rise to my cheeks at the thought. "I'm going to take a look at the yard again while you make arrangements with the landlord." I suddenly needed some fresh air. I walked onto the porch and looked at the cute little homes in the neighborhood. What kind of neighbors would we have?

At that moment, a black pickup truck drove down the road. The man behind the wheel craned his neck in my direction, a man with black, shaggy hair and a goatee. I stumbled back into the house and burst into the living room. "I just saw Shaggy driving down the street!"

Brad flew out the door, but the street was empty. "I don't see anything." He took me by the shoulders and turned me to face him. "Lex, are you sure?"

"Who else would wear hair like that on purpose?"

A crease formed between his eyes. "Did you get the license plate number?"

"I can remember it if I think hard enough."

"Good, write it down and your dad's buddies can check it out." He ran his arm along my shoulders and said, "Shall we go back in and talk to Mr. Stratton before he changes his mind?"

I nodded, took his outstretched hand, and we walked back into our future home.

EPILOGUE

★ ★ ★ ★ ★

My heart raced, moisture squeezed from my palms, and suffocating air filled my lungs. My eyes opened but couldn't see a thing. I felt my surroundings and knew I was back in the cave! I had no recollection of how I'd come into this situation; my last conscious thought was of being in Brad's arms.

My hands searched the cold walls for a way out. A crack of light squeezed out from under a wooden door, and I crawled toward it. But it was bolted shut. My balled fists pounded against the thick, heavy wood. *Bang! Bang! Bang!*

Brad shook me awake. "Breakfast is ready," he said.

I sat up in bed. My heart still raced, my hands were still moist, and my eyes searched but saw nothing. "Breakfast?"

"Yes, we told them to bring it up at 8:30."

"They?"

He chuckled. "The Anniversary Inn. They just knocked. Come on, let's eat."

Recollection seeped into my mind like slow-running molasses. How could I have forgotten I was on my honeymoon? Thick curtains hid any evidence of the sun or our room, but memories of a sparkling cider bottle lying empty next to the jetted tub, and the rest of our romantic evening came back to mind.

"Did you have another bad dream?" He ran his fingers

through the ends of my hair.

"Yes, I dreamed I was back in the cave. I'd found a door out, but it was locked."

"Look at the bright side. At least you don't have as many of those dreams now as you did when you first got out of the mountains. I imagine they'll be gone before you know it."

"You're right," I said. I lay back down in the warm covers and snuggled against Brad's chest.

He propped himself up on one elbow and shook my limp body. "Come on, Sleeping Beauty, let's eat."

"You go ahead. I'm going to sleep in." I closed my eyes, but my new husband was determined to keep me awake.

"Lex," he said softly in my ear. "What do I have to do to get you out of bed?"

A smile played on my lips. "Not that. It'll just keep us both in bed longer. But if you really must know, Sleeping Beauty can't be awakened without her true love's kiss."

"I think I can manage that." His words were muffled against my face and disappeared entirely when our lips met. "Are you awake now?" he asked when he pulled back a full minute later.

"Yes, very much." I had forgotten that I'd even had a dream.

"Good. Let's go eat! Last one down gets to give me another back rub. Oh, that'd be you." He ripped the covers from me, and I squealed at the cool air that crept over my arms and legs. He laughed so hard that he stumbled down the dark staircase from our bed to the main area below.

"Are you okay?" I asked. I didn't even try to suppress my laughter.

"I'm fine, but my toe isn't," he said. He tried not to laugh but eventually did.

Light broke into the room when he pulled in our breakfast tray from just outside the door. He clicked on a dim overhead light and carried the tray to the little glass table in the nook area. Seconds later, the morning's autumn rays entered the room when he pulled the curtains back.

I climbed out of bed and descended the spiral staircase. The aroma of a large, freshly-baked cinnamon roll and hot ham and cheese croissant teased my nostrils. I knew my husband would completely devour them if I didn't join him soon.

"I saved some for you." He swallowed a mouthful of croissant and washed it down with orange juice. "It's really good. Oh, and you'll notice when you use the bathroom next, that I put the toilet seat down."

I grinned and said, "Thanks." I pulled up a chair next to him and tore off a section of croissant.

"Are you still tired?" he asked.

"A little. I guess we had a big day yesterday."

He swallowed another mouthful of juice. "I don't know very many couples who spend an entire day on their honeymoon in downtown Salt Lake . . ."

I raised an eyebrow. "Touring the city in a horse drawn carriage, admiring the falling leaves, and walking hand-in-hand around Temple Square?"

He shook his head. "Spending hours at the Family History Center, looking for information on your deceased great-great-great-uncle."

"True, but at least we found more information supporting that he died in 1885. Still, I'd like his brother's marriage certificate or even his own death certificate. Did he even have one? Will we ever know when he died?"

"I don't know."

"Does it even matter?"

He squeezed my hand. "Yes, it matters. You've gone through a great deal of thought and work to find the truth, and someday you'll be rewarded with that knowledge. Until then, we just need to be patient. I'm positive your uncle Enoch is pleased with all you've done to find out more about him. A knowledge of his life on earth lives within you. Not to mention, I think he'd be glad to have you as his great-great-great-niece, the way you stuck up for him when Carl made that remark. I thought you were going to throw him in the fire."

"I nearly did," I said. That night by the campfire seemed like ages ago.

"You wouldn't have felt that way if you didn't love your uncle, and you love him because of all that you've done to find out about him. You should feel happy."

"Thanks. You always know what to say to help me feel better."

He smiled. "I wonder if he ever regretted seeking the gold instead of staying back and getting married. I bet he did. I know I would." His eyes looked into mine. "So, do you feel bad that you gave up all that wealth to be the wife of a poor student?"

I giggled. "I'm already the wealthiest woman alive; I've got you. Plus, I know you'll be an excellent provider once we're done with school. I can be patient until then."

He took my hand in his and played with the ring on my finger. "I know how to get back into the mine."

"What?"

"I remember exactly where it is and what it looks like. It's hard to find because it's hidden, but I remember it because it was the only way for me to get to you."

"You're not going back there."

He smiled. "I know, but if things ever get tight . . ."

"Then we'll manage like all other newlyweds."

He brought my hand to his lips. "You know, after we searched all day for information on your uncle, eating at The Roof made it all worth it."

"Oh?" I asked. The pleasant atmosphere of the restaurant at the top of the Joseph Smith Memorial Building played in my mind; the white linen tablecloths and black napkins, soft piano music in the background, good food, and the most gorgeous view of the Salt Lake Temple in the world.

"Yes, I didn't think I could be so close to heaven, sitting across the table from you, watching the sun set and the temple lights come on, knowing that we were married and sealed in that very temple; not just for time, but for all eternity. Imagine that, all eternity. . . . That's a lot of back rubs."

I laughed. How lucky I was to be married to such a wonderful man. There was no way I'd allow worldly treasures to take priority over my eternal treasure sitting before me. I was determined to do all I could to make our marriage last forever, and I knew that he was filled with that same determination.

His aquamarine eyes looked at the features of my face then moved to my lips. He smiled and slid in close. "You've got a crumb. Let me get it for you."

My lips parted in a grin. "Do I really, or do you just want to kiss me?"

His lips covered mine with a tender kiss, and I had my answer.

BOOK CLUB
★ ★ ★ Questions

1. What did Lexi learn about herself through the course of the book?

2. What were the overall themes of the book?

3. What did Lexi learn about the difference between infatuation, attraction, and love?

4. What attitudes toward money did Derek posses that contributed to his downfall?

5. What did Lexi learn from turning her heart to her ancestors?

6. How was Lexi's experience in the cave similar to the trials that we all face?

Bonus Question:

When did Enoch Rhoades really die? (If you find the answer, please let Jillayne know! She's been trying to solve this real family history mystery for years.)

BIBLIOGRAPHY
★ ★ ★ ★ ★ ★ ★ ★

Boren, Kerry Ross and Lisa Lee Boren. *The Utah Gold Rush.* Springville, UT: Council Press, 2002.

Letter from Enoch Rhoades to Thomas Rhoades Jr., July 7, 1885.

Rhoades, Gale and Boren, Kerry Ross. *Footprints in the Wilderness: A History of the Lost Rhoades Mines.* Salt Lake City, UT: Publishers Press, 1971.

Thompson, George. *Faded Footprints.* Salt Lake City, UT: Dream Garden Press, 1996.

Thompson, George A. *Lost Treasures on the Old Spanish Trail.* Salt Lake City, UT: Western Epics, 1992.

http://www.familysearch.org/eng/search/IGI/individual_record. asp?recid=500113217680&...   7/18/2008

http://www.familysearch.org/eng/search/IGI/individual_record. asp?recid=100229396364&...   7/18/2008

http://www.uintahbasin.usu.edu/johnbarton/files/usu1320notes. pdf pg. 6-7

ABOUT THE Author
★ ★ ★ ★ ★ ★

Photo courtesy of Images by Janä

Jillayne was born in Salt Lake City, Utah, but was raised primarily in Park City. However, crashing into young kids on the slopes and freezing her fingers and toes squelched any desire she may have had to ski. Instead, she spent her time playing musical instruments, drawing, and going for walks in the hills behind her home.

She attended Weber State University for two years until she fell in love with and married her husband, Greg. Together, they attended Utah State University where she received her four-year degree in Family and Human Development.

Jillayne enjoys expressing her creativity through writing and coming up with healthy, delicious whole-food recipes. She also enjoys vegetable gardening (just not the weed pulling), reading to and spending time with her four children, and going on dates with her husband.